Escaping CAMP ROOSEVELT

BRYAN T. CLARK

For more information on the Bryan T. Clark and his works, please see www.btclark.com

Fiction / Gay & Lesbian / M-M Romance / Contemporary / Publishing

First Edition

ISBN: 978-0-9970562-8-0

About the book:

"He's a bad boy—cocky and damaged. So, why can't I stop thinking about him?"

Broken Dreams

Sociable and unselfish, eighteen-year-old Tucker Graves loves two things—his darling little sister and the thrill of playing baseball. He never dreamed that he'd be homeless, but after a series of misfortunes, his life is nothing like he could have possibly imagined. Shocked and shattered, Tucker, his mother, and his baby sister now must brave the dangers of a dilapidated homeless encampment called Camp Roosevelt.

A Wounded Heart

Homeless since the age of fourteen, Dancer has mastered the tricks of living on the streets as a sex worker. The quiet, reclusive, and calculating ways of this twenty-year-old, green-eyed Adonis help him to survive. He hides his emotional scars from the world by interacting only with his clients, whose occasional bizarre requests he reluctantly fulfills. Dancer's past has taught him to trust no one.

A Second Chance

When Tucker and Dancer come face to face on a stormy night, having been thrown together under the same roof, Tucker brings out a feeling in Dancer that he didn't know still existed in him—desire.

Neither man can deny the attraction he feels for the other. But some scars run deep, causing both Tucker and Dancer to question whether falling in love is even possible, especially when survival is on the line.

Bryan T. Clark is a multi-published, Rainbow Award-winning author and LAMBDA finalist.

Dedication

The causes for homelessness in youth are many. The most common cause of youth homelessness, by far, is family conflict. However, there are many other reasons, such as psychiatric issues, drug and alcohol-related illnesses, sexual orientation, or gender identity. According to the Report from the Secretary's Task Force on Youth Suicide, twenty-six percent of gay youth who come out before the age of eighteen are kicked out of their homes and end up in the streets. LGBTQ youth are one hundred and twenty percent more likely to experience homelessness than non-LGBTQ youth. Homeless youth are frequently faced with no other option but to prostitute themselves to survive. This is referred to as "survival sex"—frightened kids in their early teens are forced to do sex work to stay alive.

To Kenny/My little brother:

It is because of you that I see the homeless man on the corner as a person, a fellow human being. Life has not been as kind to you as it has to me. Our lives may have started in a similar fashion, but our journeys have been vastly different—neither better nor worse, just different, leading us both to where we are today. Though our lives are worlds apart, this doesn't change our love for each other.

To Larkin Street Youth Services/Castro Youth Housing Initiative:

I will give 100% of the royalties from the first year of this novel's publication to the Castro Youth Housing Initiative (CYHI). The CYHI provides transitional housing in the city of San Francisco, California, U.S.A., for LGBTQ young people (ages 18-24) experiencing homelessness. Fear of being raped, abused, or murdered should not be a part of anyone's youth.

Should you, the reader, want to donate to a worthwhile cause, monetary donations can be made directly to the shelter on the book's behalf, by marking your donation with the word 'ROOSEVELT' in the memo section of your check or @: https://larkinstreetyouth.org/donate/

Address:
    HQ and Administration
    134 Golden Gate Avenue
    San Francisco, CA 94102
    Phone: (415) 673-0911
    Fax: (415) 749-3838
    Website: https://larkinstreetyouth.org/

Chapter One

Dancer tried to focus on the ticking sound of the rain as it struck the window. Like an urgent Morse code, the rapid, yet irregular, noise wasn't enough to drown out the light snore of the old man lying next to him. It was as if the two sounds were competing for his attention. His mind drifted between the rain and the old man's breathing.

It seemed as if he had been laying still for hours, but it was likely closer to thirty minutes. His eyes had long ago adjusted to the darkness. He stared up at the high ceiling flanked with elaborate crown molding. The same molding ran throughout the lavish apartment, which overlooked the east side of Chicago's sister city, Brierton. The moon, shadowed by clouds, illuminated the gray walls, changing them to a dull blue.

The old man snorted twice and then rubbed his face. Was he waking up? Dancer needed to get out of the apartment before that happened. He had been tricking with Old Man Gerhardt for six months, and on their second 'date,' the man had given him a simple nudge— a gesture that became Dancer's regular cue to leave. He never knew exactly when that was going to happen, but it always did. A silent command. These days, the twenty-year-old street hustler no longer waited for the nudge.

His butt muscles twitched as if the old man's cock was still inside him. With a bubble ass that could balance a wine glass, Dancer's five feet ten inches of natural beauty was also his Achilles's heel. Pale green eyes framed by graceful brows and a roman nose, sculpted by a fight two years ago, gave the Mississippi native a rugged, bad-boy appeal. His mother, Puerto Rican and his father German, Dancer was a modern-day street Adonis, beautiful and dangerously tempting.

From day one of his six years on the streets, Dancer had been the

1

most desirable hustler out there. These days, he worked only when he had to. He had never made love to anyone, but he'd had enough sex to last anyone a lifetime.

The number of nights Dancer spent in alleys pleasuring men had lessened since he was introduced to the old man. That night, when Gerhardt's driver stopped and approached him with a handful of questions, Dancer thought he was just another freak looking for sex. Dancer was less than engaging during the driver's probing until the man finally revealed that he was inquiring for his boss.

The pick-up was laid out like a contract instead of a date with a street hustler. For two hundred dollars, his new client required that Dancer shower upon his arrival, enjoy a proper meal in the apartment, and 'play' afterwards. Mr. Gerhardt was as vanilla as they came. After ten minutes of kissing and licking on Dancer like he was an ice cream cone and then five minutes of the old man working toward a pathetic orgasm, the sex was over. There were no fifty shades of grey here. It really was a pretty sweet gig.

Dancer turned his attention back to the rain. Watching as it drizzled down the window, he wondered just how nasty the storm was going to be when he got outside. Heat rising from the floor vent caused condensation to cover the bottom half of the window. He wondered how long it had been raining. It was the big storm everyone had been talking about for the last forty-eight hours.

This evening was a good night for a hustler to be working inside. He wasn't out in the rain trying to grab a passerby's attention or in a wet alley servicing some stranger, wondering if this was the person who would snuff him out. Instead, he was indoors, lying naked, coverless on top of soft, lavish sheets in a warm room and out of the storm. He ran his hand across the sheet, which was wrapped firmly around the large mattress. The silky feel under his fingers allowed his thoughts to drift for a second to a distant time when his own life mirrored the grandeur of this apartment. It was a time that he would banish from his thoughts forever if he could. Wealth didn't ensure safety or love.

Nowadays, Dancer's real world was sixteen floors below and two blocks over: a shabby homeless encampment called Camp Roosevelt. To lay longer in this bed only evoked memories of a time he had worked hard to forget.

A metallic taste formed in Dancer's mouth as his stomach tightened. The cause was the psychological cost of the job. The sex was revolting, but he had learned a long time ago that he didn't have to do anything but lay there while it was happening. He could zone out, go somewhere far away from what was happening to his body.

He worked to temper his angst, so he wouldn't vomit. It would be a shame to waste the gourmet meal he had eaten two hours ago. Mr. Gerhardt always had dinner waiting for him after his shower, prepared to his satisfaction. The massive porterhouse steak smothered in onions and mushrooms could have been the entire meal, but it was accompanied by a large, earthy, baked potato topped with butter, chives, bacon, and sour cream. Mr. Gerhardt had long ago stopped having any green vegetables accompany the meal since Dancer never ate them. Dancer wasn't sure which was better: the long, hot shower or the savory meal. However, it was the two hundred dollars that kept him coming back.

One evening with Gerhardt was easier than hustling multiple Johns on the street. For thirty bucks, the young hustler offered his street clientele a blowjob, and for a hundred, they got to fuck him or do anything else that suited them. If the client was arrogant, pretentious, or flaunted his good fortune, the price went up. A self-taught entrepreneur, Dancer was surviving.

He withdrew his arm from underneath the old man's sweaty neck. With one eye on Gerhardt, Dancer scooted to the edge of the king-size bed. His arm had gone numb from the weight of the old man's head. Swinging both legs out, he quietly placed his feet on the warm bamboo floor.

Naked, Dancer rose onto his tiptoes and made his way to the ornately carved mahogany highboy dresser. There, he would find the twenties the old man had placed there at the beginning of the evening—payment for services. He snickered under his breath. He was a street hustler and, if he wanted, he could rob the old man blind. But none of the stuff that filled this lavish apartment was of interest to him. He had walked away from such amenities six years ago, just as he was doing now. The shower, the meal, and the money, on top of the new clothes, were more than adequate compensation for his services. He wasn't a thief, and this high-paying gig was something he would like to keep going as long as possible.

3

Next to the dresser was the pile of new clothes he had received when he arrived this evening. He had worn them earlier for less than an hour. The old man had the clothes laid out for him to wear after his shower. After dinner, they always ended up on the floor.

He found the new pair of jeans in the pile where he had left them and pulled them up over his ass. Cinching his belt, he stuffed the money down into his front pocket. Bare chested, he scooped up the rest of his new outfit and headed to the bathroom for his old clothes. He finished getting dressed and then made his way out of the apartment.

In the elevator, he zipped up his new coat as the car rattled past each floor without stopping. The luxuries of being a penthouse owner included the exclusive use of the elevator, which bypassed all the other floors when it left the penthouse on a nonstop flight down.

He walked past the security guard at the front desk, who pretended not to notice him. Without looking at the guard, Dancer reached the front doors, leaned his slender body into the massive, brass-handled glass door, and pushed.

An explosion of cold air hit his face, causing him to tuck his head down and pick up his step. He licked his lips, tasting a slight remnant of the old man's gin—alcohol, the devil's juice. Gin was what had turned his stepfather, Robert, into a monster. He swallowed several times, trying to keep the acid in his gut from reaching his throat. He tried to push away the memories that led to the morning when he had run away. His stepfather coming into his bedroom when his mother was away from the house. From the beginning, Dancer had never felt like saying no was an option. Robert had convinced him that he was only giving Dancer what Dancer himself wanted.

Dancer had blamed himself for what happened between him and Robert. He couldn't think of a time in his life that he wasn't aware of his own sexuality, his attention to the same sex that matured into an attraction. Initially, he had relished the attention that he received from Robert. It filled the void of his father's passing two years prior. Robert was a breath of fresh air in a house of mourning. He was also a predator who took advantage of a gay fourteen-year-old who was just hitting puberty and understood nothing. When Dancer did finally resist, Robert threatened to tell his mother what they had been doing, saying that his mother would never forgive him and would choose Robert over her own son.

4

In Dancer's mind, she had already chosen Robert over him the day she married him. What option had he had six years ago but to run? He couldn't have faced his mother if she knew what he had done.

One thought led to the next: alcohol, Gerhardt, Robert, his mother… his dad. He couldn't go there, not tonight. Not in this goddamned storm.

The streets were empty. The rain had driven everyone in early as they prepared for blizzard-like conditions. With the sidewalk all to himself, Dancer pushed through the wet wind as it ripped between the giant buildings and down into the street. The farther away from the apartment he walked, the more he could put this evening's events behind him. The wind forced him to pull his hoodie down over his face and tuck his head into his chest. He didn't need to see where he was going to get home; he had walked this neighborhood since he was fourteen years old.

He didn't look up at the sound of tires as they propelled the water between the rubber and the road next to him. He sensed without looking that the lone car had slowed to a crawl for several seconds before moving forward. As the car rolled ahead, he swiped the water from his face to get a better look at it. To his surprise, it was one of Brierton's finest, patrolling the empty streets.

Thanks for the ride, assholes, he thought. Not that he would have taken it if the cops had offered. In this life, you kept as much distance as possible between yourself and those who wore badges.

Dancer rounded the corner onto Roosevelt Boulevard and nearly tripped over a body stretched across the sidewalk. Bundled in blankets, the person had taken refuge over a metal grate that pumped out a steady stream of heat. Dancer guffawed as he sidestepped the human mound. For this stranger to consider a metal grate in the middle of the sidewalk an acceptable place to crash for the night, he must be suffering from a mental illness, too much booze, or a combination of the two.

It was ironic that the boiler system designed to carry heat into offices and pretentious high-rise apartments also served to warm the homeless in a far less extravagant setting.

He couldn't walk the last two blocks to the vacant lot that contained his shelter fast enough. Camp Roosevelt had been his refuge since running away from home. The camp was where *he* controlled what happened to him. Here, he counted on no one. Three hundred and sixty-six miles from Indian Waters, Mississippi, he was safe.

Several years before Dancer's arrival, Roosevelt Heights had been considered the ghetto of downtown Brierton. Then, it had become part of the city's revitalization project. The redevelopment included combining Theodore Roosevelt County Hospital with the trauma center and moving them both into a new state-of-the-art building on the outskirts of town. They renamed the new hospital Theodore Roosevelt General. A host of financial institutions, corporate headquarters, high-end shopping malls, expensive restaurants, luxury apartments, and penthouses made up the neighborhood now. The one thing the city never factored into their revitalization plan was what to do with the established homeless population Roosevelt General once served. They moved the hospital but left the people who depended on its services behind.

There had been several unsuccessful campaigns to move the homeless to other parts of the city, but these were always met with opposition by those who didn't want the homeless in their neighborhoods. Years later, the homeless encampment known as Camp Roosevelt remained. Population: two hundred.

As Dancer once again got a rush of cold air, he ran through a mental checklist of his blankets. Thank God for the ugly sweater under his hoodie that he had inherited from the old man tonight. Using the sweater and every blanket he owned, he should manage—he would be cold but okay.

Frigid and wet, he reached the tattered chain-link fence, which was riddled with holes. He maneuvered his freezing body through the fence and entered Camp Roosevelt. The ten vacant acres where the hospital once stood was now a city: an endless arrangement of tents, cardboard shelters, and lean-tos. The city was willing to spend billions of dollars restoring the neighborhood but not a single penny to help with housing the homeless. Tired of being pushed off the streets and harassed, the homeless now took refuge inside the fence surrounding the demolished hospital.

As Dancer approached his shelter, he noticed a new tent about ten feet in front of his makeshift doorway. *Who in the hell pitched a tent that close to my door?* Whoever it was, he would deal with them in the morning. At the moment, he was too damn cold.

Chapter Two

Tucker Graves crawled out of the small opening in the igloo-shaped tent to get a better look at his surroundings. Nervousness swirled in the eighteen-year-old's gut this morning as he relieved himself along the fence line. He, his mom, Sarah, and his six-year-old sister, Mattie, had arrived at the camp after dark the night before. They had finally hit rock bottom. Irritated and cold, his focus last night had been to set up the tent that they had received from the New Beginnings shelter. Annoyed that the shelter had put them out before the onset of last night's storm, he just wanted to get everyone inside the tent before the rain started.

He hadn't slept a wink all night. Between the storm pounding their tent and the unknown looming on the other side of the thin nylon, he wasn't about to shut his eyes.

Tucker cast a glance at his mother and Mattie before pulling the zipper down as he left and securing them inside. He stood guard at the front of the tent as his eyes moved about the camp. He remembered little of what he had seen last night.

It was, indeed, a homeless encampment. He battled the urge to retreat into the tent. This place was not them; they weren't *this* homeless. Like the laundry list of places they had slept in the last year, this was temporary. They weren't staying here.

He threaded his fingers through his dirty blond hair, removing oily strands from before his eyes. The rain had done little to remove the stench of urine, garbage, and dirt from the surroundings. Though his sister and mother were just inside the tent, Tucker had never felt more alone in his life.

He stretched his six-foot frame, his arms reaching for the dark sky. His heels lifted from the pavement as he released a growl from the back of his throat. He stared up at the dark clouds that were hiding the sun. This storm was not through with them just yet. He wasn't sure how much more rain he could take.

His drawn-out stretch released a flood of endorphins, stirring his senses into wakefulness. He could smell the smoke from a campfire burning close by; the noise of rush-hour traffic on the nearby highway echoed in his ears.

They had set the tent up on what appeared to be blacktop, likely a road once upon a time. He was surrounded by tents, lean-tos, and tiny structures made of everything he could have imagined, from wooden pallets to carpet. His eyes shifted to movement in front of a structure made from stacked milk crates.

The movement's source was a person, a man bundled in a waist-length down-filled grey jacket and orange hoodie. However, it was the man's jeans, or rather the butt inside the jeans, that shifted Tucker's attention and stirred his juices. The denim molded to the man's ass like a glove. No one, except football players, had an ass like that.

Butterflies fluttered in Tucker's empty stomach, sending surges through his chest and to his neck. He felt the heat rise to his cheeks and had to look away, even though the stranger had no idea he was there. Almost immediately, his eyes returned to the unsuspecting man who was causing his pulse to race. While playing baseball in high school, Tucker had developed a fondness for tight butts. However, being hungry and homeless and watching over his mother and sister left him zero time to satisfy his fondness.

Tucker watched as the guy wrestled with the blue tarp on top of the structure of milk crates. This stranger in the nice jacket and jeans looked out of place in the camp. His clothing didn't shout homelessness. Who was he?

"Can I help you with something?" said the man. His eyes locked onto Tucker, burning into him as if he knew everything Tucker had been thinking. He released the tarp, allowing it to fall to the ground. His deep-set green eyes under his hoodie held his stare. Mysterious and partly hidden, they bored into Tucker.

Embarrassed that he had been so transparent, Tucker shrugged and shook his head. The man's aggressive tone didn't threaten him, though. It was a challenge to stare him down and, more so, an opportunity to absorb those beautiful green eyes of his.

He had never backed down from a fight, but it was his first day here. Too early to get into a fight with a stranger. Just in case, he sized up the guy, who looked slightly smaller than him, though it was hard to tell in that large jacket. Tucker kept his eyes on the stranger, waiting for him to blink first.

The young man turned his attention back to his work, picking up the tarp from the ground and hurling it over the top of the structure. Watching the wind blow the tarp back onto the young man's body, Tucker laughed loud enough to be heard.

The man struggled for another minute or two as the tarp continued to get the best of him. After a couple of tries, he again stopped. "Can you help, or are you just going to stand there and watch?"

Tucker's ear picked up on a tiny southern drawl in the man's speech. *Texas, Arkansas, Mississippi?* Tucker's infatuation with the young man stopped him from telling the stranger to screw off. It was like watching a bad movie starring a hot main actor. How could he not stick around to see how it ended?

He looked over his shoulder at his tent. Mattie would be okay; he was only moving a couple of feet. He could keep an eye on his family and help the idiot with the tarp at the same time.

The couple of inches in height he had on the guy was enough to make securing the tarp across the roof easy. "What are you holding it down with?" he asked as his long arms held it in place.

The man handed him a long two-by-four. "Put this on it."

As instructed, Tucker tossed the wood on top of the tarp. "Really, a two-by-four? Do you have any nails, a hammer? This won't—"

"Does this look like a hardware store to you?" The man picked up a brick and handed it to Tucker. "Use this." His hoodie shielded most of his face, revealing only glimpses of his striking eyes.

"Oh yeah, this should do it." Tucker laughed as he placed the small single brick on top of the tarp next to the two-by-four.

"I'm glad you think something is so funny!" The man snatched his hoodie from his head, revealing a lustrous head of loosely spiraled curls. His green eyes deepened against his sun-kissed auburn hair.

Tucker was unfazed by his aggression and motivated by the stranger's beauty as he extended his hand. "I'm Tucker."

"I don't shake." The man's eyes glanced down to Tucker's hand before looking back up. As they passed over Tucker's face, his eyes lingered.

Retracting his hand, Tucker drew a breath as he restrained his impulse to knock the little shit out. "Okay, whatever. Me neither. What's your name?" He asked only out of politeness. At this point, he didn't care.

"What are you, the cops?" The man's dark eyes showed more mistrust than the curiosity Tucker thought he had seen. His cheekbones were of a prominent type reserved for a chosen few. A reminder of how ordinary and plain the rest of the world was.

"Look, I'm not trying to start a fight with you. And I'm certainly not the cops." Tucker blushed and turned to go. It was time to walk away—not out of exasperation but to obscure his attraction to the green-eyed Adonis.

"Dancer! My name's Dancer." The man's voice caught up with him.

Keeping his stride, Tucker raised his hand and waved. "It *was* a pleasure meeting you—Dancer."

When Tucker reached the tent, he fought off the urge to look back. He had more than enough to worry about without giving any thought to a socially dysfunctional asshole.

*****

Inside the tent, wrapped in the one thin blanket they shared, Mattie lay awake next to their mother, who was still asleep. Her bright blue eyes fixed on her brother. "Where are we?" she asked as she raised her head.

"Camp Roosevelt." Tucker knew this because that's what the people at New Beginnings had called it when they gave them directions last night. He had no idea what their next move would be, but he knew he had to find a shelter for them. They couldn't stay in this tent surrounded by homeless people.

This was the lowest point in his family's yearlong downward progression toward being homeless themselves. Before this morning, yesterday had been the lowest. They had reached New Beginnings' five-day limit and were told they couldn't stay a sixth night. This information, coupled with detoxing from a lack of drugs, had caused their mother to flip out and call Ian, the director of the shelter, a faggot, a cocksucker, and several other insults. This morning, reality set in yet again. Today was the *new* worst day of his life.

"I'm hungry." Mattie lifted her little face off his mother's arm. Her blonde curly hair was matted where she had been laying on it.

They had no food. Yesterday, Ian had told them to come back this morning for a hot breakfast at seven. He looked at his watch; it was ten after nine. Scratching his forehead, he knew he had to go out and find something for Mattie to eat. He also knew he had to take Mattie with him. He couldn't trust his mother to look after her. Hell, it was because of her drug addiction that they were here.

"Okay, baby girl. Get up. Let's find you something to eat." Even if breakfast was over at New Beginnings, maybe he could still get something for Mattie to eat there.

The curls in Mattie's hair this morning were more knotted than usual. Tucker worked slowly to comb them out with his fingers, not wanting to hurt her. When he was done, he pressed his mouth against the top of her head and kissed her. If it wasn't for her, he might have struck out on his own a long time ago. But he could never leave Mattie with their mother. He would never leave her. "You set?" he asked.

"Yep." Mattie looked up at him, her sky-blue eyes sunken and dark.

"It's not raining, but take my coat, it's cold." He removed his light jacket and draped it around her. "You have to stay warm, sweetie."

Unzipping the tent, he let Mattie out first before crawling out behind her.

"Where you goin'?" Sarah mumbled. The morning light shining through the open flap caused her to close her eyes.

"Out." Tucker refused to look at her as he zipped her inside. His eyes were drawn to Dancer's shelter. *Dancer.* Was that even his real name?

He was about to take Mattie by the hand when he realized he had left his backpack inside. "Hold on." He unzipped the tent and went back in.

He grabbed his backpack and then remembered he hadn't taken

his seizure medication. He dug down into his backpack, feeling for it. Locating the amber-brown plastic bottle, he opened it up and took the last of his Depakote. He hadn't had a seizure in over a year. Hopefully, he had enough of the medication in his system to last until he could figure out how to get more.

Tossing the empty pill bottle into his pack, he grabbed his cell phone, which lay where Mattie had been sleeping. It had ten percent battery life left. Although the phone had no service, it kept the date and time and a list of phone numbers that were now of no use. He looked around for anything he should take with them. He refused to leave anything of importance with their mother. Anything they ever had of value, she sold or traded for drugs when he wasn't looking.

He stepped outside and immediately saw that Mattie was gone. "Mattie," Tucker called as he looked around. He walked around the tent, sure she was going to be there. His heart sank when he saw that she wasn't. "Mattie!" He called for her again in a louder voice as he checked around a larger tent about ten feet from theirs.

Tucker shouted this time. "Mattie!" He went back to the front of the tent, hoping she had heard him calling for her. The hair on the nape of his neck rose. She was gone.

"Mattie!" Tucker took off toward the front of the camp. He looked down every row and opening as he continued to call for her. He reached the street but told himself that she would never walk out this far alone. She had to be inside somewhere.

As he ran back toward their tent, he saw her walking on the other side of the camp. She was holding hands with someone, and their backs were to him.

"Mattie!" Tucker took off at a full sprint. In seconds, he was right behind them. "Mattie!"

She turned around just as Tucker reached them and yanked her up. "What the hell do you think you're doing?" Tucker asked the man. The man's hollow eyes instantly told Tucker that no one was home. If Tucker hadn't had Mattie in his arms, he would have laid the guy out right there.

"He said he had candy. I want some candy," Mattie whined.

"What did I tell you about going with strangers!" Tucker's blood was boiling. He wanted desperately to pound this guy into the ground. Instead, he held Mattie and walked away.

When he was about twenty yards from the stranger, he stopped and put her down. "Mattie! What did I tell you about going with strangers? You don't know him!" He knew he shouldn't be yelling at her, but the rage inside of him had to come out. This had been close. "He didn't have any candy!" Tucker sighed, exasperated.

He took Mattie by the hand again as they walked toward the front of the camp and the street. They walked to the intersection. He refused to let go of her hand as he pushed the button to change the light for them. He took a deep, cleansing breath as they distanced themselves from the camp.

"I don't feel well," Mattie mumbled.

"What's wrong?" His impulse was to ignore her. He was still mad, not at her but at himself. That had been too close. His stomach churned at just how close it had been. Never again, never ever, he told himself.

"I don't know. My stomach hurts."

Her voice told him she was being whiny. "Okay. I bet after you have something to eat, you'll feel better. You need to eat something." Neither of them had eaten since they left New Beginnings yesterday.

"We have to get Mommy something too." Mattie looked up at him with an innocence that, in him, had been shattered long ago.

"Sure." He half smiled at her, a smile that shielded the truth about their mother, a strung-out meth-head. At six, Mattie didn't need to know the truth about her.

They rounded the corner and headed down Broadway toward New Beginnings. Passing a small corner market, Tucker's eye caught the *Help Wanted* sign in the bottom corner of the window. His urge to investigate this was immediately struck down by thoughts of his seizures, migraines, and the fact that he was a high-school dropout. Also, there was no way he was leaving Mattie alone with their mother while he worked.

A rain drop landed on his cheek, causing him to look up at the dark grey clouds. Could they make it to New Beginnings and back before it rained again? Nothing ever seemed to go his way, so there was no reason to believe this storm would be any different.

"C'mon, jump on my back." Tucker slid his little sister onto his back and secured her legs around his waist. Picking up the pace, he covered the mile and a half, arriving as more drops of rain dotted the sidewalk.

13

"Hey, guys. Where's your mom?" Ian, the shelter's director, asked as he met them at the front door.

"Um, she's not feeling well this morning. Still sleeping." It was the lie he had been telling everyone for years. As a child, before he fully understood what drugs were, he had initially believed it. He had kept the lie going out of embarrassment. He didn't want people to think ill of her. She wasn't always a bad mother.

Ian's frown was a sign that he didn't believe the lie. "I'm sorry to hear that. How did the tent work out for you?"

"Okay, I guess." Tucker refrained from telling him that it was cold, damp, and too small for the three of them. He accepted Ian's gesture for them to come inside.

Inside, the dry warmth pricked at Tucker's cheeks. "We made it there before the storm and were able to get the tent up in time. I know we missed breakfast, but I was hoping you could... maybe there was something left for Mattie," Tucker stammered.

Ian looked around as if checking who might be watching. "Come with me."

Tucker took Mattie's hand and followed Ian. A sense of relief that Ian was willing to help them washed over him. After the way his mother had treated Ian yesterday, he hadn't been sure. The incident this morning with Mattie still had Tucker rattled. The more he thought about it, the madder he became at himself. He had failed to protect her. It had happened so fast that he still couldn't quite wrap his brain around it. The close call had drained the last of his energy.

Ian's office was tiny. Tucker had to step in and to the left so Ian could close the door behind him. "Let me get another chair." Ian's voice matched his relaxed demeanor.

Ian's willingness to help them caused a release of tension that ran down the back of Tucker's neck. Nothing had gone his way in years. He remembered his mother telling him two months ago, on his eighteenth birthday, "Boys do what is easy, men do what is right." Maybe she'd meant that he, now, needed to be a man. That night, she had disappeared for three days, leaving them in the motel with only a box of cereal, a case of Cups of Noodles, and what was left of his Safeway birthday cake. Last week, finding New Beginnings had been a weight lifted from his shoulders. It was five days to breathe and not think about how badly he was failing as a man.

14

Ian moved a chair from behind the door and sat it next to the one in front of his desk. "Have a seat." He offered Mattie one of the two chairs. Ian moved to the other side of his desk and opened a cabinet. He retrieved two packs of cheese and crackers and a juice box. "Do you like these?" He held them out for Mattie to take.

She looked at her big brother before nodding *yes* to Ian's offerings.

Ian held one out for Tucker.

"Um, no thanks. But if it's all right, may I take it for her later? Um, in case she gets hungry?"

Ian reached back in the cabinet and grabbed a plastic bag and filled it. "I don't have much, but I like to keep a little stash in here. They lock the pantry between meal preparations." Ian shook his head. "Stupid policies."

Tucker's eyes moved between Ian filling the bag and Mattie as she ate her breakfast of cheese and crackers and drank her fruit punch.

Ian finished filling the bag and handed it to Tucker. "Don't say anything to anybody about this." He sat behind his desk. "So, your mom's not feeling well?" His eyes shifted between Tucker and Mattie.

Tucker recognized that Ian was talking in code. So, he knew their mother was a junkie.

"Um, yeah." Tucker glanced over at Mattie, who was oblivious to their conversation. "She's been sick for a while."

"Has she seen a doctor?" Ian asked.

Treatment? Tucker shook his head no.

"Are you the one who takes care of Mattie when your mom's sick?"

Tucker nodded, though at the moment, he didn't feel like he was doing any better than his mother.

"Is she in school?"

"She was. When we lived in Saint Charles." He remembered the last two-bedroom apartment they'd had before migrating to Brierton. Although they had only been in Brierton for three months, that apartment seemed a lifetime ago.

"Saint Charles? What brought you guys here?"

Tucker wasn't sure how to explain. He decided to keep his

answer short. "The truth? We've been evicted from every place we've ever lived. We moved here and were living with some of my mom's friends."

Ian took a big breath. "You guys were living over at the Newbury Inn on Bremmer Street for a while too, right? Before you came here?"

"Yeah, a couple of weeks." Tucker wondered what exactly his mother had shared with Ian while they had been in this shelter.

"So, what happened?" Ian asked.

Tucker shrugged as he looked at Mattie. "Just hitting some hard times." He remembered the day they were evicted from their apartment on Reid Avenue, when the sheriff allowed them thirty minutes to gather their belongings and get out. But that day had been nothing compared to their months of couch surfing in different people's homes or the two weeks they'd spent in a shitty motel before being kicked out for nonpayment. As much as he wanted to blame his mother for all of it, if he hadn't gotten hurt, they wouldn't be here. Once an all-star pitcher for his high school, his stardom ended his sophomore year with a fastball to the head. Knocked out, the injury had left him with seizures and migraines. It was the end of a once-promising pitching career that would've given him and his family everything they needed. He was sure he would have been one of the youngest pitchers in the major leagues. That seemed a lifetime ago.

"Were you able to finish high school?"

"Um, no." Tucker scratched his forehead. "I… dropped out." He had gotten what they had come for. He didn't need to walk down memory lane and answer a lot of questions from a stranger. Silence filled the small space for a minute or two.

Ian spoke up. "Well, we need to get Mattie back in school. You, too, one of these days." He scribbled on a notepad for a couple of minutes before tearing the sheet from the pad. "We have a school. Well, it's not ours, but it's across the alley out back. It services most of the homeless children in the neighborhood. They won't ask a lot of questions—they understand. Since you're eighteen, you can sign her in." As Ian handed the paper to Tucker, his eyes darted to Mattie for a split second. "My good friend Cal runs the program over there. It's a good school." Ian nodded.

Tucker stood up and took the paper from him. He read through the messy handwriting, *Calvin Robertson.* Below that Ian had scribbled something else:

Terry's House
4573 M Street
They can take Mattie if you need a place to take her.

Tucker folded the paper up and stuffed it into his pocket.

"Thank you." Tucker had heard about Terry's House. It was a "safe place" for children under the age of eleven. But he wouldn't leave her with strangers. She was his to take care of. He patted Mattie, and she stood.

"You have my cell phone number as well on there." Ian nodded toward Tucker's pocket. "If you need to get a hold of me, call."

Tapping Mattie on the back, Tucker signaled that it was time to go.

"But I'm not finished." Mattie cried.

"It's okay. Let her finish." Ian leaned back in his chair and scratched at his nose before pushing his glasses closer to his face. "As you know, the shelter is closed during the day. We don't open again until dinner time, when everyone returns for the night. I'm a little short-staffed today. I could use your help if you want to volunteer for a couple of hours, until the storm lets up a little."

Tucker felt that Ian was just taking pity on them. But the reality was, they had nowhere else to go. "Okay, like, what do you need done?"

"Well, the sheets are still in the washing machines. They need to be dried and folded for issuing tonight. Breakfast dishes need to be put up, and if you can stay, we need to prep for dinner service." Ian leaned forward in his chair, resting his elbows on his desk.

"I guess. What about Mattie?"

"Why don't you take her with you? I'm sure she would love to help too." Ian winked at Tucker.

"Okay... I have another question." Tucker reached for his backpack and pulled out his empty medicine bottle. "I take seizure meds—Depakote. I took my last one this morning." Tucker held out the bottle, showing Ian his name on the label.

Ian took the bottle and examined it. "Oh... I can't give you any

17

kind of medication. We don't have that kind of stuff here. Just aspirin, Tums, and some stuff for colds." He placed his hand against his chin and looked down. "You'll have to go out to Roosevelt General. See the doctor."

"That's fine." Tucker took his bottle back. "That's where I've been getting them. It's just…" he looked away.

"Do you need bus money?" Ian asked.

"No," he lied. He was sure their mother had already spent what little money they'd received this month from the county.

Opening his desk drawer, Ian pulled out several bus passes. "Here. These should get you out there and back. Go as soon as you can, okay?"

Tucker felt Ian's genuineness. Until today, he had only seen this man as "the director," sternly reciting the checklist of do's and don'ts over and over each night as they passed through the front door. Today, he was a different person. One who really did care.

Tucker worked for several hours with Mattie by his side, first in the laundry room and then helping to set up the dining room. Tucker and Mattie ate dinner with the staff before the doors opened for the evening services. After dinner, there was a break in the rain. If they hurried, Tucker could get them back to the encampment in dry clothes.

When Tucker and Mattie arrived back at Camp Roosevelt, he put her on his back and picked up his pace. He tried to sound cheerful to distract her from the filth and garbage that lined the paths through the encampment. His stomach churned his dinner as he avoided eye contact with everyone.

In his peripheral vision, he took it all in. The shelters, bicycles with carts attached, shopping carts covered with piles of trash and junk. He swiped at his nose, trying to wipe away the stench of the camp, and the realization hit him that this was now his life.

Chapter Three

After five days of rain, the break in the storm was more than welcome. It was needed. The break allowed Dancer to repair the worn tarp, which had slipped off the roof once again. The tarp had been on the shanty ever since Dancer moved in, and it was a problem every winter. The original occupant had been known as 'the Milkman.' Dancer assumed the Milkman had gotten his name by scavenging for the milk crates used to make his shanty. Yes, he might have been a little insane, but his idea was ingenious. It was sturdy, warm, and private.

Dancer had just gone to the Walmart and picked up a new tarp with metal eyelets around the edges. He threaded a rope through the eyelets and then threaded it in and out of the holes on the milk crates until it was secured across the top of the shack.

Proud of his fix, Dancer was happy that he wouldn't have to fight with that damn tarp anymore in the middle of the night. He was admiring his work when his new neighbor with the little girl came around the corner.

Over the last week, he had seen the new strawberry-blond guy a handful of times. Being from Mississippi, Dancer knew country, and a guy with a name like Tucker, who dressed in cowboy boots, jeans, and a plaid shirt, was about as country as they came. He was surprised to find that he remembered Tucker's name.

Dancer guessed the little girl was Tucker's sister and the older woman, the junkie, was their mother. He could spot a meth-head a mile away. It was too bad, because the little girl was as cute as an angel, and well, the brother... wasn't too bad himself.

If Dancer had a type, blond hair and blue eyes would win out every time. Rarely was Dancer attracted to another man, but the red plaid shirt and boots stirred his physical desires. The sexiness of a man in boots did it for him. Nobody in this damn city wore cowboy boots. They were all city slickers, "soft sissies" as his Oma use to call them.

Dancer forced himself to look away before the guy saw him staring. The guy was way too chatty, and the last thing Dancer wanted was another conversation with him. He turned away enough to ignore them as they walked past. He held his breath until they disappeared inside their tent.

Tagged on the nose by a raindrop, Dancer looked up at the darkened sky. The clouds were almost black. The weather alert system had reported the storm coming in tonight to be a cold one from the east. The drop in the temperature in the last thirty minutes told him the alert was right on.

He was about to go inside for the night when, out of the corner of his eye, he saw Tucker reemerge through the tiny opening of their tent.

"Hey, you haven't seen my mum, have you?" Tucker asked. The tone in his voice matched the stress spread across his face.

Dancer remembered, when he came back from Walmart, seeing her talking to a guy toward the front entrance. He didn't know the guy, but he was one of the camp's resident junkies and a thief to boot. Whatever the two were doing or discussing, it wasn't any of his business.

"Yeah, I saw her about an hour ago. Up front." He stopped short of saying she was talking to another junkie, most likely looking to score something. They held each other's gaze. Tucker's sky-blue eyes were striking yet soft. They were the color of the sky on a clear day, something Dancer hadn't seen in a while.

He wasn't the type to fantasize about someone, but there was something about Tucker that piqued his interest. The first time he had met the guy was last week while fixing his tarp. He found him to be bold, perhaps a little cocky. Tucker had been indifferent to Dancer's assertive antics. People either challenged Dancer's aggressiveness or succumbed to it. This country boy had done neither.

Tucker took a step away from his tent. His long fingers rubbed at the line across his forehead. "Okay…"

The furrowed, sandy blond brows said that he was thinking. He looked past Dancer toward the front of the camp. "Thanks." He took

20

another step away from his tent before stopping. His expression sobered as he turned around and retreated inside the tent.

*****

By evening, the wind had picked up again. The second half of last night's storm had arrived. The tarp flapped above his head as the wind attacked the shelter from the front. Confident that his new tarp would hold up, Dancer prepared to settle in for the night. The inside of his tiny shanty was illuminated by a battery-operated lantern; he had everything he needed in his ten-by-ten space to get him through the storm. Over the years, he had collected several blankets to cover the twin mattress on the floor. He also had an old camping stove, a hospital urinal container, plenty of freeze-dried food, bottled water, and his tablet, which was his only possession of any real value.

He had lived through five winters at the camp. The first one had been the worst. Cold, unprepared, and fourteen years old, he had arrived in Brierton in the middle of a storm with nothing but the jacket on his back. It was his fourth day on the streets, and he was hungry and freezing. He found a place behind a dumpster in an alley to try to hide from the rain. There was no place for him to go. The buildings and dumpster provided enough shelter to keep him dry. Sleeping, he hadn't heard the trash truck as it entered the alley the next morning. If it had not been for the Milkman dumpster-diving moments before and waking him, he might have been crushed between the dumpster and wall.

He had long forgotten what made him go with the Milkman that day, but it had been the day he came to his current home.

Not a day went by that Dancer wasn't thankful for the Milkman and his shelter. He rubbed his hands up and down the arms of his salvaged chocolate-brown recliner before getting up. He dipped his finger in the pan of hot water to check the temperature. It was getting close to a boil.

Terrified of the huge population of mice and rats in the camp, Dancer kept his food supply and clothes in two of his six grey plastic bins. The other four bins, stacked along the wall, were the Milkman's. Although he had gone missing three years ago, Dancer kept them in hopes of his return.

21

Dancer dug around in the smallest of the two bins, searching through his supply of food for a beef stroganoff meal that could be boiled in its bag for dinner. The box of freeze-dried food pouches cost more than he liked to spend on food, but they were handy on nights when he couldn't get out to find dinner.

He poured hot water into a cup, and then dropped in his tea bag. Another crack of the wind above his head shook the entire shack. He froze as if expecting the walls to come down on him. When that didn't happen, he resumed his dinner preparations, dropping the cooking bag into the remaining water. He then set the timer on his tablet for five minutes.

The inside temperature had cooled, forcing him to layer another sweatshirt over his current one. Satisfied the second sweatshirt would do the trick, he took to his bed and crawled under the blankets to keep warm while he waited for his dinner.

He had about twenty minutes left of *Halloween Two* that he hadn't watched the other day because the battery in his tablet had run down before the ending. Scary movies were his thing. Blood, guts, and panic left no room in his mind to think of his own life and circumstances.

The movie resumed with Laurie's haunting screams as Michael Myers chased her into the operating room. There was an echo to her scream that caused Dancer's head to turn toward the front door. Hearing it again, his breath hitched. The screaming was coming from outside. The screech echoed again, and this time it was clear that it was a man's voice. Dancer hesitated, hoping that the wind was playing tricks.

The screams grew louder. It was someone out there. Maybe even two people. Was it a fight? This wouldn't be anything out of the norm in the camp, but in this storm? It sounded as if someone was being bludgeoned to death, like in his movie. Against his better judgement, he moved over to the door. As he slid the old accordion closet door open, he was hit with wind and rain chased by the screams.

He was shocked to see that Tucker and his sister were out there, and they were fighting to hold on to what was left of their tent. Tucker was struggling to straighten out the uprooted tent as if he could save it.

Dancer went into action and jumped in to help. He took ahold of the remains of the tent, but it couldn't be saved, at least not in the middle of this storm. "I don't think you can fix this!" Dancer yelled against the howl of the wind.

"It's all we have!" Tucker screamed.

There was little they could do to save the tent; the wind had torn it into rags. "Let it go! Come inside. When the storm passes, we'll fix it!" Dancer wiped the water-filled curls from his face so he could see.

"No!" Tucker put his foot on part of the tent to hold it.

They couldn't stand there holding the tent as they mulled over what to do. "Goddammit! Look at her!" Dancer's eyes shot down to the little girl. "You'll kill her out here! Come inside!" Dancer jerked Tucker's hands loose from the tent. "Let it go!"

Tucker turned his attention to his sister, ushering her inside the shack behind Dancer. "Watch her!" He yelled to Dancer.

By the time Dancer turned around, Tucker was gone. *Is he still trying to save the tent?*

Mattie's crying told Dancer to stay with her. "Are you okay?" He dropped to one knee and scanned her body for any obvious cuts. Other than being soaked and crying, she did not seem physically injured.

As if a frantic child wasn't enough, Tucker's return to Dancer's small enclosure drove Dancer's heart into his throat. It had been years since there had been another body inside his place. Tucker was only a couple inches taller than he, but it was enough that the low ceiling made him duck. Tucker's presence dwarfed the space, and anxiety began to swirl in Dancer's gut. He'd done something he had never done before. He knew nothing about this person, and yet he had allowed him into his sacred space. Nobody came into his space. Nobody.

Chapter Four

Dancer held his breath as the two stood face to face in the low light. Tucker was holding two backpacks. *Of course, that's what he went back for.* Dancer understood this all too well. Everything precious that you owned could fit into a backpack.

Dancer shifted his weight to his other leg and took a step back. He didn't like having anyone in his space. It no longer felt like his. "What the hell happened?" Anger gave him a voice. Not only was he pissed, he was wet and freezing. He stared into Tucker's eyes, his stare being the kryptonite that gave him power to control a situation. The water dripping from Tucker's face couldn't have been sexier. Still, he had to look away to stop himself from seeing Tucker as anything but an intrusion.

"It was the wind!" Tucker kneeled on both knees and wrapped his arms around his sister. "It will be okay." His pale face and rosy cheeks glistened from the rain water. "We were in there, and the wind hit it, and folded it up around us. It collapsed. It took forever to get out. By the time we could find the zipper and got out, it was destroyed. I thought we would die in there." Tucker held Mattie close as he rubbed her shoulders. "It's okay, baby girl. We're fine. Shhh, stop crying."

"But what about Mommy?" Mattie worked to control her hiccups.

"She'll find us. I'll keep watch for her." His brows bumped together in a scowl.

Although Dancer had no idea where their mother was, he knew what had happened out there. Tucker had pitched the tent on cement and hadn't used the stakes that came with the damn thing to anchor it. It was a wonder it had taken this long to fold up on his dumb ass. Dancer avoided eye contact. Every time he looked at Tucker, he lost the ability to focus.

24

The sound of the boiling water on the stove caught his ear. He reached down and turned off the stove, leaving the bag floating in the pot of water. Without the sound of bubbling, the place was quiet. A chill ran up the back of his spine, causing his shoulders to quiver.

They were soaked. The three of them were dripping water on his collection of rugs that covered the asphalt. "Come on, we need to get you guys into some dry clothes." Dancer grabbed a small towel and handed it to Tucker to dry his face before going into the bin that kept his clothes. He was sure he had something he could part with in case they didn't give it back.

"We're fine." Tucker rose to his feet, again lowering his head to avoid the ceiling. Bringing Mattie against his legs, he smoothed out her hair with his hand.

"Mattie?" Dancer turned to look at the little girl. Clothing-wise, he didn't have much to offer her. He pulled out a pair of cotton sweats and a sweatshirt and passed them to Tucker. "Try these on her. They'll be too big, but they're dry."

He took another look at Tucker, sizing him up for something to give him. Tucker was taller and thicker than him. Dancer's clothes wouldn't fit. Dancer grabbed one of the two blankets off his mattress. "Here… use this until I can find you something. Get out of those clothes."

Tucker handed Mattie the sweats before taking the blanket. "Thank you." He turned his back to Dancer and kneeled in front of his little sister. He pulled her wet clothes off, stripping her down to her panties. Her little body trembled as Tucker used the towel to dry her. He glanced back at Dancer and then shielded Mattie's body with his own. "Take your undies off and put these on." Again, Tucker glanced back at Dancer.

Dancer understood and looked away, focusing instead on his dinner on the stove.

It only took Tucker a second to dress her. "Thank you." His tone was filled with sincerity.

The *thank you* told Dancer it was safe to look up. It was surreal, seeing the little girl dressed in his clothes. Not wanting to stare, he looked up at Tucker. Their eyes met. Tucker's bloodshot blue eyes spiked Dancer's adrenaline, causing him to break eye contact. "You need to get out of your wet clothes too."

Tucker rose to his feet and toe-kicked his cowboy boots off. He then pulled the striped red-and-black plaid shirt up over his head. It came off in a single pull. Tucker reached for his belt. *Was Tucker going to strip right there in front of him and his little sister?*

Dancer turned away, facing his bedding along the back wall. His tablet lay on top of his mattress. He knew nothing about this guy who he had invited into his space. Keeping his back to Tucker, he slipped the tablet between the blanket and the mattress.

"You can look now." There was a laughter in Tucker's voice.

Dancer rolled his eyes at being laughed at before turning around. The sight of Tucker wrapped in his blanket stole his breath. Draped off one shoulder, it covered him from there to his knees. "I was *not* trying to look!" Dancer's eyes darted around, looking for a safe place to rest. He looked down, his eyes falling to Tucker's big bare feet. They were beautiful, long, and narrow. Dancer forced himself to look up.

Physical attraction was something that rarely happened for Dancer. His clients were nasty middle-aged men. The few who came along that were decent looking had the freakiest requests. He had stopped seeing them as anything but a body in front of him. He had learned a long time ago to shut out his emotions. Get the money and move on. But Tucker stirred something in him. Dancer felt a nervousness deep within his belly, and it made him uncomfortable. He tried to reduce Tucker to a body, but it wasn't working. He needed more than kryptonite, something stronger, to tamp down this strong reaction.

Fear fluttered in his gut. The thought of pushing Tucker out the door crossed his mind several times. This intrusion of Tucker into his space was as loud as the pot of water boiling minutes ago. Did Tucker sense his discomfort? Why was Tucker staring at him? He knew better than to look back at him, but he did. Their eyes met. He was flirting with danger. His eyes settled on Tucker's hair, which felt like the only safe place to focus. The blond curly mess had formed tiny rings that released water one drop at a time. Dancer's internal conflict rose to the next level, from uncomfortable to panicky. "Um… um." He had lost his words.

Mattie moved behind her brother. Wrestling one arm out of the blanket, Tucker shored it up around his shoulder and chest. Dancer glanced at Tucker's muscular bicep and his massive hands, which swooped around from behind and moved Mattie in front of him.

"Thank you again—um… It was Dancer, right?" Tucker extended his hand and then retracted it. "That's right, you don't shake."

"You're welcome. It's the least I could do since you helped me out with the tarp the other day." Tucker's eyes moved around the small room. Dancer was protective of his space, and Tucker's wandering eye added to his anxiety.

"Yeah, right." Tucker nodded. "I was wondering how warm these milk crates kept it inside here. But now I see." Tucker ran a hand across one of the tarps that had been hung on the inside of the shack to prevent the cold air from seeping inside.

While Tucker stared at the walls, Dancer stared at him. In the low light, the pale skin on his shoulders said they were soft. His skin was begging Dancer to touch it.

"Can we go find Mommy? I don't wanna stay here," Mattie's tiny voice trembled.

"Your mom never came back?" Dancer asked.

"No, not yet." Tucker's hand fell to the top of Mattie's head, where it rested until his blanket slipped. He caught the blanket at his waist and pulled it back up over his shoulders.

Was he naked under the blanket, or was he wearing underwear? The thought of Tucker's naked, beefy body under the blanket sent an unexpected rush of blood to Dancer's groin. Dancer tried to shake the thought as he scratched at his wet hair. The wetness was a reminder that he had to get out of his wet clothes.

"I need to change." He hesitated, seeing that Mattie was watching him. He needed to break free from the influence of Tucker's commanding presence. "Get out of my wet clothes. Can you guys turn around?"

Tucker chuckled as an acknowledgement to his request.

Dancer moved fast, finding another pair of jeans and a sweatshirt. Without drying off, he switched out of his wet clothes. "Okay, I'm done."

Tucker turned around, his eyes scanning his change in clothing.

"Can I get you something to eat or drink? Is she hungry?" Dancer softened his voice. He didn't want the kid frightened of him. "I have beef stroganoff if you're hungry."

27

"I don't like beef stroganoff." Mattie eased from behind Tucker but kept her eyes fixed on Dancer.

"Yes, you do!" Tucker looked down at Mattie. "Mum used to make it all the time." Tucker looked down in the pot. "That's stroganoff?" His lip curled up toward his nose as his brows furrowed.

Thinking of how Tucker said *Mum* instead of *Mom*, Dancer wasn't sure if he should be insulted by Tucker's facial expression at his dinner.

"I don't like it anymore," Mattie whined.

Tucker grimaced. "You're being rude."

While his attention was on his sister, Dancer stole another look at Tucker's arms and biceps. "Can I get you something to drink? Juice, hot tea… That's about all I got."

"We're fine. But I need to go back out there and get our suitcases. They're still in the tent. I need something to put on."

"Don't be crazy. You can't go back out there. Listen to how hard it's raining." His ears confirmed what he had said. The storm was hammering the outside of the shack.

"It's all we have! I'm not going to let my stuff get stolen!"

"There's no one out there. Listen to that storm." Dancer held out his hands as if stopping Tucker from leaving. "Trust me, they will be fine. You can go out there as soon as the storm lifts a little."

Tucker stuck a finger in his ear and wiggled the water out. "I can't wear this blanket."

"Why not? It'll keep you warm."

Tucker ran his fingers through his hair. "We need to find some place to go, and I'm not walking around with a blanket on me."

As Tucker spoke, Dancer watched his Adam's apple bob in his long, narrow neck. Tiny blond whiskers ran from his chin to his neck. "Where're you going? Where do you think you're going to find a place to go in this storm? Every shelter on this side of town is packed. You're not going anywhere, not tonight." Dancer regretted the words as they were leaving his mouth. "You can stay here for tonight." He nodded toward his bedding. "You two can take my bed. In the morning, you can get your stuff out there and go to the shelter or whatever."

"Um, okay. Do you want this?" Tucker started to remove the blanket.

Dancer held out his hand to stop him. "No!"

"Really?" Tucker chuckled. He pretended to release the blanket, exposing his left nipple.

Tucker's teasing sent a massive wave of fluttering butterflies to Dancer's stomach. He wanted to flee, but there was nowhere to go. How dare he do that in front of the little girl? His arrogance matched his stupidity. "I'm not interested."

"O-kay—I was only joking." Tucker's brows furrowed. "I didn't mean to offend you." He pulled the blanket over both shoulders. The embarrassment on Tucker's face confirmed that he had only been teasing.

"No offense taken. Do you want the bed or not?" Dancer's tone was taut. He didn't want to play with this guy.

"That depends." Tucker looked at him sideways. "You're not going to kill me in my sleep, are you?"

How dare this country ape continue to tease him in his own house, especially after Dancer had helped him? Dancer bit his tongue, hoping it was enough to stop him from going off. But it was Mattie, hiding behind her brother, that stopped him. He took a breath, long enough to let Tucker's teasing go. "Sorry." The apology was barely audible, but he said it. "I need my pillow, though." He snatched the other blanket and his pillow from the top of his bed.

He stepped over the stove to their side of the room. With a nod, he instructed them to move to the bed on the other side.

With them out of the way, he tossed his blanket and pillow onto the recliner. "I'll make you some hot tea. It will help you sleep." He directed his offer at Mattie.

He removed the food bag from the warm water before digging down in his food bin for a tea bag. "Do you want tea too?" he asked Tucker.

"Sure. If you have enough." Tucker's eyes followed him.

Dancer poured the lukewarm water into a cup and sunk a tea bag into it. "I don't have any sugar or anything." He looked around for something in which he could make a second cup of tea. He found a plastic cup and checked to make sure it was clean. Pouring water into the cup, he sunk his last tea bag into it and handed it to Tucker.

"Thanks." Tucker took the cup and guided Mattie onto the bed. He took a sip and then nodded. "Ah, that's good. Orange ginger?"

Dancer was surprised that Tucker recognized his favorite tea, the only flavor he bought. "That's right. I love it on a cold night like tonight."

"Aren't you having any?" Tucker extended his cup to Dancer.

"I'm good." Dancer took a seat in his chair and then remembered his tablet was in the bedding. If Tucker sat on it, he would crack the screen. "Can you hand me my tablet?"

Tucker looked around his immediate space.

"Inside." Dancer pointed to the mattress. "It's under the blanket."

Tucker leaned back and twisted his arm down under the one remaining blanket on the mattress. The blanket around Tucker pulled up, revealing enough of his inner thigh to confirm he wasn't wearing underwear while avoiding full-on exposure. Pulling the tablet out, he examined the device. "This is cool. Wireless or Jetpack?"

"Um… Internet card from Walmart." Dancer blinked before reaching out and taking the tablet. He slid it between him and the arm of the chair. He didn't want to, but he couldn't stop looking at Tucker's creamy white thigh. This man, this stranger in his house, was knocking him off his game, a game in which he was always in control. When tricking, he was in control, whether the John knew it or not. It didn't matter how much they were paying or what they wanted; he was in control. If the John moved his hand across his bare ass, Dancer might grab him by the wrist and tell him no, to show his control. It was a dangerous game, but a necessary one. If he wasn't guarded, the John had the potential to get rough.

Dancer's eyes shifted to Mattie. She worked as a distraction from the partial Full Monty in front of him. The little girl sat huddled next to her brother.

"So, how long have you lived here?" Tucker asked.

"A while." His answer was clipped. With a John, his answer would have been something they wanted to hear. This guy wasn't a John, and he wasn't a friend. Dancer had no friends.

"Do you live here by yourself?"

Dancer nodded. Another question. This was not how he had envisioned his night going an hour ago.

"How old are you?" Tucker asked.

More questions. It took a second for Dancer's true age to come to him. He had been lying about it for so many years that it had become a random number, whatever he thought the John wanted to hear. "Twenty."

"You seem older."

Tucker's comment sent heat to his cheeks. Older wasn't good in his profession. They liked them young. The younger the better.

"Tomorrow, I'll take Mattie, and we will go back over to New Beginnings. Maybe we can get in. I think the director likes me."

Dancer's ears perked. Was he insinuating something sexual about the director? First the blanket bit, and now this, another sexual innuendo? Was Dancer reading too much into it all? And what did it matter? This was a stranger who would be gone tomorrow.

"I can't believe how sturdy this place is for being made of milk crates," Tucker said as Mattie's drooping eyelids rose at the sound of his voice.

"Yeah, it's sturdy. Look, I'm not much of a talker. Do you mind?" Dancer shifted in his chair, looking for a comfortable spot. He was not willing to admit that it wasn't the chair but, rather, the vanilla thighs and hamstrings in front of him that were causing him so much anxiety.

"Yeah, yeah, I get it, dude. It's just..." Tucker's voice trailed off.

Quietly, the two sat. The only sound came from the raging storm as it attacked the camp. After about twenty minutes, seeing that Mattie's eyes had closed, Tucker gently peeled the mug from her hands. "Hey, baby girl. Lay back. You're sleeping."

Mattie resisted. "But what about Mommy? Is she coming back tonight?" Her little body swayed before reclining.

"I'll keep watch for her. Go to sleep. If she comes, I'll wake you up, okay?"

"Okay."

Dancer watched as Tucker adjusted her body in the bed and pulled the blanket up over her. His body stretched out as he leaned backwards to kiss her goodnight. The blanket that covered his body slipped from his shoulders, resting at his waist. His entire upper body was exposed as well as his long legs and bare feet. Dancer had a beautiful, naked young man in front of him, and all he wanted to do was sink into his chair until he disappeared. Tucker kissed his sister on the forehead twice and then brushed her hair out of her face. "One from Mommy and one from me. Sweet dreams."

Tucker looked up at him. "Man, I think I'll go to bed too. If that's okay?"

"Of course." A sense of relief washed over Dancer. He was exhausted from the internal conflict that had been whirling within him ever since Tucker stepped into his world. Before Tucker, Dancer had created an existence where he was in control of his feelings all the time. He didn't get emotional. No one touched him unless it was agreed upon first. He said yes or no; it was all mechanical. It was his work. His own pleasure never entered in to it. No one stirred anything in him, so why couldn't he stop himself from staring at Tucker? Tucker took his control away, and he didn't like it. More accurately, he didn't understand it. He wanted nothing more than for tonight to end.

From the corner of his eye, he tried not to watch as Tucker pulled his blanket over himself and snuggled next to his sister. When Tucker folded one arm around her, his back muscle stretched the blanket, making a wall between Dancer and Mattie.

Did he do that to protect her—from me? Dancer looked over at his unopened dinner. He would pass on dinner tonight. "Do you mind if I turn the lantern off? It runs on—"

"It's your place. Do whatever you want." Tucker's body never moved.

Dancer sat staring at the flannel blanket that covered his guest. With Tucker's back to him, his stare would go undetected. Thoughts of the men he had been with over the years played in his head. They came to him, and the power of rejection was always his. Those men were never anything other than a way to make money, to survive. A master of detachment, Dancer had no use for people other than that.

But Tucker stirred something in him, bringing his loneliness to the surface. A week ago, when he first saw Tucker, he had dismissed the lingering thoughts of him. That day, they had hardly said two words to each other that he could remember, and yet, Dancer had thought about Tucker for hours after that. Then, each time he had seen him around camp that week, his heart jumped.

A flush of adrenaline tingled through Dancer's body. His breath was shallow and rhythmic, the walls of his chest barely expanding. This was all nonsense, and he needed to put it away. He took one last glance at the back and shoulders hidden under the blanket before turning out the lantern. What he wanted was to touch the porcelain skin beneath the blanket.

Chapter Five

The sun hadn't risen yet when Tucker woke everyone with his failed attempt to be quiet. Wanting to retrieve their suitcases that had been left outside last night, he stood in front of the white bi-fold closet door that covered the shanty's entrance. Baffled, he tried several different ways to either move the door or slide it open, but it wouldn't budge. Tucker had barely escaped the simple zipper in the tent last night; the complicated locking system of the shanty was beyond his understanding.

He thought he was being quiet until, in a huff, Dancer sprang from his chair and, without a word, slammed the latches on both sides of the door and freed it.

Gone for only a few minutes, Tucker returned with three canvas suitcases. Mattie was still asleep. Dancer had returned to his chair and was covered by his blanket. Tension radiated from under the fabric. He was sure Dancer was awake under there but chose to let sleeping dogs lie.

He took a seat on the mattress, trying to be quiet as he rifled through his bag. Relieved that everything was dry, he pulled out a pair of jeans and a sweater.

Mattie stirred next to him. After a couple of minutes, her eyes opened and stared up at him. Tucker reached over and grabbed her bag, hoping her clothes were also dry. They were, and he pulled out her pink jeans and laid them in front of her. "What top do you want?" Tucker held up two different sweaters.

"The blue one." Mattie pointed to her favorite sweater. "You went to sleep last night. I saw you." Mattie took the blue sweater Tucker was holding.

"I wasn't sleeping. Just resting my eyes." He knew what she was implying. "I would've heard if she came back." Movement under the blanket caused him to stop talking as he waited for Dancer to surface.

33

Tucker hesitated for a second longer before working up the nerve to say something. "So, I imagine, somehow, I pissed you off with the door. I'm sorry." Tucker wanted to be nice to the guy since he had saved them and all.

The mound under the blanket remained still.

So, I made a little noise this morning. Is it really the end of the world? If Tucker had anywhere else to go last night, he would have gladly gone there instead of subjecting himself and Mattie to this rudeness. "Can I make coffee or something?" He stared down at the tiny propane tank attached to the ratty camping stove. He had no idea how to work the camping stove, but how hard could it be to figure out? "Are you awake?"

Like a ghost jumping from a closet, Dancer threw the blanket off and sprang from his chair for the second time.

"Goddammit!" Dancer dropped to his knees and slammed a small pot onto the stove. He filled it halfway with water from a jug and then pushed the red button several times until it lit. "It's five o'clock in the goddamn morning! Why on earth would I still be sleeping?" Dancer crawled back into his chair and flipped the blanket back over his head. He was under there less than a second before snatching it off again. "I don't have any coffee! I drink tea, and you used the last tea bag last night! Use the ones from last night!"

Five o'clock? Mortified, Tucker couldn't believe it was only five. That explained why it was still dark. He felt like an idiot for not realizing how early it was. He had only slept for a couple of hours, but sleeping on a real mattress compared to sleeping on the floor in that cramped tent the last five days, felt like they'd been upgraded to a suite. He had never stayed in an actual suite, but he'd seen them on tv enough to know they were reserved for the rich. "Look, I said I was sorry. As soon as it's light, we'll get out of here." Heat rose to his cheeks, knowing he had nowhere to go.

Dancer didn't look at him as he got up for the third time, this time to turn the lantern on. As the light illuminated the tiny room, Tucker's eyes focused on the baggy navy sweatpants that hung low from Dancer's narrow waist. He was as thin as Steven McDowell, Tucker's eighth grade crush.

He had been infatuated with Steven during the summer between the eighth and ninth grades. For two hot summer months, they had been inseparable, making out every chance they got to be alone. But to Tucker's shock, it had ended the first week of the new school year. He spotted Steven and Beverly Rice, the freshman squad leader of the cheerleading team, necking in the halls. It was as if Tucker never existed.

Dancer was far cuter then Steven. His thin body pushed up against his bins as he searched their contents. Tucker watched as Dancer shoved things around before raising his head out the bin.

"I have cocoa." His tone was flat as he showed it to Mattie. "It's the only thing I have." His voice was softer than just a second ago.

"Yes, please." Mattie mumbled before Tucker had a chance to answer.

"Here!" Dancer held out the box to Tucker. "I assume you know how to make it?"

"Yeah." Tucker's voice cracked as the word caught in his throat. He took the box of cocoa and forced a smile that only rose on one side of his mouth. He glanced over at Mattie, and if Steven McDowell wasn't enough of a reminder that he was failing in life, seeing his little sister sleeping in her clothes with a dirty face drove the point home. *What did I do to be born into such a screwed-up life?*

"And where are you going this early in the morning?" Dancer never looked up as he stared into the pot of water.

"Why do you care?" Tucker repositioned the flannel grey blanket. He debated whether he should change into his clothing now or wait.

"I care where you're planning on dragging your little sister. If you're heading over to New Beginnings, they don't serve breakfast until seven."

"By the time we get there and get in line, it'll be close. Maybe Ian will be there. Get another tent or something." Tucker picked up his jeans, which were lying next to him. He held the blanket in place as he stood up and slipped his jeans on under it. Once his jeans were on, he dropped the blanket to the floor. He glanced over at Mattie in case she needed his help.

The weight of being homeless, hungry, and dependent on others was overwhelming. He wanted to throw himself onto the mattress and toss the blanket back over his head and sleep. But with his mother gone, this wasn't an option. Anger bubbled within him. It was all his mother's fault. Every bit of what was wrong was her fault.

35

It hadn't always been this way. His early childhood memories, when it was just him and his mum, were good. That was before the drugs, before Mattie. After Mattie was born, it was never the same. He believed that was when she started using.

"It's not Walmart! Like he has some big warehouse full of tents to pass out to people." Dancer dipped his fingers in the pot of water, checking the temperature.

"Well, maybe we could get a bed and stay there again." Tucker tossed his sweater over his head and pulled it down around his stomach. He heaved a heavy sigh before dropping back onto the mattress.

Dancer shook his head. "Not likely. Not without your mom. She and Mattie were the only reason *you* got in. Women and children take priority, then seniors and people with medical issues. You're at the bottom of the totem pole." Dancer poured hot water into the cup Mattie had used last night. He extended the pot toward Tucker. "Do you want some?"

"No." Tucker's stomach was in knots. The last thing he wanted was to put something in his stomach that would run through him. Was it his meds wearing off that was making him nauseous? This would be his third day without them. He clung to the hope that maybe he didn't need them anymore and the nausea would pass.

Dancer passed the cup of hot chocolate over to Mattie. "Be careful. It's hot."

Her tiny hands cupped the mug as she blew across the top. "Thank you."

Tucker watched as Mattie took a sip. Assured it wasn't too hot for her, he sat back to wait for her to finish. He hoped she wouldn't take forever. He still had to comb her hair.

When the two of them were ready, Tucker gathered up their bags. "Can you get the door for me?" He tilted his suitcase down so he could stack his mother's suitcase on top.

Taking two steps to the door, Dancer unlatched it and moved it to the side. His arms folded across his chest, he stepped aside for them to pass.

"Thank you for letting us crash here last night. I appreciate it." Uncomfortable making eye contact, Tucker focused on a small mole above Dancer's lip. He balanced their luggage carefully as he tapped

Mattie on her shoulders, urging her to move faster. He again looked at Dancer and forced a smile, hoping somehow it would come off as sincere.

Thankfully, it wasn't raining. His lungs welcomed the fresh air outside of the shanty. It was as if he had emerged from a dark hole. But a quick glance told him he was still in Hell. Broken furniture, coolers, and garbage lined the path that led them out of the camp. He moved Mattie closer to him. They were leaving this shithole.

The walk back to New Beginnings was now a familiar one. The air outside the camp was cooler, maybe in the low thirties. Gladder to be out of the camp with each step, Tucker saw the dark clouds separating as the morning sun rose between the massive buildings of the city.

He kept an eye out for their mother. Not sure what he would do if he saw her, he tried to ignore the possibility that she was dead. He tried to switch his thoughts to baseball. He held onto that for only a second before the image of Dancer standing in his sweats this morning popped into his head. The man's wildly shaggy hair and the mole above his lip were about as sexy as it got. He was bitchy but, without question, easy on the eyes.

It took less than half an hour to walk the several blocks back to the shelter. By the time they arrived, there was a line of fifty people waiting alongside the building.

They took their place behind a young African American woman. Within seconds, Tucker realized that the woman was talking to someone who wasn't there. *Schizophrenia.* It was the one thing that made him nervous. The schizophrenics whom he had encountered always seemed agitated and ready to fight.

With people loitering all around them, he looked at everyone that could be a potential danger. Taking care of himself and Mattie was not the only problem. He was afraid that if he was arrested for fighting, Mattie would be put into the system.

Damn his mother. He'd lost count of how many times she had disappeared on them. This time, he couldn't go looking for her without someone to watch Mattie. He refused to take his sister to the places he would likely find her. The last thing Mattie needed to see was her blown out of her mind in a crack house. He'd seen it on more than one occasion, and it never got easier.

If he didn't find her in the next day or so, he could be sure she would spend every penny of the cash aid they had received from the Illinois Department of Human Services. He could kick himself in the ass for leaving the debit card with her yesterday.

"I have to pee." Mattie tugged on his hand.

"Do you have to go really bad, or can you hold it for a minute?" Tucker asked.

"I've been holding it." Mattie crossed her legs as she held herself.

Tucker turned to look at the person behind him. If Santa was homeless and in a wheelchair, this was him. There were at least another hundred people behind them. If they got out of line, there was no way any of these people would hold their spot for them. He thought for a second of letting her try to go up to the door by herself, to see if they would let her in to pee. "Just try to hold it. Can you?"

"I can't," Mattie cried.

There was nothing else he could do. He couldn't let her pee her pants. Tucker grabbed her hand and they rushed to the front door.

He pounded on the steel door several times until the door opened. Thank God, it was Ian.

"What's wrong?" There was a moment of irritation in Ian's eyes for a split second as he opened the door.

"Can I please bring Mattie inside? She has to pee really bad!" He wouldn't take no for an answer. He wouldn't let her pee on herself in the middle of the street in front of everyone.

Ian's shoulders fell as he moved away from the door. "I can let you in just to pee, but then you will have to go back outside." His brows narrowed as he looked at the crowd.

"Thank you." Tucker pushed Mattie inside and hurried her toward the restrooms across the hall from the dining room. Releasing her hand so she could go in alone, he positioned his back against the wall next to the door. From afar, he watched Ian interact with several people preparing the dining room for service.

Whatever they were cooking this morning smelled liked boiled dirty socks. He had smelled it once last week when they were staying here. He remembered someone calling it "Shit-On-A-Shingle," an awful meaty gravy served over a piece of toast. With an upset stomach, there was no chance he would eat that this morning.

Mattie took forever before coming out. She struggled to zip her little body back into her coat.

"Did you wash your hands?" Tucker pulled himself off the wall.

"Yeah," Mattie said.

"It's yes, not yeah." He grabbed her hand and headed for the front door as promised. He was doubtful that they could get their place back in line, but he would try. A couple of feet from the door, he heard his name called.

"Tucker... Tucker... Mattie!" Ian rushed up behind them. "We're opening the doors in a few minutes. Why don't you take Mattie on into the dining room? The feed line is not ready, but go on in." Ian seemed more relaxed now, the irritation across his forehead gone.

"Are you sure?" Tucker wasn't asking for any special favors. He simply didn't want Mattie to pee in her pants, which would become a lifelong memory for her. He hoped that someday this would all be either a faded memory for her or blocked out altogether. But he had little confidence in hope. It had done nothing but fail him so far.

"Sure. It's okay." Ian rested his hand on Tucker's shoulder. "I know how cold it is out there. Is your mom still outside?"

"Um, no. We haven't seen her since yesterday. When we left here, by the time we made it back to the tent, she was gone."

Ian's eyes stared into Tucker's as if trying to gather more information without him saying anything else. "Gone?"

"We haven't seen her. I was hoping that maybe she was here."

"No. We had a full house last night with the storm and all. I haven't seen her. You want me to check with some other shelters, or the police?"

Mattie's eyes widened.

"If you don't mind, could you? She might be under Sarah Miller, instead of Graves." He had no idea why she used Mattie's dad's last name. The guy was such a loser. It wasn't like they were ever serious.

Ian patted him on his shoulder, which did little to reassure him of anything. "Sure. Give me a couple of minutes. I have to get breakfast going. Get the doors open and these people inside, out of the cold. I'll come find you when I know something. Don't leave, okay?" Ian looked down at Mattie. "Go have breakfast, and I'll see if I can find your mommy for you."

Tucker squared his shoulders. "Thank you." His face said more than his words.

*****

Ian walked into the hall and stopped at the doorway. The last people in line had just been served. Those that had finished eating were taking their time with their coffee, staying inside as long as they could. Tucker raised his hand and waved in case he was looking for them. Ian acknowledged him with a nod and walked toward them.

"I hope you guys got enough to eat." Ian gestured for them to follow him. He waited a second for Tucker to gather up Mattie and their bags. "Let's talk in the hall."

Tucker followed him out into the hall, out of earshot of everyone else. He tried to read Ian's face. Was the news bad? Was he going to tell them she had been found dead? It was the same thought Tucker had every time she went missing. Would Ian say it in front of Mattie?

Ian's eyebrows rose. "She was picked up yesterday by the police." He lowered his voice to almost a mumble as he leaned close to Tucker. "Possession of drugs, prostitution, and under the influence of a controlled substance."

Tucker's heart sunk deep into his gut. This was a new all-time low. She had never been arrested. He shook his head in disbelief. "So now what? Can she get released on bail or something?"

Ian scratched the side of his head. "Well, yeah. If you could come up with bail money. I'm not sure how much it is. Is there somebody you could call?"

The question was like a knife to his heart. The only family they had in Illinois was Mattie's dad's mother. They had only met her once, and he had no idea how to get in touch with her. "No," he mumbled. His mother's parents were both dead, and he had never met his father's parents. He had one aunt, but she and his mother had fallen out when his grandmother was dying in the hospital.

"Well then, they will most likely keep her in the county jail until she goes to court. Has she been arrested before?" Ian's voice trailed off. Again, his eyes dropped to Mattie before expressing what he didn't want to say.

"No. I don't think so." Tucker still couldn't wrap his head around the thought of prostitution. His mother? Prostitutes were attractive, had long legs, and wore stripper heels and boas around their necks. That wasn't their mother. The charge made no sense.

Lost and without words, he couldn't think over the echoing in his ear from the plastic trays being dumped behind him.

"Look, I have to get back to work. I wish I had something better for you." Ian brushed his hand across the top of Mattie's head.

"No. It's fine." As bad as the news was, at least she was alive. "Um… One more thing." Tucker fell over his words, too embarrassed to ask. "Last night, the storm. It blew the tent you gave us right up from the ground. Destroyed it. Could we maybe, do you have, um, a bed for tonight—"

"Oh, I wish I did. With the storm, we're full. Even if they all don't come back this evening, I have a waiting list of twenty-five to thirty women and their children that need beds."

"How 'bout another tent?"

"I'm sorry. I don't. I'd call around for you, but everyone will be in the same boat as us, with the storm and all."

Tucker swallowed his disappointment at this latest blow. "Okay, thanks."

"Come back on Tuesday. We might be able to get you in." Ian's face revealed his grief. "So, where'd you sleep last night?"

"There's this guy, in the camp. His name is Dancer. He took us in." Tucker watched as Ian's brows rose. "You know him?"

Ian nodded. "I do."

Tucker waited for Ian to offer more, perhaps tell him Dancer was some deranged serial killer. Instead, the conversation ended.

Back outside, Tucker led Mattie by the hand. He thought about returning to Camp Roosevelt. But with no tent or shelter, there was little there that would help him. Was he going to have to take her to Terry's House? Could he get her back once he found a place for them, or would they try to keep her? He had run out of options.

It was no longer okay to sit back and wait for their mother to get her shit together. He had to take more control of their situation. It really was up to him; his mother couldn't do it. He could sleep anywhere and defend himself, but the temperature would be too cold for Mattie to sleep outside. She needed shelter. His brain was firing blanks. He couldn't think of a single option to keep her out of Terry's House. The realization that she was better off without her own flesh and blood made him sick. He turned the corner toward Camp Roosevelt, unsure why he was even heading in that direction.

41

With the storm clouds collecting above, it wouldn't be long before the rain started. The only thing he could think of was to take refuge beneath the highway overpass in the far back corner of the camp. His vision blurred as he fought back tears. He *had* to take her to Terry's House. This was too much for a six-year-old. The thought of turning her over to strangers devoured him.

Back at the camp, they made their way under the tattered fence. He stopped long enough to scan their surroundings. His sole aim was to keep Mattie safe tonight. He would take her to Terry's House in the morning. They would spend one last night together—for now.

As they neared where their tent once was, Tucker saw Dancer in front of his shelter talking to a young woman on a bicycle. Tucker's instinct told him to turn around and walk down the other row to avoid him. The last thing he needed was a confrontation.

Ian's cool response to knowing Dancer played in his head. His jaw muscles tightened like a boa constrictor strangling its prey to death. His eyes locked on Dancer. It was clear that the guy didn't like him for some reason, and yet Tucker couldn't stop looking at him.

When Dancer glanced up and looked at him, Tucker dropped his gaze to the ground. His knees wobbled underneath him, causing him to stumble. *He sees me.*

It was too late to change course now. He wouldn't say anything, just walk by. There was nothing to say anyway. It wasn't like they were friends.

Just as they were about to pass Dancer and the woman, Tucker sensed Dancer's body turn toward them.

"Hey," Dancer called to him.

His impulse was to keep walking, but the sound of Dancer's voice offered something. He had no pride to preserve; he was ready to cling to anything. Anything to keep Mattie from freezing tonight. Dancer's milk crates, an old mattress, and lukewarm tea were everything.

"You're back? Where're you going now?"

Tucker drew a breath. The words were painful to say. "Under the bridge. It's goin' to rain again." His eyes shot over to the woman next to Dancer. The scars and scabs on her arm said she was a junkie.

"New Beginnings didn't have another tent for you guys?" Dancer took a step away from the young woman, who looked to be around their age.

"No. No beds available either. We'll be fine until I can figure something out." He tried to amass some self-worth, confidence that he could take care of them.

"Oh." Dancer paused. The single word dangled as if he wasn't finished. "Did your mom ever show up?"

Embarrassed about the truth, Tucker couldn't look him in the eye. "No. Not yet."

"Look, I don't have much, but you're welcome to stay with me again." Dancer looked up at the afternoon clouds. "I think another storm is coming. After last night, I don't want to rescue your stupid ass again in the middle of the night."

Tucker felt his dignity shatter. He tried to stop himself. *Take the offer*, he told himself, *Shut up and take the offer*. His finger came up, stopping inches from Dancer's nose. "I can take care of us just fine. I don't need you to rescue me, or her!"

"You're an idiot," Dancer shot back.

The woman shifted from one foot to the other before cutting in. "I'll let you two talk. I've got to run." A nod from Dancer was enough, and she left.

Dancer looked at Mattie before turning his attention to Tucker. "You have nothing, no food or water—I'm not going to beg you." Dancer closed his arms across his chest as he turned his body away from Tucker.

Tucker knew he was being a fool. For Mattie's sake, he should take the offer. "Okay." Sleeping under the bridge in this weather would be an all-time low. "Thank you. Thank you for your help." Tucker's voice cracked.

Dancer fidgeted for a second before dropping his arms to his side. "You're still an idiot."

Tucker thought he heard a playfulness in Dancer's voice, but he wasn't willing to bet on it. Maybe the guy didn't hate him. Maybe his crabbiness was just who he was. Either way, Tucker was glad for the offer.

Chapter Six

Once again, Dancer found himself second-guessing his decision to invite someone into his space. The three of them sat around his tiny camping stove, watching the water in the pot come to a boil. The silence left him in his head. Had he extended this invitation because of what his friend Dottie had just told him? His emotions were escaping him. Dottie had Hepatitis C and HIV—she was dying. She had been sober for four months, but for what? She was going to die. They talked openly about it. She was about as close to a friend in the camp as he was comfortable having, and that friendship had taken the last twelve months to evolve.

"Are you sure you're not hungry? I have enough." Dancer removed the freeze-dried rice and chicken boil-in-bag dinner from its packaging. At three dollars a pouch, they were expensive, but it beat searching the dumpsters for food during a storm.

"No, I'm sure. We're okay. We ate at the shelter. Mattie has crackers for later." Tucker's eyes were fixed on the boiling water.

Dancer intended to only glance at Tucker as he stared down into the pot of water, but it was impossible to look away. His eyes wouldn't release the blond-haired, blue-eyed country boy. When Tucker looked up at him, the blue hue had an intensity that drew Dancer in even further.

Breaking free, his eyes went to Tucker's jeans and down his legs to his cowboy boots. It was rare to see anyone in the city in cowboy boots. He hadn't realized he missed seeing men in boots. He had never worn cowboy boots growing up, but for some reason, suddenly, he found them sexy.

Tucker's silence was noticeable. Dancer probably shouldn't have called him an idiot in front of his sister, but he held off on an apology in case it panned out that Tucker really was an idiot.

"Are you sure I can't make you some tea, or something?" Dancer turned his attention to Mattie. "How old are you?"

"Six," she stated matter-of-factly.

She wasn't the first young child he'd seen on the streets. An innocence lost to the need for survival. "Would you like some cocoa?" He tried to soften his tone.

Mattie nodded until Tucker elbowed her. "Use your words."

"Yes, please."

"Tomorrow, I'll find something for us." Tucker's voice cracked, causing him to stop and clear his throat. "Ian, down at the shelter, thought they might have beds opening up on Tuesday."

Dancer knew of Ian. Apparently, he used to be some big-shot photographer or something. Today, Ian was just a regular old Florence Nightingale around the neighborhood. Dancer had had an embarrassing interaction with Ian years ago, and shame and humiliation made him push the memory away.

"He told us to come back on Tuesday. Maybe tomorrow, I'll find something for Mattie and me, until Ian can make room for us."

"And then what?" Dancer looked around for the cup that Mattie had used this morning. He spotted it on top of a bin. He used a paper towel to wipe the cocoa residue caked at the bottom.

"What do you mean, 'and then what?'" Tucker asked. "I have no idea after that."

Dancer rolled his eyes. He shouldn't be having this conversation. It was none of his business what they did. They were here for the night. In a couple of days, they would disappear like the dozens of faces that came through the camp, never to be seen again.

"After five days at the shelter, then what? What are you going to do then?" Dancer thought of the Milkman. When the Milkman up and disappeared three years ago, it solidified Dancer's determination not to get close to people. They had lived together for three years in this tiny shanty. There was no doubt the man was mentally ill—Dancer saw it in his eyes the minute they met. But still, there was a gentleness that lay just behind those eyes, if you took an extra second to look. Dancer had done just that on the morning when the Milkman extended his hand to him and lifted him up from behind that dumpster. From the moment Dancer met him, he knew he was safe.

"I don't know. Hopefully, we'll find my mum. Maybe check

other shelters, see if they have room for us." Tucker mumbled as his eyes drifted across the room, looking at nothing in particular.

"That's hardly a plan. So, where do you think your mom went?" Dancer asked.

"Don't know."

It was only two words, but Dancer felt the lie in Tucker's voice. He looked at Mattie. Was she in on the lie as well? What else was Tucker lying about? None of it mattered. It was another reason to shut up and not care. A heavy silence settled over them, heavier than the uneasy tension this morning. Dancer didn't want to care, and yet, all he could think about was where they would go. He mentally checked off all the shelters he knew: the ones that didn't allow men, and the ones that a little girl shouldn't be in, and the ones that no one should ever have to go to.

Dancer reached in front of him, grabbed the pot of hot water, and filled their cups halfway. He returned the pot to the stove and placed the pouch of food into the remaining water to cook.

Tucker's eyes followed Dancer as he handed his sister her cup of cocoa. A whiff of chocolate filtered past his nose.

"Are you sure you're not hungry?" Dancer's question was directed at Tucker, although he was looking at Mattie.

"We're fine." Tucker leaned back and rested his body on his forearms. "I have to go to the hospital tomorrow."

"Why?" Dancer hated hospitals. They were places where people died. He had heard horror stories of the old Roosevelt Hospital. Like in the horror movie *Fragile*, the new hospital was rumored to be haunted by dead patients from the old hospital.

"I ran out of my seizure meds. The only place I can have the prescription refilled for free is at the county." Tucker paused for a second. "I think I'll try to get Mattie in this school that Ian told me about. That way, while she's in school, I can take care of the things I need to take care of."

Dancer thought of the possibility of Tucker having a seizure. He'd seen plenty of people having seizures, medication related as well as drug overdoses. The thought of Tucker having a seizure freaked him out. The only thing he knew to do when someone was having a seizure was not to hold them down. There wasn't enough room in here for this big guy to be flopping around.

He touched the side of his food pouch, assessing if his dinner had reconstituted itself into an edible state. Determining that it had, he grabbed it and sat in his chair.

He ate in silence as he listened to the chatter between Tucker and Mattie in the corner. The edge of his mouth curled upward, hearing how sweet and attentive Tucker was with her. It was a painful reminder of how much he missed his own father. He could ask his dad anything, anything in the world, and his dad would know the answer. *Would Tucker be as sweet to his own children? Did Tucker even want children?*

He let himself stare longer each time, knowing neither of them was paying attention to him. Tucker wasn't drop-dead gorgeous, but there was something about his electric blue eyes and strawberry-blond hair that was enrapturing. He studied Tucker's face, trying to figure out what exactly it was about him that quickened Dancer's pulse and sent butterflies fluttering in his stomach. This evening was turning into a roller coaster of feelings. He wasn't used to emotions and wasn't sure he liked them. It was as if his skin was burning and his insides were about to explode.

How could a guy that offered him nothing do so much to him? The poor guy had seizures, was stuck taking care of his little sister, had a crackhead for a mother, and the good sense of a wild turkey. Yet, he was confident and charming.

Tucker glanced up and caught him staring. It happened several times, and each time, a tiny smirk appeared on his face before he returned his focus to his sister. Almost always, he glanced up a second time as if to say, *Yes, I saw you looking at me.* Dancer's pulse quickened each time it happened. Was Tucker flirting with him?

Within a few minutes, his attention was drawn back. This time, it was at Tucker's milky white cheeks with their shade of rose. He and his little sister's cheeks were identical in color. Had Tucker's blond hair been as blond and curly as hers when he was her age?

If Tucker had to go out to the county hospital tomorrow for more medication, maybe Dancer would go too, if only to have something to do. He had nothing planned, and the last several days of rain had him itching to get out. He had reservations about whether Tucker could manage the two bus transfers needed to get all the way to the other side of town.

"What time do you have to have Mattie at the school?" Dancer held his stare this time without looking away.

"Um, I don't know. He didn't say." Tucker's forehead furrowed as he scratched at his chin.

Dancer tried to hold a neutral face, but Tucker's naivety would be a challenge. "How are you going to have her there if you don't know what time she needs to be there?"

"I don't know." Tucker looked down at Mattie. He wrapped an arm around her and brought her close to him.

The neutral look on Dancer's face disappeared as lines etched between his brows. Everything about Tucker either annoyed him or charged him with excitement. The lack of street smarts made him harmless in a way. Polite and simple. "She needs to be there by at least the end of breakfast. I think the kids have breakfast at the shelter and then walk over to the school afterwards." Dancer responded.

If he left it up to Tucker, Mattie might never see the inside of the classroom. "I'll go with you tomorrow. We can make sure Mattie's there in time for breakfast. We can ride out to the hospital afterwards." Dancer paused and focused on the sound of tiny drops of rain bouncing off the roof.

"I can do it myself, but thank you." Tucker's tone was anything but thankful.

Dancer's nose crinkled at Tucker's rejection. "I never said you couldn't." *Go fuck yourself,* he mumbled under his breath. "Just thought you would need the company if you're going to hang out all day at the hospital. Suit yourself."

Thunder shattered above their heads, causing Tucker to look at the patchwork of plywood that formed the ceiling. "If you want to come, that's fine. I'm saying I don't need you to come." He kept his eye on the ceiling as if waiting for it to collapse.

Dancer's cheeks puffed. "Just thought you might want company." He had kept a lot of men company but never on a bus. The thought of a plan to hang out with Tucker tomorrow started the acid swirling deep in his gut.

For the last six years, he had worked on eradicating fear, loneliness, anxiety, and any other emotion he chose not to deal with. He had carved out an existence that lacked emotions. It was essential in erasing the memories of his stepfather, Robert, and in not missing any part of the life that he had run from. It also allowed him to do what he did with strangers in alleys. Now, this stranger was undoing all of it in a matter of a few days. Dancer couldn't deny that something drew him to this man. Tucker was stirring up emotions, and Dancer knew he was playing with fire by allowing Tucker in.

Chapter Seven

Tucker had lain flat on his back listening to the rain falling for the last hour. He was too afraid to get up; he didn't want to cause a commotion like he had yesterday morning. You would have thought he set a bomb off with the attitude Dancer flung around. Tucker still couldn't believe that Dancer had blown up just because he couldn't figure out how the door opened.

Also on his mind was the vibe he had thought he felt with Dancer last night. It happened before they went to bed. Tucker was sure he had caught Dancer staring at him. It wasn't a crazy-serial-killer-before-he-stabbed-you-sixty-four-times stare; it was soft. The corners of Dancer's mouth had softened each time before he looked away.

How could he not be grateful for everything Dancer had done for him and Mattie? If it weren't for Dancer, they would have spent the other night under a bridge, in the rain. He was more than grateful for Dancer's generosity. He was indebted to the man for taking them in.

Absorbed in his thoughts, he shifted his long body on the spongy twin mattress toward the light snore coming from Dancer in his chair. In the darkness, Tucker could visualize Dancer's wildly curly auburn hair, which Dancer couldn't keep out of his face. His dark, arched brows and eyelashes were beyond pretty. His lean body lacked the muscular definition of most jocks. Yeah, *pretty* was a good word to describe him.

Unsure whether Dancer was going with him this morning to the hospital, he was less than excited to journey out there by himself. He thought of the many times he, his mom, and his little sister had spent almost an entire day sitting in a waiting room. Just thinking of his mother evoked anger in him. He wanted to blame her, even hate her, and yet all he could do was worry about whether she was okay in jail.

All he knew of jail was what he had seen on TV, and it didn't look like a place that his mother could handle. There was no way he could ensure she was okay. It was out of his hands. Although he had been taking care of Mattie since she was a baby, there was no question she was now solely his responsibility. He needed to go to the jail and get their debit card from his mother. They needed money to survive. Frustrated, he blew air from his lungs.

"You okay over there?" Dancer lifted his head from under his blanket.

"Sorry." He hadn't realized he was making noise. "Go back to sleep." He hoped he hadn't pissed Dancer off again.

Mattie's tiny body stirred. He held off saying anything else, not wanting to wake her. Tucking his head down into the top of Mattie's hair, his blood continued to boil. Their mother was dragging them deeper and deeper into despair. It was time to man up.

He knew that being off his meds and getting this upset was dangerous. He had to bring his temper under control. It had been over a year since he had a grand mal seizure, and he couldn't afford to have another one. With their mother gone, if he was unconscious, there would be no one looking after Mattie. He couldn't risk it.

After a series of deep breaths, he was able to bring his breathing under control. Although the room was dark, his eyes adjusted enough to see that Dancer was out of his chair and moving about.

"You guys need to get up. It's after six." His voice was scratchy and weak. "We have about an hour before they serve breakfast." Dancer turned on the lantern illuminating the room and revealed himself in baggy sweat bottoms that hung on his thin body.

Tucker shook Mattie's shoulders. "Baby girl, wake up. It's time to get up."

Mattie brought her hands up to her eyes and scratched them open. "Do I get to go to school today?" Her words were drawn out and grumbly.

"You do, but first we have to get you some breakfast. You have to have fuel so you have enough gas to pay attention to the teacher and get super smart." Tucker poked at her stomach to ensure she was waking up.

Dancer stood on the opposite side of the camp stove, pouring water into the pot. "Anybody want tea?"

51

As much as he needed a shot of caffeine, what Tucker wanted more was water to brush his teeth and rinse out his mouth. "Can I get a little water so we can brush our teeth?" The fact that they were sleeping in their clothes left little to do to get ready other than brush his teeth and comb his hair. "Get your toothbrush," he instructed Mattie.

"Where is it?" Mattie looked around the small room.

"In your bag, where it always is. Stop being shy and get it. Hurry now, we have to go."

Dancer held out the water bottle without looking at him. Two-thirds empty, it was plenty for them to brush their teeth with.

"Thank you." Tucker took the plastic bottle. He used the lack of eye contact with Dancer as an opportunity to look deeply at him. Dancer's thick, tousled auburn hair and furrowed brows were equally alluring. Did he know how freakishly good-looking he was? Life wasn't fair.

"Look, I'll find some place for Mattie and me for tonight." The cold silence made it clear that they had overstayed their welcome. "I'll check other shelters while Mattie's in school. Give us a few minutes, and we'll be out of here." He joined Mattie in the search for their toothbrushes.

Toothbrush in hand, he rose to his feet, nearly hitting his head on the low ceiling.

Dancer stood with his palms opened toward the warm stove. "I thought we were going to the county?" He kept his eyes on the pot of water.

We? Does that mean he is planning on going with me this morning? An unexpected release of tension drained from Tucker's neck and shoulders. "Yeah. Thank you. Mattie, let's go outside to brush our teeth."

Dancer leapt in front of them and unlatched the door. Their eyes met for the first time this morning as Tucker stepped through the doorway.

Tucker and Mattie stood between Dancer's shanty and the shelter next to it, brushing their teeth.

In the middle of brushing, Mattie stopped and looked up at her brother. "How long does Mommy have to stay in jail?"

Tucker swished the water in his mouth longer than usual,

thinking about her question. When he had the answer, he spit his water onto the wet ground. "I don't know, sweetie. But it's like a hospital inside there. They can make Mommy all better." It was a horrible lie but the only thing he had.

With his tongue, he rubbed around his mouth, rejoicing in the fresh feeling of clean teeth.

When they walked back inside, Dancer had changed out of his sweats into jeans. With his back to them, he was stuffing several items into a navy-blue backpack.

Dancer said over his shoulder, "Why don't you two go on over and eat something. By the time you get Mattie settled, I'll be there. Come outside and look for me."

"You're not going to eat with us?" Tucker returned his toothbrush to his suitcase.

"No, I have something I have to do before we head out. I'll meet you outside."

There was a vagueness in Dancer's proposal. It sounded a little sketchy, but it was also none of Tucker's business. "Um, okay."

*****

After realizing he was as comfortable as he was going to get with leaving Mattie in the school with strangers, Tucker nervously walked back out to the street. He looked in both directions for Dancer. He didn't see him until a red and black city bus moved out of the way and Dancer emerged. Once traffic was clear, Dancer jogged across the street.

"It looks like it will clear up for a bit." Dancer looked up at the morning sun, which had made its way up between the massive skyscrapers that filled downtown.

There was that smile. It was the same slight curvature of the corners of Dancer's mouth as Tucker had seen last night. As if the expression was contagious, Tucker grinned as he looked up at the sun. The little warmth it was giving out swept across his face.

"I think we missed our bus. There's another in about fifteen minutes." Dancer stepped up next to him and halted. He put his thumbs between the straps of his backpack and hiked it higher onto his back. His hair was wet, and there was a freshness to him.

53

A hint of soap permeated the air under Tucker's nose. The realization that Dancer had taken a shower surprised him. Tucker hadn't had a shower since they left the shelter last week. With Dancer clean, he was now more aware of how bad he smelled.

"Did you get your stuff done?" Tucker asked. A shower was something he never would have envisioned being jealous of, but now it was. He wanted to ask about it but held off, concerned that it would come across as prying.

"I did." Wrapped in a gunmetal jacket and scarf, Dancer appeared relaxed.

Tucker stared at the expensive-looking waist-length jacket. He knew the backpack was expensive. He'd seen the Swiss Gear logo on it and knew anything Swiss Gear was out of his price range. Dancer didn't look or smell like someone homeless. He worked to brush off his jealousy over the mysterious shower as he moved over to the Plexiglas bus stop.

Tucker took a seat on the metal bench inside the enclosure, leaving enough room for Dancer, who remained standing. "Ian asked about you," said Tucker. "I told him you were meeting me after breakfast." Tucker looked up as an older salt-and-pepper gentleman snapped their picture from across the street. When the guy realized he was being watched, he tucked his camera into his coat.

"Hmm." Dancer's response was barely audible. He, too, was watching as the guy adjusted the camera under his coat and scurried away.

Tucker had his own thoughts about the pervert taking their picture, but they seemed less important than Dancer's lukewarm response to the conversation about Ian. "What's up with you two?" Tucker asked. "He seems like a nice guy, but I get the feeling you don't like him."

"Why do you say that?" Dancer turned his back on Tucker and stepped out from under the Plexiglas. He shoved both hands into the side pockets of his jacket and looked up the street.

Tucker gazed at Dancer's frame as Dancer stepped away from him. The heavy coat concealed the lean body he had been admiring this morning. The memory of the bulging veins that ran down Dancer's narrow feet sent blood flooding into his groin. Dancer was freaking adorable.

Dancer spun on his heels, and their eyes met. As if playing Rock-Paper-Scissors, Dancer tapped a fist on his open hand as he held Tucker's stare. "What did he say when you told him you were meeting me?"

"Um, um, he said nothing." Tucker's throat constricted at the agitation in Dancer's voice. He had never been around anyone who ran so hot and cold.

The conversation stalled, leaving Tucker wondering if he should say anything else on the topic. An elderly woman pushing a small metal shopping cart made her way toward them. Placing his elbows on his legs, Tucker leaned over, stretching his neck to look past Dancer at the old woman.

Dancer removed his hands from his pockets and adjusted his brown Burberry print scarf around his neck. "I'm surprised."

"Surprised?" It took Tucker a second to piece the conversation back together. "Why? What do you think he said about you?" There was something Dancer wasn't telling him. Was he afraid of something? "Seems like you're hiding something."

Dancer's face wrinkled. "I'm not hiding anything. He's opinionated. Just don't like the dude." His eyes shifted to the old woman as she passed him and parked her cart next to the bench.

Tucker scooted over to make room for her. The old woman's presence ended the conversation.

The three of them waited in silence until another red and black metro bus rounded the corner and pulled up in front of them. Tucker rose, waiting for the old woman to gather her purse and cart. He stepped behind her and waited in case she needed help as she boarded the bus.

The woman dragged the small cart up the three steps and stopped in front of the driver. Tucker patiently waited on the step behind her as she dug around in her purse. It took her a minute to find her bus pass. She scanned it and put it back into her purse before moving to her seat.

Tucker had the voucher Ian had given him ready to go. Before holding it up against the scanner, he glanced out the front window, looking for Dancer on the sidewalk. He was still standing in the same spot. Tucker's stomach knotted. His breakfast wanted to rise into his throat.

"Are you riding or not?" The driver's booming voice startled Tucker. He scanned his voucher and moved past her. Wrapped in thought, he hurried, bumping the old woman's cart, which was in the aisle next to her.

He reached the empty seats in the rear of the bus as it pulled away from the curb. His legs wobbly from the movement of the bus, he braced his feet on the floor as he spun into his seat.

"Slide over."

Tucker recognized the voice. His heart thumped when he saw Dancer standing in the aisle. A renewed energy filled him as he slid to the window seat.

They had gone through several stops before Dancer spoke. "He doesn't like what I do."

Tucker knew who *he* was. What he wanted to know was what Dancer did that *he* didn't like. His eyes cast over the people sitting in front of him, Tucker's mind went to drugs. *If Dancer is a drug dealer, it wouldn't be a shocker.* "What is it that you do that he doesn't like?" Tucker wasn't sure he wanted to know, but it didn't stop him from asking.

"I do what I have to do to survive." Dancer's response was clipped.

"And what do you have to do to survive?" Tucker knew he was pushing, but Dancer's elusive answers only drove his need to know.

"I entertain men," Dancer said with a mirthless laugh. He said it openly, with little concern for the other passengers. As if he was a banker or a mechanic.

It took a second for Tucker to process what he had said. He looked at Dancer. *Surely he's kidding.* Tucker's mother was sitting in jail for prostitution. If this was a joke, it wasn't funny.

The corner of Dancer's mouth turned up.

Tucker took it as a grin. *He is joking.* "Be serious."

"I am." Dancer's expression dulled. His eyes confirmed his words.

"You mean, like a prostitute?" Tucker asked. The thought of him being a prostitute was better than his being a drug dealer. He had known one or two small-time dealers back in high school. A metallic taste formed in his mouth. *He entertains men. Does that mean he is gay?*

56

Dancer lowered his voice and sat up. "Prostitute is such a bad word. Why is your face all red?"

Heat flushed through Tucker's body, sending prickles up the back of his neck. He was unsure what was more of a shocker—Dancer being a prostitute or his being gay. The two stared at one another as if playing chicken until Tucker turned away toward the window.

He had visions of girls walking up and down the street in high heels, tight shorts, and pink boas around their necks. Did Dancer mean that he was more like a male escort? Tucker turned back toward Dancer but paused long enough to frame his question. "Do you work for someone? Do you go to their house? Are you like a male escort?" He had a lot of questions in his head.

Dancer adjusted himself in his seat, turning toward Tucker. He tucked one foot between the seat and his butt. "Dude, you watch too much TV. Not quite that glamorous." He laughed as he leaned back into his seat. "I take care of myself."

"Is that what you had to do this morning?" Tucker stopped short of asking the real question.

"This morning?" Dancer looked up as if trying to recall what he had done. "This morning?" He repeated as if trying to figure out what Tucker was asking.

"Yeah, this morning. Back at your place, you said you would meet me because you had something to do. What did you do?"

"Oh! Nothing, I wanted to get cleaned up. Get some of that dirt and grime off me." Dancer's face softened.

"Get cleaned up. To meet someone?" Dancer's admission explained where the fancy tea, the food, and the clothes came from.

"No! Not this morning." Dancer laughed as if the question was absurd. "I took a shower."

Tucker didn't understand the laughter in Dancer's voice. What was funny about the conversation? A dozen more questions came to mind. "Where?"

"Where what?"

"Where'd you shower?" *Was the place a client's?*

"At Chinn's."

"What's Chinn's?"

"Chinn's?" Dancer paused. "You know, that little Chinese hole in the wall down on the corner of Sixth and Elm."

"They have a shower?" Tucker's shoulders dropped as he cocked his head. This wasn't making sense.

"Well, kind of. It's a small tub in a closet where they keep the mop bucket and stuff. But it works."

"And they let you come and take a shower there?"

"Yeah." Dancer rolled his eyes as he released a breath of air. "Okay, enough with the questions. This is starting to feel like an interrogation."

Tucker's attention fell back to the real bombshell. He had so many questions, but heard the irritation in Dancer's voice. "Can I just ask one more?"

Dancer's head cocked to one side. "What!"

"What do you call yourself?"

"What do I call myself? You mean like a stage name?"

"If you don't like 'prostitute,' what do you call yourself? A hooker, a hustler?" The word *whore* came to mind. If Dancer was a whore than so was Tucker's mother.

Dancer lowered his foot to the floor as the bus came to a stop. He watched as a line of people boarded the already-crowded bus. "Yeah, I'm not into titles. Call it what you want. I'm trying to survive." Dancer leaned in as a heavyset man scooted sideways down the center of the bus past him. "But if you need a title, call me a survivalist."

Tucker looked up at the large man as he passed, eyeing the massive suit jacket that covered his body. *Was he going to work?* He looked at everyone around him. *Were they all going to work—trying to survive? Why did Tucker's survival look so much different from everyone else's?* Tucker turned back toward the window. In the glass, he envisioned Dancer on his knees, sucking some dude off. He fought to keep images of his mother doing the same out of his head.

So much had changed in the last couple of years. His old life didn't even feel like it was his. It was like baseball was someone else's life. The accident had changed everything. Not only could he no longer play ball, but he couldn't work because of the seizures. And then the meds. They made him tired all the time. The first year was a blur, and when he woke up, this was his life. It had been over a year since he'd had a seizure, yet he felt as if it would happen at any minute.

He stared out the window of the bus. The grey skies were so damn depressing. Depression clung to him like an infection, something he couldn't shake. This last year, he had been barely living. He had watched from the sidelines as his mother's addiction spiraled out of control. He'd done nothing but watch it happen as if someone else would come in and fix it. Every day, it was a struggle just to get up. Some days were better than others. There were days when his focus was on Mattie and not his own emptiness, and days he faked his happiness to shield her from the sad reality. But these last few weeks, it was as if he was being buried alive. He felt as if he was suffocating.

As the bus pulled into a large terminal, Tucker eyed the line of city buses that flanked the turnabout. He and Dancer exited the bus and walked past several others before locating their connecting bus. Tucker followed Dancer onto the bus—no questions asked, he just followed.

Chapter Eight

After signing in at the clinic's front desk, Tucker took a seat next to Dancer in the corner of the overcrowded waiting room. It wasn't even nine o'clock, and his past experiences with clinics told him they would be here all morning. He and Dancer hadn't said more than two words to each other in the last hour.

Dancer wasn't his problem. Whatever Dancer did with his body, however he made his money, was his own business. Tucker had to get his medication and find a place for him and Mattie to sleep. He had to get his life together.

"Mr. Graves." The receptionist called for him just as he started to get comfortable. He approached the counter, impressed that they had called him so fast.

"Mr. Graves, do you have a parent with you?" the small brunet in pink scrubs asked him.

"My parents? No. I'm eighteen." He didn't wait for her to ask for his I.D. He retrieved his Illinois identification card from his wallet and slid it in front of her. He stood at the counter for several minutes while she located his Medicaid eligibility benefits. Once satisfied, she handed him a clipboard with several forms to complete. Tucker took the clipboard back to his seat to fill out.

"Did she say how long?" Dancer dropped the three-year-old *National Geographic* magazine that shielded his face.

"No, but I have to fill out all these damn forms first. There's like thirty names ahead of me too." Tucker took ten minutes to complete the forms, leaving a third of the questions blank. He either didn't understand them or didn't know the answers. His mother usually filled out the forms.

After returning the forms to the receptionist, Tucker took his seat again. He watched as Dancer laid the magazine down and plugged his tablet into a nearby socket. He followed Dancer's lead and plugged his cellphone charger in next to it.

"I didn't know you had a phone," Dancer said, staring at it.

"Yeah. I don't have any service, but it keeps my contacts and stuff." Leaning over, he shuffled through the stack of magazines on the end table. His face brightened at the discovery of the *Sports Illustrated* with the cover of Izzy Fernandez. It was an old cover, but he hadn't seen it before, and he was in love with the pitcher for the Seattle Mariners.

"Maybe you should have a seizure right here. That would get you in." Snickering, Dancer lay his magazine across his lap.

Tucker rolled his eyes. There was nothing funny about faking a seizure. Sinking down into his chair, he stretched his legs out in front of him and flipped through the magazine, looking for Izzy.

He tried to read the article, but his thoughts were occupied with plans for this afternoon. He would go to the police station and see if he could get their debit card from his mom's property. Tomorrow was the first of the month. Human Services would be downloading another four hundred and twenty-five dollars onto their debit card. He needed that card. Then he would get them a room at a motel he had seen while walking to the shelter. That would buy him several days until he could find a job.

"I faked a seizure once." Dancer picked up his magazine but didn't lift it to his face. "I saw a guy do it a couple of years ago. The police were about to haul him away. But instead of going to jail, he got a trip to the hospital."

As much as Tucker wanted to ignore this stupid conversation, the sound of Dancer's voice kept him out of his own head. "Why would you want to go to the hospital?"

"You've never been to jail, have you?" Dancer asked.

"No."

"It's a good thing God made you cute. You're as dumb as hell." Dancer laughed.

Tucker's hands folded into fists as Dancer went into his story about his fake seizure. He tuned out what Dancer was saying, still stuck on Dancer's earlier comment. Initially, Tucker had wanted to punch his lights out for calling him dumb. But then Dancer's words replayed in his head—*Dumb... Cute... Really?* His heart leaped. Was

Dancer being serious when he called him cute, or taunting him? His eyes scanned over the same sentence in the article about the pitcher as if reading it three times wasn't enough.

His eyes were on Izzy, but his thoughts were of Dancer. "So—are you gay?" The real question he wanted to ask was whether Dancer really thought he was cute.

"No, I just let strangers fuck me in the ass for the money."

Tucker squirmed at Dancer's crudeness. Was he serious? He didn't know how to respond if that was the case. Everything about this guy unnerved him. He had never met anyone so in-your-face. Tucker sat up and leaned away from Dancer. "So, are you?"

"Yeah. And?" Dancer's eyes locked onto him. "Don't worry, I'm not into straight guys. You don't have to worry about me checking you out when you're not looking."

A lump formed in Tucker's throat. "I'm not straight."

Dancer's eyes widened as his elbow slipped off the metal frame of the chair. "Oh? I'd never have guessed."

"Are you being serious or being mean? I can't tell." Dammit, why couldn't he figure this guy out?

"No, I'm being serious. I wouldn't have guessed. You're like this big-ass cowboy."

For the first time, Tucker could read Dancer's face. He was being serious. "So... I guess it makes it easier to do what you do—because you're gay?"

"Are you kidding or just stupid? Would you have sex with that old dude over there for money if he wanted to?" Dancer nodded toward a frail old man sitting with his wife on the other side of the room. With his oxygen being supplied through a tube in his nose, the man looked to be in his eighties or nineties.

"Quit calling me stupid. I'm not stupid!"

"Would you?"

"No. That's nasty."

"Why not? You said you're gay."

"Because it's nasty. The dude is like eighty years old."

"You're right, it's nasty. My skin crawls every time someone touches me. It's called survival sex."

"So how can you stand to do it?"

"If your stomach is empty and you're drinking out of a bathroom sink, you'd be surprised what you would do when there's a man in your face offering you money."

Tucker pictured himself doing it. Could he?

"You'll put your pride in your pocket, then bury it somewhere when you're done. Become numb to what you're doing. You become someone else so you don't feel anything." Dancer's voice trailed off as he turned his head away.

Tucker stared at the back of his head, waiting for him to turn back around. Was that what Tucker's mother did as well? He wanted to believe this had been her first time. Maybe she hadn't had sex with anyone—maybe it was an undercover cop who arrested her. This was survival, and it was ugly. They were living in a shanty made of milk crates and sleeping on a mattress on the floor. The world didn't seem to care that two young guys and a six-year-old were living on the streets.

Although he didn't know Dancer's pain, he knew what it felt like to be rejected. Rejected by a man who never met him. Tucker had never stopped wondering why his father didn't want them. There wasn't anything in Tucker's life that caused him anything other than pain. Perhaps, long ago, as a young kid, it was different, but those memories were fading.

The two sat in silence, watching as patient after patient was called to be seen. They had been sitting for three hours when the nurse opened the door and called for Tucker. Startled by the sound of his name, Tucker realized he had been dozing. He wondered how long had he been sleeping: twenty minutes, thirty minutes? He looked at Dancer as he rose to his feet. "I didn't mean to piss you off. I'm sorry if I did," he mumbled.

Without looking up, Dancer nodded.

The sudden realization that Dancer wouldn't be here when he came out forced him to take a deep breath. He was pretty sure he had pissed Dancer off with all his questions. At this point, he couldn't take them back. He hated leaving things with Dancer unsettled. For a split-second, Tucker thought of not following the nurse, but her eyes drew him toward her as he stepped through the door and it closed.

Chapter Nine

Dancer watched as Tucker disappeared behind the door with the nurse. He rolled his eyes, trying to brush off his attraction to him. Tucker was a dork but a sweet dork. His love for Mattie was sappy and adorable to watch.

If Dancer was smart, he knew, he would get up and walk out of the waiting room, run as far as he could from this situation. It was what he did. It's what had saved him six years ago. Over the years, he had found that it was easier to avoid relationships with people than to get hurt by them. Relationships equaled pain. His brain told him to get up. Falling for someone didn't fit into his life. He had been on his own for six years and was doing fine. But a longing whispered through him and coiled down his spine, causing him to sink further down into the chair.

Tucker had nothing except for a sister whom he couldn't take care of. Why would Dancer invite that into his life? He would help him out with his meds today and then let him go. It wasn't his problem that Tucker had no plan and that he and Mattie would most likely be on the street tonight.

Dancer pushed away the idea that Mattie was his responsibility. Neither of them were. So why was he still sitting there? He tapped two fingers against his lips, waiting for the answer to come to him.

Two hours later, Tucker emerged from the back. Dancer watched as he stopped at the nurse's counter to check out. The sight of Tucker made his heart skip a beat. Tucker was tall, thoughtful, and tender. There was no denying that he was falling for this guy. He stood up, ensuring that Tucker saw him. "Hey, did you get your meds?"

Tucker did a double take, his eyes widening. "I didn't think you would still be out here." He slung his green camouflage backpack across his back.

"Yeah, that makes two of us." The light freckles that peppered Tucker's nose caught Dancer's attention. How had he not noticed them before? Heat rose to his cheeks at the discovery. The adorable freckles were reason enough to make him glad he had stayed.

"Huh?"

"Not important. Did you get your drugs?" His eyes went to Tucker's stained backpack.

"Yep, thirty days. The doctor wants me back in thirty days to see how I'm doing." Tucker tilted his head from side to side, popping his neck.

"That's gross." The sound of three snaps sent a shudder through Dancer. He couldn't believe the sound had come from someone's neck. "Let's get out of here. Are you hungry? I'm starving."

"I was planning on going over to the Living Hope mission. Maybe they have room for me and Mattie. I wanted to do it before I picked her up."

"Oh, not that place! It's full of crackheads and parolees!" Dancer stopped in his tracks. "I wouldn't sleep on those cots if I were dying and about to take my last breath."

"Really? What about Saint Anne's next to it?"

"They only take women. With a dick between your legs, you're not getting two feet inside there."

Tucker exhaled an exasperated sigh. "What about the one on Ninth?"

"Family Ties?" Dancer gasped. "That's a rehab center for women. Let's go eat, and then you can go over to Living Hope." Dancer knew that Tucker had few options. He felt conflicted by this. If Tucker and his sister were able to get into Living Hope, they would be gone. Dancer realized he didn't want Tucker to be gone. So then, what did he want? They would go to lunch; that was as much as Dancer was willing to admit to himself. *It's only lunch.*

The look on Tucker's face said he was reluctant. Dancer slapped his shoulder, hoping the extra push would help. "Come on, let's go." Not waiting, Tucker fell in behind him.

The bus ride back into downtown Brierton was quiet. Other than the occasional verbal exchange about the weather or when he was watching a person on the street, Tucker stared toward the front of the bus. Dancer watched Tucker out the corner of his eye. What was he thinking? His blank stare didn't say it was anything painful, but still, he didn't want to interrupt.

Back on Main Street, the bus rolled past Camp Roosevelt before coming to a stop at the corner. Storm clouds above had turned the sky to a dark grey. Any plans of Dancer working tonight were erased by the possibility of more rain. He would leave the streets to the junkies and the desperate. Working in the rain was miserable.

He had spent less than half of what he made the other night from Old Man Gerhardt. It would be a week before he had to go back out, unless the old man called for him sooner. He could spend a little on lunch today.

As the two stepped off the bus, Dancer looked around at their options. He gazed over the crowds of people moving about. There were countless restaurants for the more discriminating of palates to choose from, as well as a Subway, the Mexican place next to it, and Chinn's.

Chinn's was out, and he was unsure of the Mexican place. "Do you like Subway?"

"Yeah, that's fine," Tucker mumbled.

As soon as they walked into the narrow shop, the eyes of the woman behind the counter picked them out. Subway was one of the few places that allowed the homeless to come in, but there was always the chance that whoever was working would ask them to leave.

For most businesses, the uneasiness that the homeless caused their other customers was not worth the few dollars they spent. Complaints that they stunk and that the mentally ill made others uncomfortable rendered their dollars useless. Even with a shower, Dancer was still one of them. He never visited any store other than the neighborhood Walmart. There, in such a massive store, he could get everything he needed and go undetected.

"Good afternoon." The woman was speaking to them, but her eyes darted over to her other customers sitting in the dining area.

Dancer's eyes followed hers, seeing a man and woman at one table and four guys at another. His eyes caught one of the guys staring at him. He knew the look. *The closeted gay guy with his straight friends.* They were clueless as their friend held Dancer's stare a second or two longer than he should have.

He hoped the woman's greeting meant she would let them stay. The lit menu board above her head displayed all their choices, from a foot-long sandwich to the six-inch combo. For the price of the sandwich, Dancer could buy a small loaf of bread and some salami and eat for a few days.

"I'll have the roast beef on white bread. Plain, nothing on it but the meat." He refused to pay for a sandwich packed with a bunch of lettuce and junk. He moved to one side, allowing Tucker step up to the counter.

"Can I have the… are the meatballs hot?" Tucker asked the woman.

"Yes." She gave him a frosty look.

"Okay, can I have the meatball sandwich with everything?"

They found a table toward the back of the store, next to the restrooms. Dancer took a seat that allowed him to watch who came through the front door. The admirer with his friends glanced up at him several times. Each time their eyes met, Dancer looked away first.

Tucker unwrapped his sandwich and went to work. After several bites, he slowed his pace. A grin plastered on his face, he kept his eyes on the sandwich. "I haven't had a sandwich in forever."

Dancer wondered just how long his forever was. His roast beef wasn't anything to get excited about.

"I'll pay you back." His eyes bored into Dancer as if he wanted to say something but couldn't. "I… I…"

"What?" Dancer wasn't sure he wanted to know what Tucker was trying to ask, but he couldn't help himself.

"I can't believe you have sex with other men and get paid for it." Tucker licked mustard from the back of his hand.

The statement caught Dancer off guard. He had never talked about what he was doing with anyone. He hesitated long enough to figure out how much he wanted to talk about. "It depends on what you think sex is. They mostly want another guy's lips on their cock. Five, ten minutes at max, and then I'm out of there."

"Where do you go, I mean to do that?"

"Around—wherever." Dancer grimaced, accepting that they were going to talk more about his work.

"Do you do it every night?"

67

"No, not anymore. I have two or three regulars that pay better than normal. It depends."

Tucker took another bite of his sandwich. With a mouth full of bread, he fired another question. "Are you from here?"

"Mississippi. A little swamp town called Indian Waters." It was three hundred miles away, yet upon saying where he was from, he felt as if he was standing in his bedroom, watching his stepdad come toward him.

"So that explains that cute little southern drawl that slips out every now and then. How long have you been out here, on the streets?"

"About six years." He wasn't certain it had been six years; it could have been five. Very little of the last couple of years stood out in his memory. The days and nights all ran together. He forced himself to take another bite of his sandwich, but his appetite was rapidly escaping him.

Tucker stopped his interrogation long enough to take several bites of his sandwich. The six-inch sandwich was no match for him. With a single bite left, Tucker came up for air. "Do you ever see your family?"

"No." He didn't want to talk about his family. He didn't want to share any more about himself.

"Why not?"

Tucker was a book of questions, one after another. This was the reason Dancer would rather be alone in this world. He answered to no one. "My dad died when I was twelve. My mother remarried her manager."

"Her manager? What does she do?"

Dancer guffawed. "She writes books." He questioned why he hadn't cut off the Q&A session yet. How was Tucker able to draw so much out of him?

"Your mom is a writer? That's cool. What does she write—murder mysteries, suspense, horror?"

Dancer chuckled. "Romance."

"Like the books with the hot guy with long hair on the cover sweeping the girl off her feet?" A beaming smile crossed Tucker's face.

"Yep, those are the books. If you knew my mother, though, she is anything but romantic. Bitch of a businesswoman. At least, she used to be." He could picture his mom sitting behind her laptop in her office. He couldn't remember the last time he'd had such a vivid image of her.

"What's her name?" Tucker's voice trailed off as if it wasn't a real question.

"Joaquina... Ziegler." Dancer watched for the reaction.

Tucker's eyes widened. "No way! Your mom's Joaquina Ziegler? She's like Oprah's best friend—after that other lady." Tucker twirled his finger around in the air as if trying to catch the name of the woman that had escaped him.

Dancer nodded. "Yep." Tucker's pale, pink lips caught his eye. Tucker's top lip curved like Cupid's bow, symmetrical to the bottom lip. They were shaped as perfectly as anyone's lips could be. First the freckles and now the lips. It was as if Tucker was spinning a web of attraction and Dancer was inching closer to the center.

"What the hell are you doing out here? Y'all are, like, super rich. I've seen your mom's picture everywhere."

"Yep." This disclosure reminded Dancer more of who he was then he cared to remember. He turned his attention to his thumbnail for a second before going to work on it.

"Does she know where you're at? That you're out here?"

Dancer shrugged as he debated taking more of the nail off. It was a better option then talking about his mother.

"So where did you get the name Dancer?"

The question killed his appetite for fingernail. "You know, I'm kind of done with this conversation." He wasn't shooting for silence, which would only allow him to dwell on what he was trying to dodge. "What about you? What happened with you? Why are you guys out here?"

A grimace washed over Tucker's face as if he'd been kicked in the gut. "Um... um." The question caused him to sputter. "I don't know. My mum couldn't keep it together."

Dancer heard the pain in Tucker's voice. "What about your dad?"

"Never knew him." Tucker's eyes looked at him for a second before looking down at the table. Several seconds of silence passed before Tucker spoke again. "I know it's sad and all that your dad died, but at least you knew him."

69

"Huh?" Dancer murmured.

"Yeah, I hate that whenever I see a guy in his forties with blond hair and blue eyes, I can't stop from asking myself, 'Is that him?' I used to tell myself that, if I could get that guy to look at me, I'd know by their reaction to seeing me. You know, like a father would know his son, and there would be no disguising his reaction."

Dancer thought about Tucker seeing his father on the streets. Was it true that two people would just know? Dancer tried to piece together an image of his own father's face. It was a memory buried so long ago and so deep that he struggled to bring it into focus.

"As much as I hated my dad for not being around," Tucker continued, "There was always the thought that, if he was around, maybe things would be better. Maybe mum would have been happier… if I could just meet him." Tucker's voice trailed off.

"So, you and your sister don't share the same father?"

"God, no. But he was never around, either." Tucker looked at Dancer's sandwich.

"You want it? I'm not going to eat it." Dancer pushed his sandwich across the table. "Here."

"Are you sure?" Tucker pulled the paper placemat closer and took the sandwich.

Several questions came to Dancer. "Your seizures, were you born with them?"

Tucker picked up Dancer's sandwich and stared at the stack of meat between the roll. "No. A baseball hit me in the head. Knocked me out. The sucker meant to do it. If I hadn't been knocked out, I would've kicked his ass. It was bad. Luckily, the protective shell inside my helmet took most of the force. But the hit left me with grand mals. It took a while to find the right medicine to stop the seizures and migraines."

"So, you're a jock and not a cowboy. You play baseball." Dancer savored his correct assessment.

"Played. That ended everything for me."

"Was that, like, your big plan in life? Go—what do they call it, pro?" He pushed away the creeping thoughts of the dancing career he never had.

A snicker escaped the edge of Tucker's mouth. "Major league. But yeah, I was good enough. I know I was."

"So, you couldn't play baseball after that?"

"I couldn't do anything."

It sounded like a copout to Dancer. As if playing a stupid game was everything. "So, you gave up on life? That's weak." He certainly wasn't sitting around crying that he wasn't dancing anymore.

"Excuse me—Not everyone can live out their dreams like you." Glaring at Dancer, Tucker ripped a big bite from his sandwich and starting chewing.

The hair lifted on Dancer's neck. Tucker's words stung. He deserved it, even if it was a shitty thing to say.

They sat in silence as Tucker picked at the rest of Dancer's sandwich. Dancer wished he could take back his words. He wished he wasn't the reason for the miserable look that dominated the muscles in Tucker's face.

Finishing the sandwich, Tucker balled the soiled paper up and stuffed it and his napkins into the plastic bag. "I got to go. I have stuff I need to do before I pick up Mattie. I'll come by later to get our stuff." Tucker stood up. "Thanks for lunch. Like I said, I'll pay you back."

Dancer watched as Tucker swung his backpack over his shoulders and turned around to leave. Was he going to let him walk out? Had he subconsciously orchestrated the end of their friendship?

Tucker plowed through the front door, nearly taking it from its hinges. Part of Dancer said to let him go. But he knew Tucker didn't deserve to be shit on like that. He owed him an apology.

71

Chapter Ten

Dancer grabbed his coat, scarf, and backpack. There was no time to put them on as he bolted out onto the street after Tucker.

"Hey! Hey!" Dancer yelled out to Tucker's back as he moved closer with every stride. "Hold on. I'm sorry."

Tucker didn't turn around as he kept his pace, moving between the shoppers moseying along the storefronts.

When he was close enough, Dancer reached out and grabbed Tucker's arm from the back. "Hold on. I'm sorry." He positioned himself in front of Tucker. "I'm sorry!"

Tucker said nothing. He looked over the top of Dancer's head. His body wiggled as if he was trying to break free of his grip, but not too hard. "For what?"

Dancer held him in place, waiting for Tucker to look at him. The tiny blond whiskers that tried to shield his jawline were barely more than stubble. His beautiful pink lips—Dancer wanted to kiss those lips. His heart pounded in his chest as his heels left the ground. He took a deep swallow and pushed his heels back down. "For being an ass. I didn't mean it."

"Then why'd you say it?" The aggression in Tucker's voice reverberated in his throat.

The idea of kissing Tucker scared the shit out of him. Dancer couldn't remember the last time something had scared him like this. He didn't kiss a John unless he had to. He tried to keep it out of the deal. But all he wanted at this moment was to kiss the most magnificent pair of lips he had ever seen.

Without thinking a second longer, he stood on his toes and kissed Tucker as hard as he could. His heart was racing.

Tucker pushed him down. The look in his eyes was as if he had never seen Dancer before. "What are you doing?" He took a step back.

It was a question Dancer couldn't answer. A question he should have been asking himself. *What am I doing?* He wanted to kiss him again, but Tucker's glare said no. "I don't know. I don't know what I'm doing. But I don't want you to go."

"Why'd you kiss me?" The muscles in Tucker's face relaxed.

A passerby bumped into Dancer's back, throwing him into Tucker. The clash of their bodies together made Dancer hyper-sensitive to his inability to pull away. He had no control of his own body.

Tucker helped Dancer back onto his feet but held his grip on him. The two stood inches apart, their eyes locked onto one another. "You kissed me," Tucker muttered.

"I don't want you to go. I don't know." Dancer scrambled for words. "I like you. I'm sorry for kissing you. I shouldn't have."

"I didn't say you shouldn't have. It surprised me. I didn't know." Tucker's tongue moistened his lips before it ran over the spot Dancer's had just been.

Tucker's tongue was entrancing, drawing Dancer's focus onto his mouth. Lips he wanted to kiss again. "Then come back with me. To my place."

"Me and Mattie?" Tucker pulled back.

It wasn't what Dancer was asking, but yes. "You guys can stay with me for a couple of days until you figure things out." Even if it included Mattie, he would take what he could get.

Tucker looked at the time on his phone. "Are you sure?"

"Yes, I'm sure. It's okay." As Dancer finished his sentence, thunder cracked over their heads, unleashing the storm that had been holding back all morning.

"I hate this rain!" Tucker shouted over the sudden downpour.

Throwing his hood over his head, Dancer tried to shield himself from the rain. "Come on! Let's get out of here!"

The two ran through the wet streets, weaving around people until they reached the camp. Soaked from head to toe, Dancer's heart was racing, not because of the run but the prospect of what was to come. With the door closed, he turned to look at Tucker. He was adorable with wet hair. A tiny giggle escaped under Dancer's breath as he admired the water falling from Tucker's hair and face.

Tucker's body shook as he crossed his arms around his chest. "Do you have heat in here?"

The question was so absurd that it wasn't even funny. "No. Get out of your wet clothes." He tore the blanket from the top of his mattress. "Take this!" This was déjà vu, all over again. He handed Tucker the blanket.

The sight of Tucker wrapped in one of his blankets five days ago played out in his head. The thought of Tucker's beautiful arms holding him stoked a tiny fire in Dancer.

Tucker took the blanket and used it as a towel to wipe his face. "I have dry clothes." He handed the blanket back to Dancer and looked around until he spotted his suitcase.

Tucker brushed against Dancer as he moved past him to retrieve his dry clothes. His light touch raised the hair on the nape of Dancer's neck. His eyes followed Tucker as he kneeled in front of his suitcase.

Dancer was unsure if he could keep himself from watching Tucker undress. He ached at the thought of seeing him naked as his own body responded, the blood thickening in his groin.

With his back to Dancer, Tucker peeled off the wet shirt. His back muscles flexed as he rummaged through the small suitcase until he found a sweatshirt to put on.

Dancer's eyes followed the sweatshirt as it dropped down his back, stopping about two inches from the waistline of his wet jeans. The way Tucker squatted over his suitcase, the back of his jeans had pulled away from his skin, revealing the crack of his ass. Dancer swallowed a gulp of air, pushing it down into his lungs. When Tucker rose to his feet with another pair of jeans in hand, Dancer looked away before he could be caught. To his surprise, Tucker never turned around. He toe-kicked his boots off and wrestled out of his wet jeans. He was commando, standing bare ass with his back to Dancer.

Dancer's heart raced at the sight of Tucker's ass. It was elongated, his butt cheeks perfectly symmetrical. Shaped like two half-moons, each cheek had an adorable dimple in the middle of the muscle. Yes, it was the most beautiful ass he had ever seen. He had to force air down into his lungs to be able to say what he wanted to say. "I like you." The words echoed in Dancer's head as if he hadn't been the one who said them.

With his jeans in hand, Tucker turned around. He gave Dancer a curious glance. "Is that why you invited me back?"

Dancer's eyes fell to Tucker's flaccid cock, which laid against a set of balls that matched the length of his penis. "No… Yes… I mean, no, that's not the reason." It was a lie. "I'm sorry about kissing you like that."

"I told you not to be sorry. I'm cool with it." Tucker put one leg into his dry jeans and then hobbled a step forward as he sunk his other leg down into his pants.

The moment had passed. Tucker was in dry clothes. Had he said he was *cool* with it? As if Dancer had offered him a soda or something? "I'm not sure why I invited you back." Mattie and his mother complicated things.

The sensation of Tucker's hands on his waist was enough to shake Dancer back to the present. Tucker's six-one frame was standing inches in front of him, his eyes staring down at Dancer's. "You're an odd duck. I enjoyed the kiss. But…"

Dancer tried to stop himself, biting down on the *but*. "But what?" He took a deep breath, pushing down the lump of excitement that was trying to form in his throat.

"Nothing."

"Just say it."

"Okay. That was messed up, what you said at lunch about me giving up on life. Baseball was my life, and I didn't give up on it, someone took it from me. I was hit in the head by a damn ball and almost died."

"But you didn't." Dancer stared up into Tucker's eyes. The heat coming off Tucker's body radiated out into the room.

"There are days I wish I had. With seizures, the medicine, the headaches, I can't hold down a job. And… my sister, I'm all she has. What would happen if…"

Their faces were inches apart. Dancer was realizing that Tucker was a person who put others first. Despite all his own problems, he still put his sister first. Tucker was kindhearted and gentle. Heat coursed through Dancer's veins at the thought of Tucker kissing him.

"You like me?" The corner of Tucker's mouth creased. "I'm good with that." There was a hint of laughter in his voice.

Lost for words, Dancer hunched his shoulders. He liked this guy, and the emotions it was stirring in him were flying everywhere. The kiss had been more spontaneous than anything he'd ever done before. He always calculated everything, and now this spontaneous kiss seemed like it hadn't been such a good idea. It was impulsive and stupid. He had lost count of how many guys he had been with in the last six years. There had been so many that, at some point, they stopped having faces. Mr. Gerhardt and Mr. Chinn were the exceptions. He tried to push away the thoughts of what he did for them. He freed himself from Tucker's hold, but Tucker immediately pulled him back in. The force of Tucker's hand controlled his entire body as it pulled him up into Tucker's chest.

Tucker's hand moved across Dancer's neck and under his chin. Tucker's grip was stopping him from fleeing. Dancer had to escape his grip so he could breathe. This dance they were doing was overwhelming him. Tucker's grip made him feel pinned. There was no need for Tucker to hold him at all. He had to breathe. Tucker was trying to control him—Tucker was breaching his defenses.

Dancer needed to be in control, and the only way to be in control was to break free. He pulled back hard enough to escape from Tucker's hold and took a step back. He gasped for breath.

Tucker stared at him. His eyes conveyed worry, searching for what went wrong.

In a panic, Dancer knew he owed him an explanation. It was too much, too fast. He'd had Johns in the past that became aggressive with him when he pulled back. But Tucker wasn't a John. "It's just that I never—" He questioned whether he could allow himself to be vulnerable by telling the truth. He took a deep breath to collect himself, trying to corral the rampant thoughts swirling in his head.

"What?" The concern in Tucker's voice was unmistakable.

"Can we just talk?" Dancer tried to slow his breathing. His face was still burning.

Tucker scratched his forehead. His eyes locked on Dancer, brows waiting for an explanation.

"Other than you and your sister, I've never invited anybody in here." The truth was, other than the Milkman, no one had ever been in his place, nor had he ever kissed anyone who was not a John. He'd had sex in cars, motels, apartments, back alleys, and even someone's office. In the last six years, he'd yielded to the most bizarre requests, ranging from pretending to be dead, to wearing masks, to being dominant. Nowadays, he was relieved when the John just wanted a blowjob or anal sex.

76

"Oh. So where do you go?" Tucker looked around the room.

"Where do I go? For what?" Dancer's thoughts were scattered. He knew this was bigger than letting someone into his place. He was on the verge of letting him into his heart. Heat rose into his cheeks as his skin begin to tingle.

"When you have sex?" Tucker's brow further narrowed, confusion on his face. "You have sex for a living, so where do you take them?"

"Not here. I've never brought anyone here." Dancer focused on their conversation.

"Not even a boyfriend or something?" Tucker fell back in the recliner as if his legs had given out on him.

"No."

Tucker stared at him as if trying to read his mind. "But you've had boyfriends—right?"

"Well…" There was no 'well'; the answer was no. He had never been with anyone other than a John. "Not really," Dancer murmured.

"That's a trip! You have sex for a living, but you've never had a boyfriend. How is that possible?"

Tucker's questions gave him a second to think. Sex wasn't at all what he wanted from Tucker. And yet it seemed as if whatever they were talking about was the same. "Well, I'm not into people. I prefer to be by myself." Dancer moved over, creating more distance between them. Tucker was staring at him as if waiting for him to continue.

"Let's see if I can change that." Tucker stood back up.

"Change what?" There was no changing anything. This whole thing was stupid. He wasn't looking to hook up with Tucker, if that's what he wanted. To have sex with Tucker would make him like every other slimy, disgusting man looking to get off. Was that what Tucker was looking for, to get off?

"I invited you back here because…" *I thought you were different. I thought you liked me.* "I don't know why, I just did. But now…"

"What?" Confusion riddled Tucker's face.

How could he get out of this mess he had created? "Um, I told you, I'm not into people. I don't know what I'm doing." Dancer stood to create distance. *I like you. I do, but—I can't have sex with you.*

"You keep saying 'but'—but what?" Tucker replied, his voice low and husky.

Dancer didn't know how to say that the thought of having sex with Tucker made his skin crawl. That he wanted no one to touch him. He wasn't a child any more. He controlled what happened to him now. But there was no way of telling Tucker the truth without having to revisit a place he refused to go. He'd worked too hard to put it away for good. And what about Tucker's mother and Mattie? It felt like more than Dancer was ready for.

"Wow, okay. I get it. You're not into people." Tucker rubbed his hand across his face. "Let me get our stuff, and I'll be out of here."

"No!" That wasn't at all what Dancer wanted. "Go get your sister. Come back here. I meant it." He had promised Tucker a place to stay. He wouldn't go back on his offer. "You guys can chill here for a couple of days, until something comes through for you."

"You don't have to do that. We'll be fine."

Dancer's heart was racing. There was a part of him that said, *Let him go*. "No, It's fine." He crossed his arms over his chest.

Tucker stepped over the camping stove between them. "I'm having a hard time figuring you out. Are you asking me to stay because you're worried about me and Mattie out there, or because you like me?"

Dancer's heart stopped as Tucker stepped into his space. Before he could step back, Tucker's hands dropped to Dancer's waist, encircling him, pulling him up into his body.

"I want to think it's because you like me," Tucker whispered.

The surge of desire from being pressed into Tucker's body told Dancer why he didn't want him to walk out that door. Dancer's heels rose, his body arching up into Tucker's chest. To steady his legs, he reached up and clutched Tucker's biceps. Tucker was not that much heavier than him, at most twenty pounds, but his firmness sent a wave of excitement through him. Body heat moved between them as a swirl of emotions that had been buried deep within Dancer rose to the surface. He gasped as his lungs released air that had been trapped.

"You need to answer my question," Tucker murmured.

Dancer couldn't talk. He was fearful that his voice would waver. His body was on fire. Why was it so freaking hot in here?

"I don't know what it is you're trying to tell me." Tucker's voice trailed off.

"I like you. I'm just not ready to have sex with you." It surprised Dancer that he could get the words out.

Tucker studied him. "It's okay. It's okay to like me. We don't have to have sex." Tucker ran his thumbs across Dancer's eyebrows before kissing him again.

It wasn't just about the sex. "What about your mother? What if she returns, then what?" She was a junkie. He avoided junkies. They were thieves, liars, and always bad news. Bile rumbled in Dancer's stomach as he pulled away from Tucker.

"What about her?" Tucker placed two fingers under Dancer's chin and raised his head.

Staring into the sea of blue that was Tucker's eyes, Dancer would have fallen if not for the hold Tucker had on him. "Your mom. What are you going to do if she shows up tomorrow—or the next day?"

"I don't know, but I don't trust her. I don't want to leave Mattie with her while she gets high or does whatever it is she does with guys. I have to protect Mattie! I don't know what the hell I'm supposed to do!"

"Are you staying with them to protect Mattie?" Dancer already knew the answer to that.

"Look, I've been crazy about you since I met you. Since I saw you, when you were messing around with the tarp. You were trying to be all butch and badass. You're not butch or a badass. I think you're scared."

Dancer cringed. Tucker's words punched him in the gut. "You know nothing about me!" *And if you did, you wouldn't like me.* "I just met you."

"I was joking. You're so serious. For right now, I'm good with you liking me and me liking you." His face reddened. "Look, I have about an hour before I have to go get Mattie. Do you want to go to the police station with me? I have to get our debit card."

"Now? You're going right now?" Shifting his mindset, Dancer grappled with everything, trying to make sense of any tiny piece of their conversation.

"No," he finally said. "Go do what you have to do and get your sister." Dancer looked around his small space. He would give them his bed and he would take the Milkman's chair again. Would they eat at the shelter before coming back? He needed food for Mattie. If it were just him, that sandwich would have tided him over for the night. But it wasn't anymore. How quickly his little world had expanded. There was a knot in his gut as he questioned again what he was doing.

Surprised and jolted from his thoughts, Tucker pulled Dancer back up into his chest. "Why are you frowning?"

Unaware that he was, Dancer faked a smile. "I was thinking. I should probably wash the sheets for you guys." Because of the storms, it had been over a week since his last trip to Mr. Bubbles Laundromat.

"You don't have to. It's just a few days. I don't want you fussing over us."

The warmth of Tucker's breath pressed across Dancer's face. His words reminded him that yes, it was only for a few days. The knot in his gut grew.

Still holding him, Tucker laid a tiny kiss on his bottom lip. It felt as if a stone travelled through his mouth, down his throat, and blocked air from escaping his lungs. He had been strong the last several years, doing everything by himself, but now, it all was colliding with desire. Tucker possessed the ability to rock his world and change everything.

Chapter Eleven

Relieved that he had made it back from Walmart before Tucker and Mattie returned, Dancer dropped the three shopping bags on the floor. The kiss—it was impossible not to think about, and he could not bring himself to admit that it was the reason for his giddiness. If he did, it would mean he cared. He thought of himself as strong. Tucker was compromising his strength.

Dancer stripped the bedding off his mattress as his mind raced at the possibilities of what could occur on this bed. He knew that he was overthinking, forgetting about Mattie. He tossed the dirty sheets and blanket on his chair to use later that evening. Between new sheets, disposable razors, shaving cream, toothpaste, baby wipes, and stuff from the deli for tonight's dinner, he had spent almost all his money.

He worked quickly to make the bed, trying hard to push his excitement down. He didn't want Tucker thinking he was making a big deal about them staying, but wanted them to be comfortable—he wanted it to be nice. After fixing the bed, he fluffed his two sofa pillows and propped them against the wall. He laid out the hygiene products next to the pillow.

Dancer folded the old sheets and blanket on the chair and placed them on top of the bins in case someone wanted to sit there. He debated leaving the rotisserie chicken and bag of BBQ potato chips he had bought for dinner in the bag or setting them out. He decided he would leave them in the bag and put the large bag of M&Ms, a box of orange ginger tea, and the hot cocoa mix into his food bin. They didn't need to know that he had bought those for them as well.

It was after six when Tucker shouted his name from outside, alerting Dancer that he was back. Dancer's heart leapt in his chest. He was unsure if he was ready for this.

He unlocked the door and pushed it to the side. The tightness in his stomach felt as if someone was wringing out his intestines. He was standing in his own home, yet he felt uncertain about what to do.

Affection glowed in Tucker's eyes as their gazes met. Had he been this beautiful when he left? "Were you able to get that card from your mother's things?" Dancer asked. He didn't know what else to say. What he wanted was another kiss. In all his years as a sex worker, his body had never responded to a kiss the way it had today.

Tucker nudged Mattie to go inside. "No. They said they couldn't release anything to me out of her property." He followed his sister as they entered the shanty.

"Why not?" Dancer waited, ready in case Tucker wanted to kiss him.

"They said she would have to send it. They couldn't give me anything out of her property. The cop was an asshole."

Dancer's eyes bounced from Tucker, to Mattie, and then back to Tucker at the curse word. There was no reaction from Mattie to his foul language. He moved toward the food he had purchased. "Did you guys eat already?"

Tucker nodded. "They fed her right before I got there. The school's nice. I met her teacher too." Tucker helped Mattie with her coat as she twirled out of it. He tucked the coat between his legs and then took his jacket off. "What have you been up to?

"Nothing. I ran out to pick up a few things—while it wasn't raining. I think it's supposed to rain again later tonight." Things were awkward now, with Mattie in the room. It was like the kiss had never happened, and he was searching for something to talk about.

He reached out, took the coats from Tucker, and hung them on a hook protruding from the wall. Tucker looked surprised that the hook was there. "They're all around," he said. "What about you? Are you hungry? I have food if you're hungry."

Dancer pulled the package of chicken and bag of chips from the bag. "I didn't know what to get." He laid them on top of the bin as if it was a table.

Tucker leaned toward the food as he eyed it. "I'll take the chips. Thanks. Mattie, you want some potato chips?"

"No." She clung to her brother's side.

"Did you have time to see your mother at least—to let her know you needed the card?" Dancer watched as Mattie followed Tucker's nod to sit down on the mattress. He wished he had something for her to do. Why hadn't he thought about picking up a doll or something for her to play with?

"No. They said I had to fill out a visitor's application, and it would take four days to be approved." Tucker started in on the bag of chips.

"Are you going to be okay with no money?" Dancer stopped short of offering to help.

"Ian told me to go down to the welfare office and ask for a new one. Let them know we lost it."

Why hadn't he thought of that? Of course, Ian had thought of it. Dancer tried not to roll his eyes. "You saw Ian?"

"Yeah, after I picked up Mattie. We went over to the shelter. I wanted to see if they had any room for us. They're full. He came into the dining room to say hi." Chips in hand, Tucker took a seat next to Mattie on the mattress.

"I thought you were okay with staying here." Had Tucker already had a change of heart? Was that the coolness Dancer was sensing?

"I am, but I'm also trying to figure things out. I have to do something to get us off the streets. I need a job."

It made little sense to Dancer. Why would Tucker want to stay in a shelter instead of here, with him? He was about to sit back in his chair when Tucker nodded at him.

"Come here." Tucker's eyes steadied on him as he nodded again.

Sit next to him? And Mattie? Unsure what to expect, Dancer stepped over the camping stove and eased down next to Tucker, leaving several inches between them.

Tucker leaned over and, with a mouth full of chips, gave Dancer a tiny peck on the lips. Dancer licked his lips, tasting the spice and salt from the chips. He was about to kiss Tucker again but stopped. Movement on the other side of Tucker reminded him that Mattie was sitting there.

Tucker chuckled. "It's a kiss. She's seen two guys kiss before."

To Dancer, it didn't seem as innocent as just two guys kissing. The flutter in his stomach, the dry mouth... He was never nervous with a John. This was more than two guys kissing. "Oh, okay." He adjusted himself on his own bed. It didn't feel like his bed anymore.

83

"She knows we like each other. She knows what gay is." Tucker stuffed his mouth with several more chips.

He was so open about it, so matter of fact. Was it really okay? Dancer's mind went to all the things he did with other men. Some he wished hadn't come to mind, but he couldn't shut it off. How much had Tucker told her?

Mattie pulled out several sheets of white paper from her tiny pink backpack. She reached deep inside and pulled out a purple crayon. Dancer watched as she started coloring on what looked like a page from a coloring book. "Did she like her first day at school?" He wasn't sure why he was asking Tucker instead of her, but it was safer to speak to him.

"Yeah. She loves school." Tucker patted her on her head then stroked her hair.

Her hair was oily, strung together by dirt. Dancer looked at her pants and tiny shoes, and they too were soiled. She needed clean clothes. He had clean clothes. He always had clean clothes. He bathed every other day, sometimes daily at Chinn's. He knew what dirty was, he lived all around it, but looking at Mattie, he felt a desire to make it better for her. "Do you guys have clean clothes?"

Tucker looked down at his shirt and then at Dancer. His brows furrowed. "What do you mean? We have our stuff in our bags."

Dancer's question had not come out as he intended. "I mean, like, more stuff somewhere else. Like in storage or something?"

Tucker shook his head. "No. We lost everything. Every time we moved, we took less and less. This is all we have."

Dancer looked at the two medium and one small suitcases. "Does she have something clean for tomorrow?" Dancer looked around the tiny space. He didn't have much, but he had all he needed. He didn't want for anything. Although he'd spent almost all his money today shopping, there was always more where that came from. He knew how to get more; he could get as much as he needed. Men wanting sex was a sure thing.

"I think so. Mattie, hand me your bag." Tucker pointed to her bag on the other side of Dancer.

Mattie put down her crayon and pulled herself up. With a few steps, she crossed in front of Dancer and grabbed the handle of her bag. Tilting it down, she wheeled the suitcase over to her brother.

Unzipping the bag, Tucker pulled out two sweaters, two pairs of pastel-colored pants, underwear, and several pairs of socks. "Yeah, she has lots of clean stuff."

"Can I wear this tomorrow?" Mattie snatched up the pink pastel pants and floral print sweater that Tucker had tossed on the bed.

"Yeah." Tucker took the pants and sweater and put them to the side. "I have less than she does. I need to wash some of my stuff. I could use a shower too." Tucker's eye's fell on Dancer's pants.

For the first time in his life, Dancer was embarrassed that he was clean. "After you drop Mattie off in the morning, we can go to the laundromat. There's a place you can get cleaned up." Then he hesitated, questioning whether he should say it. "After we pick her up tomorrow, we can take Mattie over there, so she can have a bath too." Dancer wasn't sure how that would work with Mr. Chinn. It made him nervous, but it was the only solution he had.

"Cool. That would be great. I'd love a shower." The excitement in Tucker's voice escalated as he licked salt from his fingers.

Dancer was kicking himself for suggesting going to Chinn's. It was a bad idea. He had invited Tucker deeper into his world. Would Tucker be okay with it? Surely not. His stomach turned.

"Can I ask you something?" Tucker crumpled the empty bag of chips and lay it in front of them.

"Sure." Dancer surprised himself with how easily he agreed without even knowing the question. He cleared his throat as he prepared himself for what Tucker might ask in front of Mattie.

"Where'd you get the name Dancer?" Tucker slid his large hand across Dancer's thigh and squeezed his leg.

The harmless question caused more of an internal conflict than it should have. Dancer had left his old life in the past, somewhere in a motel, the back seat of a car, or in an alley. This was now his life, but somehow, Tucker was merging the two. "My Oma, she called me Dancer. Ever since I can remember." Dancer crossed his arms and released a sigh. "I used to dance. Like you, I had dreams. I wanted to go to Juilliard in New York or the Royal Ballet School in London." Yes, he used to dance. He could feel a buoyancy in his body thinking about how light he was on his toes when he danced. He would sail in the air doing a grand allegro, a combination of jumps that took him from one side of the stage to the other.

He recoiled a little with the thought of his Oma. She had fried catfish and hushpuppies every Friday until the day she died. "When I first came here, someone asked me what my name was. For some reason, I said Dancer. It's been Dancer ever since."

Tucker leaned into him, and their shoulders touched. "That's cool. So, you were a dancer. What's your real name?"

Tucker didn't understand what he was asking. Dancer hadn't said his name in years. That was a different person. "My name's Dancer." His voice trailed off. He wasn't going there with someone he barely knew. Silence fell between them, a welcomed silence that only lasted a couple of seconds.

"Oma. I had a friend who called his grandma Oma. They were German." Tucker spoke up again. "Are you German?"

A scratch in his throat delayed Dancer's answer for a second. "Half. My real dad was."

"I would've thought Italian. Your dark features make you look more Italian than German."

"My mom's from Puerto Rico. I take after my mom." He sniffled, hoping to pull back emotions that were struggling to free themselves. "You ask a hell of a lot of questions." He shouldn't have cursed, but it slipped out. "What are you going to do about your mom?" He would turn the tables; it was the easiest way out of this trip down memory lane.

Tucker shrugged. "Dunno."

Dunno was a lame answer. Would Dancer let him off the hook that easy? "What if she shows up tomorrow?" He wanted to know how she fit into whatever this was. He stood up and walked over to where he had left the chicken on top of the bin. He took it and sat back down next to Tucker. "Dig in."

Tucker grinned. "Did you get all this for us?"

He had, but that wasn't what he wanted to talk about. Dancer wasn't willing to be a surrogate for Tucker's mother. He watched as Tucker tore into the cavity of the chicken and ripped off the right drumstick and thigh. The grease from the chicken skin coated his fingers.

Tucker leaned over and puckered his lips. His greasy lips waited for his kiss. Dancer wasn't used to such playful affection. Hesitantly, he obliged the request. A faint hint of meat and grease wafted either across his nose or taste buds, he wasn't sure. Where it came from was lost in the chaos in his brain. What was Tucker expecting from him? They hadn't talked about it. Stuck in his head, he accepted the second and third lingering kiss but resisted when Tucker tried to pry his mouth open with his tongue. Dancer couldn't do that. Mattie was right there, and what about their mother?

Tucker pulled back, ending the kiss. "What?" A slight frown creased above Tucker's eyes.

"I can't." Dancer didn't mean to look over at Mattie, but it was an involuntary response as he juggled the many thoughts racing through his head.

Tucker turned to look at Mattie, who wasn't paying them any mind as she scribbled purple across the paper, which she held in place with her other hand. The crease in Tucker's forehead deepened.

"It's just..." Dancer sat up, creating a little separation between them. "We should talk." He clawed at his throat, flustered by what it was that he wanted. There wasn't anything he wanted to talk about; he just didn't want to make out in front of a child.

Things were so simple with a John. A one-minute greeting and then straight into the negotiations of services and price. From there it was off to wherever they would complete the deal. It was the same each and every time. He knew when a John was bad news. He could lean in against the car window and see in their eyes if they were trouble. It was a matter of survival. He'd had his ass kicked enough to be able to spot trouble. But Tucker wasn't playing by his rules. He was changing the game. "I put fresh sheets on the bed for you and Mattie." His hand trembled as he ran it across the bedding.

"You didn't have to." Tucker cocked his head to the side. "What is it you want to talk about?"

Dancer knew nothing about Tucker. He tried to pull away, but Tucker's soft tone and blue eyes brought him back and held him. "I want to get to know you better. I don't know much about you." Dancer broke eye contact, trying to retreat again. "Earlier, when I asked how you guys ended up on the streets, you said your mother couldn't keep it together. What did you mean?"

Tucker smirked and nodded. "Well... for as long as I can remember, we moved a lot. Apartment after apartment, sometimes living with friends, other times with whomever mum was sleeping with. When I was little, she worked for the county. It was the only real job I remember her ever having. That's where she hooked up with Mattie's dad and got pregnant. After she had Mattie, something happened, and she lost her job. I think that's when she might have started using more than weed. We moved out of the first real house we'd ever had back into an apartment. We were there about a year before we got kicked out. And then my accident happened. After that, things really fell apart. We spent a couple of months living with different people. She messed that up every time, and they would throw us out. Then we ended up moving here and lived with some friends. When that didn't work out, we moved into this motel over on Bremmer Street. We were there for about three weeks, then got kicked out of there, too, and ended up at the shelter."

"So, where's Mattie's dad?" Dancer asked.

"He's never been around. The only time he ever saw Mattie was the day she was born. I remember seeing him at the hospital. He spoke to me, and he and my mum were all happy and shit. Never saw him again."

Tucker's story was completely different from his but just as tragic. He couldn't imagine living with a junkie. Tucker's story said he was a caretaker. If it wasn't for him, who knew what could happen to Mattie? He stared at the bulky chocolate chair in front of him, his bed for the night. The Milkman had given up the mattress when Dancer first arrived, too. He took care of him when there was no one else. The least he could do was give his bed to Tucker tonight. Taking the chair was the natural thing to do.

Tucker licked the drumstick clean before tossing it on top of the stack of chicken bones that was beginning to resemble an archeology dig. "That was good. Thank you."

"You're welcome." Dancer placed the lid back on the plastic container and slid it out of the way. The container couldn't stay in here overnight. The rats would come in. The Milkman had taught him that everything either went in a bin or out the door. Tucker's presence brought back so many memories of the Milkman. Dancer pushed down a lump forming in his throat and then took a big, cleansing breath. He smiled, remembering how the Milkman didn't speak but communicated a lot, and quite well, with his body language and facial expressions. He had truly been Dancer's savior in this very dark world.

Tucker continued talking about his childhood, allowing Dancer's thoughts of the Milkman to fade into thoughts of Tucker as a child. There were sporadic periods of time when life was good. Almost as if he was bragging, the inflection in his voice rose when the conversation turned to baseball. Dancer knew next to nothing about the sport, a fact that appeared to excite Tucker more. The light from the lantern cast a glow onto Tucker's face as he explained the goal of a pitcher. The skin on his cheeks gleamed like silk, and the rhythmic tone in his voice said he wanted nothing from Dancer other than his ear.

Mattie found the conversation less interesting. Her little body was still sitting up, but her head and torso slumped over into her lap as she slept.

"Should you put her to bed?" Dancer nodded at her.

"Yeah, I guess. I should've made her brush her teeth before she fell asleep." Tucker lifted her arms, raising her torso, and slid her sweater off.

To get out of the way, Dancer rose and picked up the plastic container that held the skeleton of the chicken. The rats would be pissed that Tucker had picked them as clean as he did. "I'm going to dump this. When I come back, I'll fix some tea. Do you want some?" His heart fluttered as he watched Tucker lift Mattie's limp body, tucking her into his bed.

"Orange ginger?" Tucker asked as he lifted the covers up around Mattie's neck and smoothed them out.

Dancer anticipated Tucker's answer as he pulled the lid from his food bin and retrieved the box of tea he had just bought. "Yeah."

Tucker rose to his feet and stepped away from the bed, closer to Dancer. "You need help?"

"No, I'll be right back." Dancer gathered up the trash they had accumulated over the evening. Gone less than a minute, he shook the cold from his shoulders as he came in and went to work prepping the hot water for their tea. The sound of the flame buzzed as he lit the tiny camping stove and moved the pot over the flame.

He could feel Tucker's eyes on him. As much as he wanted to look up, he focused on the pot of water, nervously waiting for it to boil. He knew what Tucker was thinking—furthermore, what he wanted. Now that Mattie was asleep, what would happen?

Tucker's light touch to his shoulder caused him to flinch, sending a quiver down through him. Was this it? His stomach knotted as he stared down into the pot of water.

"Didn't your mother tell you a watched pot never boils?" Tucker squatted down into a catcher's position and dipped a finger in the water.

"I've never heard that." A nervous laugh escaped as he took comfort in the added distance Tucker created just by squatting.

"It's a joke, a saying. You know, like if you're waiting for something, it won't happen." Tucker rose and ran his fingers up Dancer's spine.

Dancer's body jerked at Tucker's touch. It felt like his stepfather coming up behind him. He moved out from under his touch, hoping to end the flashback. "That itches."

"Is something wrong?" Tucker's brows raised.

"No. I don't like people touching me." He created a separation between them with another half step.

"Oh, that's right. Sorry about that, I just..." Tucker's voice trailed off. Their eyes fixed on one another. "So how do we... You know, if you don't like being touched?"

"How do we what?" He knew what Tucker was asking.

"I'm a touchy-feely kind of person. I like touching you. But if it makes you uncomfortable, then I won't." Tucker's jaw clenched.

Dancer recoiled. He hadn't expected to react to the touch as strongly as he had. It was more complicated than he was ready to go into with someone he had just met. He fell back into his chair, hoping the extra space between them would help. A chill ran up through the back of Dancer's neck and down into the pit of his gut.

Tucker tapped Dancer's knee, signaling him to let him sit down. Dancer told himself there was not enough room in the chair for two people. If he did nothing, Tucker would get the message and abandon the idea.

"Come on, let me sit down." Tucker squeezed down into the chair. His voice squeaked. "Let's start with just sitting together. You don't have to do anything or say anything. I'm good just sitting next to you."

The hammering in Dancer's chest slowed. He could do this. The two sat in the Milkman's chair, the warmth of their bodies passing through one another. Without thinking, Dancer lay his head against Tucker's shoulder. His breathing slowed as he let go of another breath. He stared at Mattie sleeping across the room. Because of Tucker, she was safe.

Peace washed over him as the nervous energy was dispelled from his body. He wasn't sure how long he could sit there, so close to Tucker. The sound of rain outside played in his ear. He could hear it hitting the tarp and the speed with which it was falling. The sound of drops became louder, dominating his last thoughts as he drifted off to sleep.

Chapter Twelve

Tucker stirred at the sound of rush hour traffic picking up. The rain had stopped, and the buzz of the passing cars on the freeway echoed louder. They were still in the chair. Sometime during the night, Dancer had laid his head in the pit of Tucker's arm and chest. Tucker thought about how bad his pits must smell. He drew a breath that caused his nose to twitch. Yep, that was him.

If that wasn't reason enough to move, it was time to get Mattie up. He had to have her at the shelter early enough to have breakfast before school started. It had been nice yesterday, not having to worry about her for several hours. He couldn't remember the last time he had spent any amount of time without her. It was fun hanging out with Dancer, going to lunch, and just chilling.

He wasn't sure what had set Dancer off last night, but the fact that he let Tucker hold him all night indicated that Tucker wasn't the problem. With the top of Dancer's head under his chin, he caught a light scent of soap in his hair. The shower Dancer had offered last night couldn't come soon enough. Having clean clothes and washing the stench of dirt away from his body would be a dream come true.

He shifted his body enough to cause Dancer's head to stir, lifting slightly and then collapsing back into him. "Hey, sleepy, we have to get up." Tucker shrugged, causing Dancer's head to bob. Tucker was in love with his wild hair, his eyes. Dancer was the kind of dude that never paid any attention to people like him for the simple reason that he was way out of Tucker's league. Dancer was so cute sleeping, that Tucker hesitated to nudge him again.

He needed to step it up. He needed a job. He lay there for several minutes before sliding out from under Dancer's limp body so he could stand up.

"Mattie." Tucker stepped over to the mattress and bent down

over his little sister. "Hey, Mattie." He rocked her shoulders, waking her. "It's time to get up. We need to eat and get you to school."

Mattie's eyes opened at the mention of school. She was excited about going. He was thankful for Ian's help. She had missed months of school while they bounced from place to place over the last year.

With Mattie up, for the first time, Tucker opened the front door by himself. Quietly they went out and brushed their teeth, and they both relieved themselves over along the fence line.

When they returned, Dancer was up, digging around in one of his bins.

"Good morning." Tucker walked up behind him and wrapped one arm around his waist. Dancer tried to wiggle out of his arm, but Tucker pressed tighter, wrapping his other arm around Dancer's other side. He wasn't going to let him run.

"Can you let me go?" Dancer squirmed again. "Do you want tea?"

"Why don't you drink coffee?" Tucker refused to let him go, placing a kiss on the back of his neck as if it was a game.

"Because I like tea." Dancer twisted his neck away from Tucker's lips.

"Okay then, tea it is. You know I'm not going to let you go until you tell me good morning."

"Okay, good morning," Dancer groaned.

"Now tell me you like my kisses." Tucker grinned as he kissed him again across the nape of his neck.

"Can you let me go?" Dancer freed himself.

Tucker stared at him, unsure if Dancer was joking or in a bad mood. "Then I won't do that. Sorry. Are you okay?" Tucker held his gaze, still trying to make sense of what had just happened.

"I'm fine." Dancer's body language said he was anything but fine.

It was clear to Tucker that Dancer wasn't going to talk about it. Certain he must have done something more then just touching Dancer to set him off like that, he was unsure Dancer had accepted his apology. Embarrassed, Tucker got Mattie dressed faster than normal, and with little conversation, the two left.

*****

In the alley, Mattie released her brother's hand and never looked back as she passed through the doors and into the school. He stood in the alley, between the shelter and the school, not sure what to do next. He had no money and nowhere to go. Returning so soon to camp didn't seem like a good option. Maybe Dancer needed a little space.

He thought about looking around, seeing if he could find some 'Help Wanted' signs. This morning was as good a time as any to look for work. His schedule was wide open. As much as he was falling for Dancer, it was possible that Dancer didn't want a boyfriend. Maybe sex with anonymous people was his thing, and that was all he wanted. He said he wasn't a people person. Maybe that included Tucker. He couldn't figure out how someone could have sex for a living and refuse to be touched.

It wasn't long before he spotted his first *Help Wanted* sign. In the window of the Napoleon's Pizzeria hung the answer to all his problems. He pushed on the glass door to go in, but it was locked. The hours of operation posted in the window said it wasn't opening until eleven. That was hours away.

He turned on his heels and walked back toward the camp. He would return after his shower. That made more sense anyway. He needed to be clean and shaven to get the job.

When he arrived back at the shanty, Dancer was still in his sweatpants and hoodie. As adorable as he was in his baggy sweats, it was a bad idea to try anything romantic. Tucker opted for conversation. "Did I do something wrong this morning?"

"No. I just don't like to be grabbed." Dancer turned his shoulders away.

"I didn't grab you, I was—"

"You did grab me, and I told you I don't like to be touched," Dancer replied.

Tucker felt the aggression behind Dancer's tone. Who was this devilishly hot man hiding behind the movie star hair and seductively green eyes that was so broken? His words, his behavior, were a cheap mask hiding fear and pain. What had been done to him for this to be? The thought of someone abusing Dancer made Tucker sad. Who had damaged this work of art? There was no mistaking what Dancer was telling him, nor room for any negotiation. "Sorry." Tucker felt like an ass realizing how oblivious he had been this morning. Dancer wasn't

94

just being bitchy earlier, he really didn't like to be touched—and yet Tucker had kept touching him—hugging him—trying to cuddle.

Silence filled the room as Dancer punched several pieces of clothing into a black garbage bag. When he was finished, he grabbed several items from one of the bins and stuffed them into his backpack.

"Did you still want to get cleaned up and wash your clothes?"

"Yeah, I guess." Tucker scratched at his head trying to make sense of the mood swings. "Give me a minute to get our things."

Dancer held out the bag in front of him. "Here, put 'em in here."

Tucker took the bag, their eyes meeting for less than a second before Dancer looked away.

Within minutes, they were at the laundromat and had three washers going. Tucker had come to terms with the fact they weren't talking. Whatever Dancer was pissed about, he was going to keep it a secret. He watched as Dancer transferred the clothes from the washers to the dryers.

Dancer finally broke the silence. "I don't mean to be bitchy. I just... I told you, I'm not a people person. I don't know what I was thinking when I kissed you yesterday. We should have never—"

"Don't say it! You're lying. You're afraid of something." Tucker refused to allow him to walk back what had happened. There was something there; he felt the chemistry between them. He wanted to believe that Dancer wasn't broken beyond repair. "I don't know jack shit about you. But I know you slept in my arms last night and never moved. I know you didn't invite me to spend the night because you're not into people."

Dancer closed the lid on the dryer and slipped his card into the slot to start it. His not looking at Tucker did little to prove him wrong.

"Come on, Dancer, talk to me. I like you, and you admitted that you like me. Is it that you're scared to get involved with me because of my mum? Is it because of Mattie? Because I don't have a job? What is it?" He didn't dare throw out the other possibility, that maybe Dancer had been abused. Tucker tried to imagine how deep that emotional wound would be.

"No! It's because of you! I've never done this. I live alone, I have sex for a living with strangers. And I don't like to be touched by people!"

Tucker would not judge Dancer based on his profession. But it

95

made no sense how he could have sex for a living and not liked to be touched. What did he mean, saying it was because of Tucker? What had he done? "I don't understand. Did I do something to you, to make you change your mind? If you give me a chance—"

"I'm screwed up. I don't need to complicate your life any more than it already has been."

Tucker laughed. "What life are you talking about? I have no home, no job, and no money. I can't wash my clothes without your help. Can you mess up my life any worse than it already is?"

Dancer folded his arms across his chest. His nostrils flared. "You think you can handle it?" Dancer's eyes were sharp and steely as he stared at him. "I have sex for a living with guys I don't know. They're nasty-ass dudes who don't give a shit about me. Can you deal with being with someone who does that?"

Tucker's expression sobered. "I don't know."

"That's what I thought. The last thing I want is to get involved with you knowing you won't be able to deal with what I do."

Tucker wished he had said 'yes' instead of 'I don't know' to Dancer's question. But he really didn't know. He also didn't know where his next meal was coming from, or if he was going to have a seizure in the middle of the night, or when his mum was coming home. With all the unknowns, he was sure about one thing: he wanted to be with Dancer, period. He had given no thought to what he did, where he lived, or what he had. He wanted to be with Dancer. They had known each other for less than two weeks, and yet he was head over heels about Dancer.

This whole conversation had Tucker's brain on overload. He thought about what he could say to fix it. Maybe if Dancer didn't have to do what he did, things might be different. "Will you always be doing that? I mean, like, instead of a real job? You said you didn't enjoy it. Why do it then?"

Dancer's face contorted, and Tucker knew he shouldn't have said it.

"Because I fucking have to eat!"

Tucker wasn't that naïve. He knew Dancer had to work, but why this? Why had this been the only option? There was little doubt this option had served him well. To someone other than Tucker, Dancer may have looked like he had nothing, but it was a lot more than

Tucker had. If not for Dancer, he wouldn't have had a place to stay last night. It seemed a lifetime ago that he was at home, in his room, thinking about his next game. Once upon a time, that was all he thought about.

"Your shower, it's not for free, either. There's nothing for free in this life." Dancer removed a stack of clothes from the last washer and tossed them into an empty dryer.

Tucker was unsure whether he wanted to know what Dancer meant. Something told him Dancer wasn't talking about money. "What do I have to do for the shower?"

Dancer leaned back on the dryer he had just started. He folded his arms across his chest and just stared at Tucker.

"Tell me what I have to do." Tucker was tired of his games.

"He likes to watch."

"Who is *he*?"

Dancer fidgeted. "Mr. Chinn."

"Is that all?" Tucker knew there was more. He wanted Dancer to talk to him. Some old fart watching him take a shower was nothing. There had to be more.

"Sometimes… when his wife isn't there, he wants to play."

"What does that mean?" Tucker knew damn well what it meant, but he needed Dancer to say it.

"He likes to watch me touch myself—while he jerks off." Dancer's eyes burned into him.

"Will his wife be there?" Tucker stared down at the dirt under his fingernails.

"I don't know."

"I'm not taking Mattie there!" Tucker was reminded of the mentally ill man that had tried to take Mattie last week. There hadn't been a day since that happened that he hadn't kicked himself in the ass for leaving her outside by herself. It was only two seconds, but it was enough time to possibly change her life forever. For the first time in all of this, he questioned what he was doing.

Dancer rolled his eyes. "He's not interested in little girls. Anyway, his wife and kids are almost always there after school."

"I don't care! I'm not taking her there!" That would never happen, never ever. He wasn't sure he would go himself now. He imagined himself punching Chinn in the face, not for looking at

97

Tucker but for what he had most likely done to Dancer. Rage crept up his spine, bringing heat to the back of his neck. He turned to the dryer and stared at the tumbling clothes through the bubbled window.

The sound of the dryers filled his head as he thought about his life. It was a mess. Could he ask this Chinn person for money? If he wanted to watch, why shouldn't he make him pay?

The first dryer came to a stop. Dancer opened the door and ran his hand through the pile of hot clothes. He removed most of them from the dryer and tossed them onto the narrow metal table in the middle of the room. The rest of the clothes he merged with those in another dryer that was still running.

Tucker walked around to the other side of the table. He tried to fight back the words he was about to say. Leaving wasn't at all what he wanted. "Look, if you want me to leave, I'm cool with it. You don't owe me a shower or anything. You've done more than enough already. I thought—"

"No, I don't want you to leave. Don't be stupid!"

"How is that being stupid? You're pushing me away. You say it's not me, that you're afraid I can't handle any of this. Like I don't know what I'm getting myself into. That sounds like it is me." Tucker waited for Dancer to say something, anything. When it didn't happen, he took that as his answer and began folding his and Mattie's clothes.

Dancer folded what little he had to fold and stuffed it into the black garbage bag. He backed away from the table and propped his back and foot against the wall. "I don't want you to go." He seemed to wrestle with what he wanted to say. "I've got issues." He paused for a second. "It's not you, I swear. I'm used to being alone. Then you come along, and being alone is the last thing I want. You're funny. You make me laugh. But I don't know if I can do this."

He pushed off the wall and walked over to the vending machine in the back of the laundromat. "Do you want something to drink?"

"No, thank you." Tucker stared at Dancer's back as he fed the machine two dollars. What did he mean, saying that he didn't know if he could do this?

Dancer sipped his soda and then held it out to Tucker anyway. "You make me feel alive," he said, "and I don't know if I want to feel that."

Tucker took the can as he thought about that. The cold soda ran through his body. He hadn't realized he was so dehydrated. "What do you mean, you don't know if you want to feel alive? I don't get it." Tucker smacked his lips and handed the can back. Their fingers brushed together lightly.

"I really am fucked up. There is so much you don't understand about me."

"Will you ever tell me?" Tucker asked.

Dancer shrugged. "I don't know."

Everything inside of Tucker ached at what Dancer wasn't saying. Whatever it was, it was horrible.

Chapter Thirteen

The door swung open to the tiny restaurant. Chinn's had been in the neighborhood long before the city's revitalization, and it was one of the few original businesses that remained. Thanks to their large portions and cheap prices, it was a lunchtime favorite for the busy men and women who worked in the area. Their business in the evening came from takeout orders to the many who lived high above the ground in the new luxury apartments.

The old brick building still stood because of its landmark preservation status, a maneuver by the Chinns' lawyers to beat the city at their own game. Chinn's restaurant occupied the lower floor. Narrow from front to back, the kitchen opened to a back alley filled with dumpsters.

On the walk over, Dancer prepped Tucker for what Mr. Chinn might want and that they would tell him no. Mr. Chinn owed Dancer more than a free shower.

Tucker's eyes moved around the empty restaurant as he followed Dancer. They passed through the main dining room and through a set of swinging doors that led into the kitchen. A tiny Asian man sat on a stool in front of the counter, chopping carrots. As soon as he saw them, he stood, revealing how short he was. "Why-you-here?" His words ran together as if they were one word.

"This is my friend Tucker. If it's okay, he'd like to use your shower." Dancer moved closer to Mr. Chinn, took one of the carrots he was chopping, and snapped it off in his mouth. "If that's okay?"

Mr. Chinn's eyes shifted from the carrot in Dancer's mouth to Tucker. He held his stare, evaluating Tucker, assessing value over risk.

Tucker could crush the little guy with one hand, choke the life out of him within minutes, but that wasn't how this was going to go.

100

"Him-take-shower?" Mr. Chinn's head turned to the back door, which was open for airflow.

"Yeah, if that's okay," Dancer replied.

Tucker watched as Mr. Chinn leaned in and whispered something to Dancer.

"No." Dancer shook his head. "I'll come by later this week." His lashes fluttered as he ran his finger up Mr. Chinn's chest.

"Go-now. Hurry!" Mr. Chinn's face was cold as he waved them on. "You-hurry! Five minutes only!"

Dancer appeared to ignore the man's request for urgency as he sauntered past him. "Come on. Before his wife gets back." Dancer signaled for Tucker to follow.

The two walked through a door and into what appeared to be a storage room. The tiny shower, concealed by a curtain, was tucked in the corner of the room. Tucker was surprised; he had assumed the shower would be in a real bathroom, upstairs in the apartment. Mildew filled his nose. The place smelled of a wet mop.

"There." Dancer pointed to the shower. "Hurry." He stepped away from the shower and leaned his body against the door.

Kicking off his boots, Tucker worked to unfasten his belt and the zipper on his jeans. Within seconds, he was standing nude in front of Dancer.

Tucker twisted his body to turn the water on, causing his waist to narrow, and his pale ass to thrust out. He looked under his arm, glancing back at Dancer. Although nothing had been settled, they were at least smiling at one another again. "Are you enjoying the view?" Tucker asked.

Dancer cleared his throat over the sound of the pipes vibrating in the wall. "You have the most beautiful ass I've ever seen." Dancer's gaze traveled up Tucker's body.

"I thought you said you weren't sure you could do this." Tucker turned and smirked at him. "Sounds like you're ready to *do this*." Smiling, Tucker grabbed his right butt cheek and squeezed it in his hand.

Dancer's gaze stayed on him. "It's a nice ass. I think I can be persuaded."

"Well it's going to have to wait. You've had your chance, now I want the shower." Tucker ran his hand under the running water. "Does this get hot?"

Dancer chuckled. "Give it a minute. It gets hot. Trust me."

"I'm sure it does, but what about the water?" Tucker joked as he arched his ass out before stepping into the shower.

The water, as it hit his face, cascaded down his shoulders and caused him to forget their playful banter. He closed his eyes, shutting out everything but the warm water hitting his back. There was more than dirt being washed away; the water was stripping away frustration, anxiety, and anger. He moved to allow it to hit his upper neck, and his shoulders relaxed. The warmth of the water propelled him into a dreamlike state as blood rushed to his head. The endless cleansing waterfall stripped days of drama from his soul.

"You-finish-up-you-come-out!" A muffled voice barked from the other side of the door, causing Tucker to open his eyes.

He scrubbed down his body with the tiny bit of soap that smelled of rancid oil. He squeezed the soap between the pits of his arms and his neck, chest, and butt. He then wiped down his legs and feet with the bar before rinsing off.

Rejuvenated, Tucker pulled back the curtain to find Dancer still against the door. "Okay, all done!"

Dancer lifted his head, but his eyes fell back down to Tucker's groin. He pushed away from the door and grabbed a dish towel from a small stack of towels next to the shower. "Here." His face brightened with a look of approval in his eyes.

"Thanks. It feels so good to be clean again." The two made eye contact as he took the small towel.

"Come on. Hurry and get dressed." Dancer's voice was low as if he was talking to himself.

Tucker finished drying off and moved over to the trash bag that contained his clean clothes. "That was amazing! Thank you."

"Glad it worked for you." Dancer's voice was barely audible as he watched Tucker slip on his jeans over his bare ass.

Tucker smirked at Dancer's visible attraction. "So, that Mr. Chinn guy, did he want to watch me scrub my big heavy balls?"

Dancer's eyes rolled. "Did you want him to?"

"That shower felt so good that, if he wanted to, I think I'd let him."

"Well, I'll remember that next time." Dancer rolled his eyes again. "I'll heat water for Mattie when she gets home tonight. You can help her get cleaned up. I'll hang outside."

Tucker had forgotten about the plan to bring Mattie. He was relieved that Dancer had a better plan; he would never have brought her here. The flirting with Dancer and the warm shower had stirred up his primal needs. The thought of going back to Dancer's place and having sex stretched the front of his jeans. Could their first time also count as make-up sex? "What time is it?" How much time did he have before having to get Mattie?

"It's almost noon. Why?"

"Just wondering…" A surge of electricity pulsed through his gut and down into his groin. He tried to play it cool as he pulled a clean sweatshirt over his head and then tousled his hair, finger-combing it away from the front of his face.

Once Tucker was dressed, they made their way toward the kitchen. They spotted Mr. Chinn in the dining room taking an order and used the opportunity to escape out the back door and into the alley.

The shower did more than Tucker had expected. More than clean, he felt alive again. He had felt embarrassed when people took a step back from him as it was a constant reminder that he stank. Clean versus dirty seemed like such a small distinction, yet dirtiness evoked fear, skepticism, and contempt in people. They seldom hid their reactions.

*****

On the walk back to camp, the possibility of having sex with Dancer was a constant thought. Being commando didn't work when you were in an aroused state. Sure that everyone they passed could see his erection, he kept shifting to make it less noticeable.

He watched over Dancer's shoulder as he unbolted the door. Tucker thought about Dancer's compliments of his ass back at Chinn's and the look in his eyes on seeing Tucker naked. He was pretty sure Dancer wanted to have sex too. He wasn't buying that Dancer didn't like to be kissed. He was a phenomenal kisser. The thought of kissing Dancer caused his shoulders to jolt.

As much as Tucker wanted to have sex with him, he would let Dancer make the first move. As much as he didn't want to admit it, the fact that Dancer had sex for a living was as intimidating as it was intriguing. He was probably phenomenal at that too.

103

With the door closed, Tucker anticipated Dancer would jump him immediately. When it didn't happen, he stumbled over the ball of nerves in his gut. He couldn't be the one who made the first move. He was too chicken. Even with the way Dancer had looked at him, it wasn't enough. "I want to know more about you. I still can't believe your mum is Joaquina Ziegler, and that you used to be a ballerina." His nervousness caused him to ramble.

"First of all, I wasn't a ballerina. That's a girl. I was studying ballet." Dancer backed up and took a seat on his mattress.

"Did you like it?" Dancer sitting on the mattress instead of in the chair gave Tucker hope that something would happen yet.

"I loved it. I'd dance for hours. It was all I wanted, once upon a time." His voice trailed off.

"Would you dance for me one day?" Tucker joined him on the mattress, leaving about a foot between them.

"That was a long time ago." Dancer moved over, creating a little more distance.

"I get it. Baseball was a long time ago for me. What made you get into it?" Had Dancer moved over because Tucker was too close?

Dancer looked as if he had to think about it. "I don't know. When I lived at home, I don't remember a time when I wasn't dancing. When I was little, I was in a dance troupe. Later, I started my real training at La Bella."

"What's that?"

"It's a dance school. We did local productions and competitions around the state." Dancer lay on his back, stretching the end of his shirt out of his pants, exposing his abdomen.

Tucker tried not to look. "Were you good?" His eyes shot down at the bare skin across Dancer's flat abdomen. A dark patch of hair ran from beneath his jeans up to his belly button. Tucker wanted to see more, to touch it, to do something nasty to it, like lick it.

Without looking at him, Dancer nodded as he stared at the ceiling.

Tucker's nasty thoughts were like a drug that had just kicked in. "Now, don't take this the wrong way, but I think you guys are super-hot in those pants you wear. They're damn near see-through." His eyes fell to the bulge in the front of Dancer's jeans. "Was your dad cool with it?" What if it was his dad who abused him—maybe because he was gay? Was that why he lived on the streets?

"My real dad was amazing." Dancer looked over at him. "My dad drove me to all of my practices. He would stay for hours watching."

"How old were you when he died?" The front of Tucker's pants tightened as he thought of what lay beneath Dancer's zipper. *Should I make the first move? Should I just reach over and start kissing him?* Tucker wasn't sure what the first move was. It had been easy with Steven McDowell. Steven, the aggressor during their summer tryst, initiated when, where, and what they did.

"Twelve. They diagnosed him with pancreatic cancer. It all happened so quick. He was gone in six months." The glimmer in Dancer's eyes faded. The muscles in his jaw tightened as he turned his eyes up at the ceiling.

Tucker wanted to know more but saw the hurt in Dancer's face and decided not to ask anything else about his father. He thought for a moment how to frame his next question. It was something that had plagued him for the last couple of days. He thought about Mr. Chinn and the shower today. "Could I go out with you one of these days?"

"Out where?"

"You know, to make money." He wasn't convinced he could do it, but he was willing to try. There was a small part of him that couldn't deny that it would be pretty cool to get paid to have sex. He needed money, and he needed to take care of Mattie. It didn't seem to have destroyed Dancer. It had provided a roof over his head, food, money in his pocket, and a tablet with freaking Wi-Fi.

"And what about your little sister? What are you going to do with her while you're sucking off some old man in an alley?"

The picture Dancer painted sent bile up into Tucker's throat. Maybe it wouldn't be as cool as he thought. Dancer also raised another good point: what would he do with Mattie? The thought of strange men doing... whatever with his mother made him doubt again the notion that he wanted any part in it.

Dancer's brows rose as his head lifted. The green in his eyes glistened as they bore into him. "You don't want to do it. You need to find a 'real job' as you put it earlier." Dancer winked at him. "Has your mother always used?"

He had never discussed his mother's drug addiction with anyone. "No, or at least, I don't think so." As bad as the last year had been for them, he did remember a happier time. Before Mattie was born, it was just the two of them. She had doted over him to the point that he could do no wrong in her eyes, and he knew it.

"I'm sorry." Dancer's hand slid across the mattress. Palm up, it stopped halfway between them.

Tucker hesitated, questioning if Dancer was asking for his hand. Slowly, he took it and felt Dancer's fingers clasp around his.

"You can kiss me if you want." Dancer's voice quivered.

Tucker wasn't sure he had heard him right. The gleam in Dancer's eyes confirmed it. "Can I touch you?" Tucker asked.

"A little, but no funny stuff." Dancer's mouth curved into a tiny grin.

Tucker moved closer to Dancer, their faces inches apart. "No funny stuff. Got it." He thought he knew what funny stuff was, but now was not the time to clarify.

Dancer's head was angled to the side as their lips came closer and closer together. He brushed Dancer's lips with his.

Dancer's exhale startled him, causing him to pull back. Had he moved too fast? They stared at each other, deep into each other's eyes. The yearning green flecks in Dancer's eyes said to be careful with him.

Tucker whispered, "No funny stuff." He savored the syllables of each word between delicate butterfly kisses. Slow and soft, comforting, just as Dancer's eyes had asked.

"No funny stuff." Dancer murmured the words back as his lips followed Tucker's. His hand touched Tucker's ear as their breath mingled.

Tucker's fingers softly traveled down Dancer's spine, pulling him closer until they were chest to chest with no space between them. Dancer's heart hammered against his, the beats in sync. Unable to contain himself anymore, Tucker pressed his mouth tighter against Dancer's as he rolled Dancer on top of him. The weight of Dancer sent a warmth throughout his entire body, stoking the fire into a passionate kiss.

He worked his hands around Dancer's body, feeling each crevice, each line along his perfect physique. A moan escaped Tucker's lips. Dancer's firm ass through his jeans caused his fingers to grip harder as he pressed Dancer's body even tighter against his.

"What would you like?" Dancer uttered from the back of his throat.

He wasn't sure. He wanted everything. Whatever Dancer would allow, he wanted to do. "I don't know. Whatever you want." Tucker rolled Dancer off him and climbed on top. He covered Dancer's body with his own as he nuzzled his lips into Dancer's neck, laying soft kisses. "I want what you want." Whatever that was, Tucker was more than happy to take it.

Dancer moaned each time Tucker touched him. They were the rhythmic sounds that one makes when pleasured. With each kiss, Dancer murmured just a little louder.

They continued kissing, fighting to stay on the tiny mattress as their bodies rolled back and forth, trading who was on top every few minutes. The raw intensity built as their breathing became so shallow that they fought to breathe. With every kiss, the world melted away. Their mouths fit together as if they had been lovers for years.

One button at a time, Dancer removed Tucker's shirt before ripping his own off. Tucker savored every moment of Dancer's intoxicating breath during their frantic kissing while grinding against each other through their jeans. Several times, Tucker edged and had to slow himself down. If he came, it would be over. He didn't want it to end, not yet, not ever. In all the years he'd masturbated, it had never come close to feeling anything like this.

"You feel so good," Tucker groaned as their bodies continued to grind against each other.

Dancer reached between them and first freed himself from his jeans. He then worked to unzip Tucker, freeing his cock. When they pressed together, it was like a hot rod pressed against Tucker's belly. The two shifted their bodies against one another as they each made soft noises in the other's ear. Tucker rode the high as long as he could until the friction between their skin became unbearable. He could no longer hold it, spilling between them and everywhere.

Dancer had taken his breath away. Exhausted and in a euphoric state, he buried his head down into the side of Dancer's neck. His breathing ragged and shallow; he couldn't get enough air into his lungs with his face pressed into the mattress. He tried to move, but his body wasn't cooperating.

"Did you come?" Tucker asked. It had been fast and furious. From start to finish, he had lasted less than fifteen minutes. His head was spinning as the muscles in his thighs continued to twitch.

"No." Dancer moaned, his breathing ragged. He looked down between them. "Jesus! Is this all you?"

Tucker's eyes narrowed as, embarrassed, he looked down at all the goo covering Dancer's belly. "Sorry."

A smile curled the corner of Dancer's mouth. His eyes flickered a deep green. "Hand me a paper towel."

Without moving from the mattress, Tucker stretched his long arms across the floor to reach the roll of paper towels. He tore off two sheets and swabbed Dancer's flat abdomen clean. He had to use several more sheets to clean himself.

When he finished, Dancer reached up and swept the back of his hand across Tucker's flushed cheeks.

Dancer's light touch sent a rousing pulse deep into Tucker's back, causing his body to jerk. It was more than amazing. It was incredible. Tucker lowered his head enough that Dancer could kiss his neck. Each kiss radiated heat at the spot where his lips touched.

"Just for the record, I think you stole my heart." Tucker brushed the long curls away from Dancer's eyes. He would never tire of glancing into those magnetic green eyes. He loved the way the emerald glimmered when they gazed up at him. Dancer's eyes had the power to hypnotize him within seconds.

Dancer's eyes widened, the tiny grin becoming a little more prominent. "Do you want it back?"

Tucker laughed. "No, you can keep it, but no funny stuff."

"Okay. No funny stuff."

"Thank you."

"For what?" Dancer asked.

"For being the way you are." His voice wavered, still reeling from what had happened. He had so much to thank Dancer for, but for now, he would start there. Tucker rolled to his side so he could look at Dancer.

Dancer's hands stroked the hair on Tucker's neck. His eyes were steady. "It was nice. I like kissing you." Dancer propped his body up against Tucker's. He kissed him again before falling onto his back.

The last thing Tucker remembered was feeling Dancer's body snuggled up against his, and his arms folding over Dancer. His eyes remained open for a second before they both drifted off to sleep in the middle of the afternoon.

Chapter Fourteen

"Tucker! Mattie baby! Are you guys in there?" Three rapid thumps to his door shook him from a deep sleep. Dancer's brain told him it was one of his neighbors fighting, to ignore it. Within seconds, three more pounds on the door shook the entire structure, jarring his eyes open.

Tucker was wrapped under his arm, and it took a second for Dancer to put together that the body next to him wasn't a John. In fact, he was in his own bed. Half asleep, he knew the knocks weren't a cheated wife or the police interrupting him and a client. Nevertheless, it was someone who wanted in.

"Mattie! It's Momma, let me in!"

Three more thumps not only shook the structure, but also his reality. It was Tucker's mother.

"Come on, Tucker! Let me in! I know you guys are in there!"

Just as Dancer was about to shake Tucker, he woke up on his own. He looked like he had seen a ghost, his eyes wide. Unsure if Tucker grasped what was happening, Dancer shook him. "It's your mom. She's outside!"

Tucker cleared his throat as he rubbed at his eyes.

"Tucker!" Dancer needed him to wake up. "Get the hell up! Your mom's outside!"

Tucker sat up as three more knocks jarred him completely awake. "Hold on. I'm coming!" He stumbled as he looked around for his shirt. "Can you get the door?"

"You need to go outside!" Dancer demanded.

"I am!" Tucker jammed his shirt down the front of his jeans to organize things before moving. "Just wait! I'm coming out!"

Dancer moved over to the door and unlatched it. The sunlight flooding into the shack caused Dancer to squint and look down. His eyes caught Tucker's big narrow bare feet as he brushed past him.

Tucker stopped just outside the door. "What are you doing here? When did you get out?"

"Last night. They released me. I'm over at Family Ties. It's sober living. I'd have come here last night, but it was late. They lock the doors at nine, and I wouldn't have been able to get back in. Where's Mattie?" She looked past Tucker and into the shack.

"She's in school." Tucker tried to smooth his hair to one side. "What happened? How'd you get released?"

"It was bullshit! They made me plead guilty to possession if I agreed to treatment!"

"How did you know we were here?"

"The chick down the…"

Their voices faded as Dancer stepped away from the door, not wanting to listen to any more of their conversation. He couldn't move far enough away to avoid her high-pitched whine as she complained about the jail and the horrible food. He was glad that Tucker had stepped outside. The last thing he wanted was her to come in. Now that she was back, would Tucker leave? She wasn't staying here; there was no way in hell he would offer to let her stay with them. Her presence was causing his blood to boil.

He felt a knot in his stomach as he propped the door closed. Was Tucker leaving? Everything he didn't want to feel bubbled to the surface: remorse for allowing himself to feel something for someone.

He tried to occupy his thoughts by making the bed and cleaning up a little. His life was once completely organized. Everything in its proper place. Now, everything was in disarray. It was as if someone had kicked him in the gut, knocking out every ounce of oxygen in his lungs. *What could they possibly be talking about?* He wished he had listened to what his gut had been telling him all along.

A quiet tap on the door before it slid open sent his heart into his throat. He prepared himself for both Tucker and his mother to come through the door.

Tucker appeared in the doorway, his face flushed, eyes bloodshot. He didn't make eye contact. Instead, he moved over to their bags. "I need to get—"

Dancer cut him off. "That's fine." His eyes bore into Tucker, waiting for him to meet his eyes. If Tucker was about to destroy him, then he should at least look at him while he did it. "Don't be a coward!" He hadn't intended to say it, it just came out.

"What?" Tucker came to a stop. "I was just getting their stuff, and my boots. They're going to some sober living place." His forehead creased. He looked confused as his eyes rose to meet Dancer's. "Um, I can't stay there. Only women and children."

Dancer knew that. *Of course.* Tucker wasn't leaving. He squeezed his eyes shut, thankful for the answer to a prayer he vaguely recalled making.

"Do you want me out?" Terror flashed in Tucker's eyes as he stood still.

"Whatever you want is fine." That was a lie. Dancer turned away to break eye contact with him.

"What does that mean?" Tucker came up behind him. "Turn around. Look at me. What do you mean, whatever I want is fine? Do you not want me here? I thought—"

Dancer spun around. His words flowed faster than his brain could control them. "Of course I do. I just don't want to get hurt. When you finally leave, I know I'm going to get hurt. I don't want to get hurt."

"I'm not going to hurt you. I'm staying. I want to be with you." Tucker took him by the arms but quickly released him. "I gave you my word. No funny stuff, you remember? My word is the only thing I have worth anything. It's everything I have, and I gave it to you. I'm not going to hurt you. In fact, I'd beat the shit out of anyone who looked like they were going to hurt you."

Tucker's words echoed in Dancer's brain. It wasn't as simple as believing him. Dancer cleared his throat several times, pushing down the emotions that were bubbling up. "I don't need protecting. I can take care of myself."

Tucker grabbed him by his elbows and pulled him close. "I didn't say you couldn't. I said I will. Let me get them settled, and I'll be back. We can talk when I get back."

Dancer nodded, knowing his voice was going to fail him if he tried to speak.

With one hand, Tucker hooked the back of Dancer's neck and brought their heads together. With a gentle kiss on Dancer's forehead, Tucker held his lips against his skin for a second before pulling back. "I'll be back. But I have to know where Mattie will be."

Dancer's eyes swam with tears.

111

Tucker looked around until he spotted his boots. "I'll be—"

"Tucker! Are you coming?" His mother appeared at the door.

Dancer glanced over Tucker's shoulder at her. It was a quick look but long enough to reaffirm his suspicions about her.

"Yeah. I'm coming!" Tucker barely looked back at her. "Let me take her down to the school to get Mattie." Tucker rubbed at his temple. His eyes conveyed his worry. "I'll be back."

*****

The eeriness of the surrounding stillness was becoming unbearable. A week ago, sitting in this room by himself had been the norm, but now, Dancer felt alone. In the last six years, he couldn't recall a single day when he had been lonely. He had mastered the ability to live a life of isolation, and now, Tucker's absence was causing him anxiety.

He wanted to hold on to the memory of what had occurred between them less than three hours ago. It wasn't a dream, it had happened, but it was going to take some convincing for him to believe it. He and Tucker had made love on this mattress. Tucker had kissed him like he had never been kissed. He didn't know people like Tucker existed. Tucker was gentle and attentive and asked for nothing in return.

He jarred his brain trying to remember the details. The beginning was clear; he remembered asking Tucker what he wanted. Dancer was prepared to please him. When Tucker shushed him instead of telling him what he wanted, it confused him, until he realized what it meant. Tucker wanted nothing but his love.

There had never been a John that didn't want something. It was why they came to him. His sole task was to please them, and yet, Tucker asked for nothing. He had said their lovemaking was amazing. It was more than amazing, it was mind-blowing, awesome. Weightless euphoria surged through Dancer as he laughed at Tucker calling it amazing.

Never had he experienced anything like it. He liked this guy. His heart sped up thinking of him, just as it had when Tucker was lying on him. He wanted to know what made their sex so amazing for Tucker. He couldn't deny it. The euphoria was unbelievable.

Tucker's absence was squeezing his chest with so much pressure that he couldn't breathe. This space, his room, these walls, had once protected him. Now they were aiding in his suffocation. He had to get out, get some fresh air, take a walk.

He threw his tablet into his backpack, grabbed his jacket, and was out the door. The cool air rushed into his lungs as if he had been drowning. He held it for a second and gasped. He glanced around, prepared to dismiss any stares. The old man sitting in the broken chair across the way, the three men huddled around a fire burning in a barrel, none of them were paying any attention to him.

He knew almost everybody in the camp, but they were not his friends. Camp Roosevelt wasn't a place where people mingled with one another. Any talking was about an immediate need, a problem that needed resolution, a conundrum, and none of them could help him with this.

He picked up his step, heading toward the front of the camp. He traveled down the street and turned the corner that marked the three city blocks that contained Brierton's sex workers. After four in the afternoon, men looking for gay sex started to troll the streets.

Would Tucker let Mattie go? He kept his head down, avoiding the world as he hurried toward the corner.

Dancer lifted his hoodie above his eyes enough to ensure he had the green light to cross the street. His eyes shifted from the light to a man standing on the opposite side of the street. He tried to place where he knew the man from. Dancer stepped off the curb and into the street when it hit him that this was the same guy who had taken his picture last week. He had seen this same guy in Walmart the other day. He remembered him because he had thought the man was cruising him.

The sound of brakes screeched as a black sedan entered Dancer's peripheral vision. Dancer held out his hand as if he could stop the car. Smoke billowed from the car's tires as it stopped within inches of him. With his hand touching the hood of the car, Dancer shot an evil look at the man behind the wheel before realizing it was Mr. Gerhardt's driver.

The man stuck his head out the window. "Jesus, kid! I've been looking for you for the last two days! Get in!"

Dancer looked toward where he had seen the familiar man on the corner. He was gone. Rattled between the mysterious man and nearly being plowed down by Mr. Gerhardt's driver, he walked over to the driver's window. "Not tonight. I can't." He had never told Old Man Gerhardt no. The money would have come in handy. He was damn near broke because of the money he had been spending on Tucker and Mattie. "Can I come by tomorrow night?"

"Mr. Gerhardt is leaving town in the morning. He'll be gone for three weeks. He wanted to see you before he leaves. Tonight's it."

The blaring sound of the horn coming from the taxis behind them stopped the conversation, causing both of them to look in that direction.

"Goddammit! Wait a minute!" Gerhardt's driver shot his middle finger at the taxis behind him.

This diversion was the two seconds Dancer needed to escape. "I can't. Sorry." He held his breath as he walked toward the sidewalk. Had he done the right thing? Would this anger Gerhardt? Would he call for him again? Every time he called for him, the payment for that one night kept him off the streets for two weeks. The thought of Tucker on the streets with him made him sick. There was no way he would turn someone out.

There was so much that Tucker didn't know about him. So much not to like.

Within ten minutes, New Beginnings was in his sight. Surprised that he was actually chasing someone, he felt adrenaline surging through his body like a panic attack. He couldn't deny he was crazy about Tucker, and it scared the hell out of him. His body shivered, but he was anything but cold.

As he got closer to the shelter, he saw the long line of people waiting to go inside. It had to be getting close to dinnertime and the shelter's opening for the evening. Several men were sprawled across the sidewalk, some of them sleeping, while others just congregated in groups. Ian was standing in the doorway talking to a woman with two children.

Dancer had hoped to avoid running into Ian. If he continued ahead, there would be no avoiding him. He pulled his hoodie down over his face and turned around. His heart pounded in his chest. He hadn't had a panic attack in years, not since running away. His airway began to close and his chest tightened. He had to get back to his place, where he felt safe. He jammed his hands deep into his jacket and picked up his step.

Chapter Fifteen

Dancer tried to concentrate on the movie. He had seen *Silence of the Lambs* enough times that it didn't require his full attention anyway. Detective Starling didn't need to see Buffalo Bill to be able to put a bullet in him. The sound of the killer's gun cocking in pitch darkness was enough to tell her to fire. It was now or never. The blast of the gun caused a flutter in Dancer's belly. The killer was dead, and there was just resolution. His eyes gleamed, knowing the bad guy was dead. No matter how scary the movie, there was satisfaction when the bad guy got it in the end.

The credits were almost over when his front door jarred open. Dancer quickly powered down his tablet and tossed it to the side.

"Hey, are you in there?" Tucker slid the door open and entered. "Why are you sitting in the dark?"

"I was watching a movie. I didn't realize it was dark." Dancer stood up, wanting to hear what had happened.

Tucker secured the door. "What movie?"

He sensed a casualness in Tucker's voice. "*Silence of the Lambs.*"

"I loved Jodie Foster in that movie!" Tucker stepped over the camping stove and into Dancer's personal space. "I'm sorry about my mum." He leaned down and kissed Dancer once on his bottom lip and then used his tongue to wipe moisture from his own lips.

The kiss welled up in Dancer's heart. He didn't dare move, just in case Tucker wanted to kiss him again. "Did you get to see Mattie?"

"I did. She was sad that I wasn't going with them, but I promised I'd visit. I walked them over to Family Ties. It's not far from here. On Tenth. I couldn't go in, but the lady said they have Family Day on Saturdays. How're you doing?"

"Fine." He was anything but fine.

Tucker kissed him again. "You look madder than an old wet hen. What's wrong?" Tucker brushed his hand up and down Dancer's shoulders. "Talk to me."

In a matter of days, Dancer had fallen for a guy he barely knew. He didn't know where to begin. "Do you want some light?" Dancer tried to change the subject. He flicked on the lantern and placed it on top of the bins.

Tucker stood still, his eyes following Dancer about the room. "Um… Okay, so…" He scratched his head. "It's obvious you're not okay. Can I ask… Are *we* okay?" The anguish on his face said more than his words.

"We're fine." Dancer wasn't sure if he was answering Tucker's question or convincing himself. Was this all too much?

Tucker walked over to the Milkman's chair and sat down.

"So, you got them settled. It's a rehab center, so that's a good thing." Dancer tried again to change the subject.

"Mum's never been in rehab. They even have a program for the kids where Mattie can go to school while my mum is in, like, counseling or rehab during the day. Mattie's missed so much school."

Dancer heard the excitement in Tucker's voice. He wished he could be as hopeful, but he had observed the failures of drug rehab firsthand. His friend Dottie had been in and out of so many rehabs that he had lost count.

Tucker pushed back on the chair, elevating his feet as the back reclined. "Have you ever been tested?"

The question came out of nowhere. *Tested?* He knew Tucker was referring to HIV. Why was that any of his business? "No." He hesitated. Tucker's question felt more like judgment than concern. "I've never been sick a day in my life. Why? Are you afraid I'm gonna give you something?"

Tucker's head tilted as his brows narrowed. "No, I never said that. Don't put words in my mouth."

"You didn't have to. But it's cool. I get it." The muscles in his neck stiffened. It was as if he was talking to a John. Everyone wants to know if the whore is negative. He winced at the taste of humiliation.

"Get what? If I'm going to be accused of something then I think I should have at least said it. I was asking because of my mum. I was thinking about her… Never mind."

Embarrassed at the realization that Tucker's question had nothing to do with him, Dancer squeezed his eyes closed. He owed Tucker an apology. It took a minute for him to gather his words. "I'm sure she's fine." He wasn't sure why he said this instead of the apology. It was a lie. If he was willing to forgo a condom to satisfy a John, a junkie was almost always willing to go without one for drugs. He thought about Dottie. "I'm sorry, I shouldn't have jumped all over you like that."

"It's all right. But just so you know, I'm not worried about HIV. I'd sleep with you. I'd do it in a heartbeat. But one, you haven't asked, and two, I've never done it."

A virgin? Had he just said he was a virgin? Dancer was shocked. "How old did you say you were?"

"I didn't, but I'm eighteen." Tucker's voice proclaimed the number as if it was an attribute.

Eighteen. A laugh escaped Dancer. He had assumed Tucker was older. Now his naivety made sense.

Tucker turned to his side in the chair. "So, if we're done fighting, I saw Ian for a minute at the shelter. I told him I was still staying with you. Are you ever going to tell me what it is about you and him? He's a nice guy."

There was so much that Tucker didn't know. So much Dancer would rather he never knew. His past with Ian wasn't where he wanted to start. "Well, the truth is, I don't like anybody. You're the first person I've let in here. Other than Dottie, that woman I was talking to the other day when you guys came back, I don't talk to anyone." This was an easy admission. Living with the Milkman for three years made it easy not to have to talk.

"How can you go through life not liking anybody? You like me." Tucker grinned.

This was a little harder to admit. "Yeah. So, Ian said nothing about me?" He wanted to know what Tucker already knew.

"Like what?"

"I don't know. Like some bullshit story." Dancer inspected his fingernails before going to work on a cuticle.

"Like what? What would the *bullshit* story be?"

Dancer was satisfied Tucker knew nothing. It was just like 'Mr. Wonder Bread' to keep their secret. "I don't know, maybe..." He

117

propped himself up on the arm of the chair. "When I first got here, I'd gone to the shelter a couple of times." Dancer paused, realizing what he was about to say, assessing whether he was ready to go there. "I had just started tricking." Dancer stood up and took a step away from the chair. "Ian let me come in and clean up, though I wasn't staying there. I don't know why, but I guess I thought he might be interested, so one day… I told him I needed to talk to him after my shower. He told me to meet him in his office." Dancer bit down on the side of his fingernail as he thought about how he was going to tell this story. He tore at a tiny piece of his cuticle, and a sharp pain ricocheted between the nail and his tongue. "Ouch!"

Tucker was oblivious to Dancer's botched manicure or stall tactic. "And?"

The pain subsided enough to allow Dancer to refocus on what he was saying. "After my shower…" He had never told this story to anyone. The humiliation of telling Tucker was almost worse than the night itself.

He took a second to find his words. "So, anyway, I made my way down to his office. He wasn't there, so I stripped and laid back in his chair and waited." The embarrassment of what he was about to say came out as a snicker. "When Ian came in, it was as if he had seen a ghost. I don't remember what all was said, but he basically kicked me out of there. He ordered me to put my clothes on. He said he would wait on the other side of the door while I got dressed. I don't know why—maybe I was embarrassed, maybe it was despair, maybe stupidity, but I snatched a stack of gift cards that were on top of his desk."

Tucker gasped. "Did he catch you?"

"No, but I know he knows I took them." Dancer was mortified and couldn't look in Tucker's direction.

"What kind of cards were they?"

"They were five-dollar McDonald's gift cards. It scared me to use them, so I sold them."

"How old were you?" Tucker pushed forward in the chair and sat up.

Dancer held on to the arms of the chair, trying to balance himself as it moved. "I hadn't been here but a couple of months, so I was around fourteen."

"Damn, that's young. You were…" Tucker paused. "…doing it at fourteen?" He bent over and, with both hands, he pulled his boots off. He tossed the first clunky cowboy boot in the corner before removing and tossing the other. "That's it?" Tucker cocked his head to one side.

So, is that it? Was Tucker referring to Dancer's prostituting himself or his ripping Ian off? Did neither matter to him? He glanced at Tucker's giant boots in the corner.

Tucker was a breath of fresh air in his stagnant life. He would never forget how safe he'd felt laying in his bed with Tucker earlier. He appreciated the gentleness with which Tucker treated him. He was used to being treated like shit. People had said things to him you wouldn't say to a dog on the street. He had come to believe those things about himself. He glanced over at Tucker, who was clueless as to what he was getting himself into.

Tucker stood up and walked over to Dancer. He took him by the waist as his mouth curved into a smile. "Do you know what?"

"What?" *Please, no more bombshell disclosures.*

"As much as I'll miss Mattie tonight, we're all by ourselves—all night." The look on Tucker's face left little doubt what he meant.

Tucker was gorgeous, but despite having sex for a living, having sex with Tucker was not what Dancer wanted. He'd had sex with a lot of people. He had never slept with any of them, except for a few minutes next to Old Man Gerhardt.

He looked into Tucker's eyes. A sea of ocean blue, they were a gentle compliment to his milky white skin. Tucker was neither Gerhardt nor a John. Dancer wanted to wiggle free but held his stance. "I don't want to have sex with you."

"Oh… O-kay." Tucker released him and took a step back. "I'm confused."

"Well, although you didn't say it, I *should* get tested before we do anything." The thought of having to be tested was a reminder of what he was.

"I'm not afraid of that. We could use a condom. Condoms are safe." Tucker stepped forward, filling the space between them.

Tucker had shot a hole in Dancer's attempt to make this sound like it was about safe sex. He was right; condoms, for the most part, were safe. He'd been having unprotected sex for years. It had never mattered if the person wore a condom or not as long as he got paid.

119

He needed to get tested, but that wasn't the reason he couldn't have sex with Tucker right now. Sex would change everything between them. He was trying to prevent Tucker from becoming like every other guy in his life. Tucker didn't know that what he was asking for could mean the end of them.

Dancer didn't enjoy sex, and there was no reason to believe having sex with Tucker would change that. He liked Tucker, more than he should. Tucker was an open book; he wore his heart and his thoughts on his sleeve. His motives were pure, but they were not harmless. To add sex could ruin everything.

Chapter Sixteen

They laid in each other's arms all night, talking in the dark. In a moment that felt safe, Dancer revealed what had driven him to the streets six years ago. Tucker was silent, listening as Dancer exposed a part of himself that he had never talked about and worked hard to eradicate from his thoughts. He didn't go into detail, that would have been too painful, but he exposed his stepfather for the monster that he was, and his anger toward his mother. Over the next several hours, a wall came down with the touch of Tucker's fingers as they caressed Dancer's shoulders. From Tucker's touch, Dancer drew the courage to bear the pain that came with admitting to Tucker the anger he also felt toward his father for dying. This opened another set of floodgates.

"You know, I use to have this little Chihuahua named Tamale. My mother brought her home from the pound after my dad passed away. I think she thought it was going to cheer me up or something." As plain as day, Dancer could see his tiny chocolate and white Tamale on his bed while he dressed for school in the morning. He was pretty sure she crawled under the covers to stay warm once he left the house.

"Was it a puppy?" Tucker asked.

"No, the people at the SPCA said they thought she was two or three. She was actually kind of cute." He shifted his arm from under Tucker's head.

Tucker rolled onto his side, facing Dancer. "You know, they use dogs in the old folks' home to help with depression. It's a scientific fact that the presence of animals helps."

Dancer went on. "I tried to take her with me when I ran that morning. I wasn't going to leave her with them. When I tried to get on the bus with her, they said she had to be in a carrying cage. They wouldn't let me take her."

"So, what happened to her?"

"I got back off the bus. I didn't know what I was going to do. Then this older lady came out of nowhere and wanted to pet her. When she said she used to have one just like her, I offered Tamale to her. It happened so fast. It was like I couldn't even look at Tamale or say goodbye. I just handed her over and jumped back on the bus." He wiped a single tear from his cheek. He hadn't cried in years and couldn't understand why he was getting all choked up over a damn dog. He squeezed his eyes closed, trying to tamp down the grief that was swelling with every breath.

"I can't believe they wouldn't let you take your dog on the bus." Tucker repositioned Dancer's arm around him as he nestled in under him. "Do you think she's still alive?"

Dancer thought for a second or two. "Yeah. I'm sure she spends her days in that lady's lap." Even if it wasn't true, it made what he'd had to do seem okay.

In the wee hours of the morning, silence finally overtook them. Tucker lay in his arms asleep as Dancer's mind continued to stretch back into the past. He squeezed his eyes closed, trying to calm his anxiety. An endless emotional marathon wrapped itself around his heart. With all the talking, he had somehow stripped himself of the ability to shut off his emotions. His insides quivered as he fought off the cost of burying such pain.

Without waking, Tucker slid one leg between Dancer's legs and nuzzled in closer. He buried his face in Dancer's chest as he slung his arm over Dancer's body. Wide awake, Dancer lay listening to the sound of Tucker's breathing.

The thought of being tested crept into Dancer's thoughts. What would happen if he was positive? He wished he had always used protection, but it wasn't an option when you were trying to survive. This was a lie that he had come to believe as the truth. His allowing a John to take him bareback had more to do with his lack of self-worth then he cared to acknowledge. It was an easy lie to believe because there was a premium for those who wanted it without a condom. If they were willing to pay, who was he to argue?

In his six years of living on the streets, there was little to be grateful about. It was just one bad day after the next. People died every day out here. Going without a condom had been the least of his worries, especially if it earned him more money.

At some point, the avalanche of emotions wore him down and pushed him into a deep, hard sleep. He woke in a state of confusion. Pressed between Tucker and the wall, he didn't recognize the room initially. He shook the fog from his head. "Hey, we've got to get up." He pushed Tucker to wake him. A twin mattress wasn't going to work for them. He sat up and waited for Tucker to wake.

Tucker brushed his hair back out of his face and rubbed his eyes open. "Oh my God, I slept so good!" With a yawn and a funky wiggle of his body, he rolled his head toward Dancer. "How are you?"

"Okay, I guess."

"Are you sure?" Tucker reached down into his jeans and repositioned himself.

"Too much talking. I had a hard time shutting my brain off after that." Dancer's eyes followed Tucker's hand as it shifted what he presumed was morning wood behind the zipper. He could visualize Tucker's cock. There was an instant when he was willing to have sex with Tucker right then and there. It was a hollow in his heart that begged to be filled. He pushed the thought back as hard as he could, knowing it was a dangerous road he shouldn't travel. He forced himself to look away, waiting for the moment to pass.

"I'm sorry this world is so messed up. If I met your stepfather, I'd whoop his ass. Only a punk does that to a child." Tucker's hands tightened into a fist as his eyes shot sparks.

Not wanting to revisit those bad memories again, Dancer instead focused on Tucker saying *whoop* instead of *whip*. He tried not to show his amusement as he climbed over Tucker and out the bed. "Do you want tea?"

"Noooo... I want coffee! I want you to have coffee in this goddamn house!" Tucker groaned, high pitched and whiny.

"Okay, get up, and we can go get coffee. I have to use the bathroom anyway." The need to use the bathroom was only an excuse to get Tucker up.

"Really! You will buy me coffee?" He sat up and stretched his arms toward the ceiling, wiggling his long fingers.

"You're not getting Starbucks. There's a McDonald's over on Twelfth." Unsure if he had enough money for a coffee, he hoped it was on their dollar menu.

Tucker jumped out of bed. "I'll take it!" He reached down into

123

his bag and grabbed his toothbrush. He was about to take the half bottle of water that Dancer had used last night but stopped. "Can I use some of that water to brush my teeth?" His eyebrows rose waiting for the answer.

"This isn't the Ritz. I'll show you how to do it without water." Dancer brushed his teeth without the water and then swallowed everything that was in his mouth. He rubbed his tongue against his teeth, wiping them clean.

While Tucker did as he was shown, Dancer grabbed a clean shirt from a bin. He pulled off the dirty shirt and was about to put on a clean shirt when Tucker stopped him.

"What happened?" He was pointing at Dancer's scar between his belly button and the top of his groin.

He had forgotten about the scar. "Oh, I had appendicitis when I was ten. They had to remove my appendix."

"Damn, that is ugly." Tucker's face twisted as if he'd seen a car accident.

"Really!" Dancer couldn't believe he had insulted him. "Do you want your coffee or not?"

"No, I meant that it looks like it hurt. Not that the scar is ugly. I saw it yesterday but didn't want to ask." Tucker moved toward him and put his hand on Dancer's abdomen.

Tucker's cold hands on his stomach caused Dancer to inhale. His proximity sent a flutter of butterflies to his stomach. He knew what was to come.

"Everything about you is beautiful. Your green eyes, your ears," Tucker's hand reached behind Dancer's ear, tucking strands of hair behind it as his thumb caressed his cheek. "Your beautiful nose, your lips." Tucker kissed his bottom lip.

The moment their lips touched, air escaped from Dancer's lungs. Focused on his words, he hadn't had time to inhale before Tucker kissed him again. Tucker's tender touch made Dancer's heart pound harder.

To regain control, he pulled back, against the gravity that was pulling him into an abyss. "Come on. Let's get you some coffee." Not wanting Tucker to notice his swelling erection, he turned away and quickly adjusted himself. He was never attracted to anyone to the point of a spontaneous erection. This was something he usually had to focus on achieving for the client. Tucker caused it with just a simple touch. Dancer couldn't stop the corners of his mouth from turning up.

Tucker reached down and took hold of Dancer's bulging crotch. "So, you like my kisses?"

"Stop it." Dancer pushed his hand away. "If you want coffee, let's go." Although he didn't say it, Dancer would have gladly taken another kiss.

*****

The five-minute walk to McDonald's cooled them both down. The morning air was frosty with a light wind that cut between the buildings. Before going to bed last night, Dancer had checked the weather forecast for the week. The next four days were going to be dry and cold, and a light storm was due by Saturday.

If he was going to make any money, he would have to take advantage of the clear nights. He was unsure how he was going to approach this subject with Tucker. It didn't sit well with him that he now was accountable to someone. He tried to convince himself that he didn't owe Tucker an explanation or need his approval, but it sure felt like he did.

The two stepped up to the counter, where a skinny young Asian boy greeted them. "What can I get for you two this morning?"

Dancer hesitated, waiting for Tucker to order his coffee. Instead, Tucker turned and whispered to him, "Do you have enough so I can get a cheeseburger too?"

Surprised at the last-minute addition, Dancer glanced at the menu board. Cheeseburgers and coffee were both on the dollar menu. "Sure."

After the boy rang them up, Dancer noted what was in his wallet. Eight dollars was all he had left from his visit with Mr. Gerhardt. He second-guessed his decision to decline Gerhardt's last offer.

At the table, Tucker devoured his burger in five bites before starting in on his drink. "Aww, this coffee is so good."

While Tucker relished his cup of coffee, Dancer slipped into his pragmatic mode. He tried not to let the weight of the results from the looming HIV test occupy his thoughts, but the longer he sat there, the more he began to overthink things. If the test was positive, he might lose Tucker. Plus, he was damn near broke, and although he was almost sure the testing was free, he still needed money.

He estimated he needed about fifty bucks: thirty for a new internet card for his tablet and another twenty for basic supplies that he had run through with two extra guests.

That would be a quick night's work, providing there was limited competition on the streets. With clear skies, he was sure that horny Johns would be trolling the streets this evening looking for sex. His best hope for a quick night and good money was that his regulars showed up.

"Hey. What are you thinking about?" Tucker asked.

His voice jarred Dancer out of his head. "Nothing."

"I said, do you know only two percent of the world has green eyes? They're my favorite."

"Well I'm glad I could satisfy you with my eyes." Dancer winked at him.

Tucker leaned over the table and kissed him. His mouth tasted of coffee, his lips warm to the touch. How was it he had lived twenty years not knowing the decadence of a kiss? He licked his lips, tasting Tucker one last time as he savored the tang of coffee that slid across this tongue.

"Thank you for breakfast." Affection glowing in his eyes, Tucker tossed him a come-hither look.

"You're welcome. And stop looking at me like that! It makes me think nasty thoughts." Dancer massaged the back of his neck, trying to prevent himself from being hypnotized by the sapphire-blue eyes that bored into him.

"What's wrong with nasty thoughts?" Tucker gave a suggestive grin.

To collect himself, Dancer blinked away from Tucker's vain attempt to seduce him. "Can we talk for a sec?" The corners of his lips fought a smile at the mischief in Tucker's eyes.

Defeated, Tucker sank down in his chair, hanging his head low with a semi-pout. He winked at Dancer.

Dancer ignored Tucker's last attempt. "I have to go out tonight. We need cash." Unsure how much he had to tell Tucker, he stopped to compose his next sentence.

"Okay. I'll go with you."

That was a hard no. There was no way Dancer would take him out. Dancer leaned back in his chair. "No! You don't need to go. I'll be quick. Two hours at most."

"But why can't I go? We don't have Mattie!"

"Because." Dancer paused. There was no simple answer as to why. "I don't want you going!"

"Why?"

Dancer sunk his head into his hands. "It's dangerous, and I don't want to be responsible if something happens to you. You're not going!" Without saying it, he couldn't be the reason Tucker turned to tricking on the streets. He couldn't be that person.

Tucker's eyes narrowed as he scowled at Dancer.

Ready for the next round, Dancer braced himself. He watched as Tucker got up and refilled his coffee. When he returned, he yanked his chair out and plopped down. "Okay. I guess I'll go get a job today. I saw a help wanted sign at this pizza parlor on Seventh that I want to check out. Can I borrow a nicer shirt?"

Relieved that he had won the fight, Dancer was willing to give Tucker anything he needed for his job hunt. But he was unsure if Tucker could fit into any of his shirts. "Sure."

The prospect of Tucker getting a job was a greater accomplishment than he'd ever achieved. At fourteen, there was no chance of anyone hiring him and, by sixteen, he was already working the streets, making the money he needed to survive.

The two sat in silence while Tucker drank his second cup of coffee. People were coming and going. Dancer looked around for a clock. Not seeing one, he remembered Tucker had his phone. "What time is it?"

Tucker maneuvered his hand down into his jeans and pulled up his phone. "It's almost eight."

"Okay." Dancer stroked several curls away from his eye.

"Are you ready?" Tucker asked.

"Yeah. I'll meet you back at the house." Stressed, he needed to go to the clinic by himself. If it didn't go well, he wanted to be alone. "I'm going to the clinic and then by Chinn's."

Tucker grimaced, letting him know he understood what that meant. "Would he pay you if you asked?" Tucker's voice faltered.

"Nah, he's too cheap, but we'll get dinner for tonight."

Tucker stood up and pushed his pant legs down his thighs. "I'm ready."

Dancer wasn't okay with how things were ending, but what was he supposed to do? A week ago, he would have cussed someone out if they tried to control him. He was a free bird, his actions were his, and he was not accountable to anyone. He had isolated himself for years; he didn't have close relationships. Dottie, Mr. Gerhardt, Mr. Chinn, and a handful of regular Johns were about as close as people got.

Dancer pushed out his chair and stood. "Hey, before I go out tonight, maybe... How 'bout we, you know..." He had never had a problem offering himself to someone, but it was caught in his throat.

"What?" Tucker's face brightened as he looked at him.

"You know, celebrate, after the test this afternoon." He wanted to ease Tucker's sadness and didn't know any other way but with sex. He would give Tucker what he wanted. He loved kissing Tucker. His body responded to him, which said something.

Chapter Seventeen

That afternoon, Tucker made it back to Camp Roosevelt before Dancer. Humiliated and feeling about as low as one could get, he wanted to crash. Excited at the idea of having a job, he had learned why no one would hire him.

After being told "No, we're not hiring" or "You have to apply online" countless times, the lady at Gift's Emporia said they were hiring and invited him to fill out their application. He sat down to do so and realized he had no address, no phone number, no references, no past jobs, not even a high school diploma. He turned in the application with little more than his name and date of birth.

He had decided to take a nap, hoping it would get him out of his funky mood and excited again about his and Dancer's rendezvous that afternoon. He was still sleeping when Dancer came in holding a large pizza box. He sat up as if he had been awake, propping himself up on the mattress as Dancer tossed the box on the bed. "Here, I found us something to eat for today."

As the world came into focus, he recognized Dancer was in a foul mood. *Had he done something wrong? Was he upset that he was sleeping? What happened to the Chinese food?*

Tucker contemplated what to say as he opened the pizza box. It was from the same restaurant that he had tried to apply for a job at earlier. They had all but laughed at him. He looked down at the untouched pizza, cold with all the sauce and toppings mangled and stuck to the top of the box. "How did everything go?" He would test the water with an easy question before hinting that he was ready to play.

"Not good. I couldn't get the test, and Chinn wasn't there when I went by."

"How come you couldn't get the test?" Tucker stood up but was unsure if he should try to kiss him with his mood. It looked risky.

"The free testing shit is bullshit! They wanted a hundred and eighty-nine dollars for something called an anonymous test. They wouldn't need my name, and I would get immediate results. The only free testing required my name, and it takes two days to get my results. They're not getting my name. No way! I'll get the money tonight and go back tomorrow."

Yep, he was in a mood. Tucker wondered if that meant that Dancer was reneging on his offer to play? "Thank you for dinner. What happened at Chinn's?"

"He wasn't there! His wife was there with the kids. Something about he was out shopping or some shit!" Dancer sat in his chair and banged his head back into the padding.

"Did you buy this pizza?" Tucker looked at the cold pizza again.

"No. I found it in the dumpster in the alley behind Giovanni's." Dancer kicked out the foot rest on the chair and pushed back, reclining in the chair.

"A whole pizza? Why would someone throw away a whole pizza?"

"Because it's crap pizza. They make a bunch ahead of time. If they don't sell them, they just toss 'em. They're in there all the time. They throw away a lot of stuff right after lunch."

"Do you want some?" Tucker took a slice and tried to mash some congealed cheese and toppings on to it. He held it up, offering the first piece to Dancer.

"No. I'm not hungry. Go ahead and eat. Tonight, as soon as I make enough for the test and to carry us for a couple of days, I'll come home."

Tucker was ready to take a bite out of the piece in his hand but stopped. If Dancer wasn't in the mood to have sex with him, how could he go out and have sex with total strangers? "You're still going out tonight?" Tucker asked.

"I have to."

Tucker hesitated, knowing he shouldn't say it, but he couldn't stop himself. "It seems a little weird that I'm supposed to stay home tonight while my boyfriend goes out and has sex with a bunch of people." As the words left his mouth, he knew he was in trouble.

Dancer closed his eyes. The strain caused a vein to pop on his forehead. He released a gasp as if someone had stabbed him in his gut. His eyes remained shut as his hands rubbed his face.

Tucker waited for him to say something. It was coming. His mind shot to the worst-case scenario: Dancer would throw him out. A sickening sensation starting from his belly, increasing in strength, spreading like fire in the wind. "I'm sorry!" he said. It wasn't going to be enough, but it might decrease the inferno that was heading his way.

Dancer lowered the leg rest and placed both feet on the ground. He stopped short of getting up, leaning forward in the chair. His right hand swept back the long curls that dangled in front of his right eye. "So, I'm your boyfriend now? Did you decide that on your own, or am I forgetting a conversation we had?" His green eyes shot sparks.

"I'm sorry. I didn't mean that. Not that you're not my boyfriend, but what I said about other people. I'm sorry," Tucker begged. He tossed the pizza back in the box and stood up. He hesitated, debating if he should move closer. He moved next to Dancer and kneeled on both knees. "I'm sorry."

Dancer leaned back in the chair. "Look, if there's any chance you can't handle this, what I am, then don't pretend that you can. I need to know now. There is no such thing as a fairytale. Happily-ever-after doesn't exist except in my mom's stupid books!"

Tucker shook his head. "That's not true!" He drew in a long breath, preparing to fight for what he believed. "In this chaotic, messed up world, if you're lucky enough to find love, why would you throw it away? Why wouldn't you try?"

"Because you'll only get hurt!"

"Is that what you're afraid of, getting hurt by me? I love you!" Tucker couldn't believe he had said the L word. He meant it, but it was too soon to tell him. For him, it had been love at first sight. Watching Dancer repair his tarp as the wind tried to take it away. Dancer's bark when he tried to scare Tucker away was nothing short of adorable. He saw through him. Cupid had shot the arrow right into his heart, and it had exploded.

"You can't love me," said Dancer.

"Why? Because you don't think you can be loved? Is that it?"

Dancer stood up and stepped away from him.

Tucker wasn't going to let him run. "You have all this bullshit in your head. Shit that's real to you, but it's not all accurate. You say you don't like to be kissed, you don't like to be touched, you don't

131

like to talk. But I feel it when we kiss. I feel your heart." Tucker reached out and seized him by his waist. "I don't like the idea of someone touching you. Of you having to do what you do. I'm sorry for what I said, but I'm not sorry for loving you so much that I want you all to myself. Please don't hate me!"

Dancer brushed the hair out of his face again. "I don't hate you. I have to survive."

"But surviving doesn't mean you have to be alone."

"But this isn't going to work if you can't handle me going out."

"I don't know, but I'll never hurt you. I can't promise I won't disappoint you sometimes, but I'll never hurt you. Go tonight. Do what you have to do. Let me work on me, and I'll be right here when you get back." Tucker leaned in and kissed him. "I trust you, and in time, you'll learn to trust me."

Tucker didn't want to fight anymore. He didn't have it in him. This was not at all how he planned his afternoon going. He wasn't keen about their first time being make-up sex anymore. They leaned against one another. Quiet and subdued, Tucker rested his head on Dancer's shoulders. His eyes blurred as he sniffled back a tear. His mum had always told him that, if he wanted to be a real baseball player, he had to stop being so sensitive. He wasn't sure how to do that. It came from his heart, not his brain.

Instead of a celebration, the two settled for a nap. Clothed, they nestled together on the mattress and fell into an effortless sleep.

Chapter Eighteen

It was after two a.m. when Dancer returned that evening. His place was dark. Maybe Tucker couldn't find the lantern. Maybe he was gone.

He switched on the lantern and saw that Tucker was curled in a ball, sleeping on top of the bedding. Although it was strange coming home and seeing someone in his bed, it was better than the alternative. A sense of comfort washed over him, seeing that Tucker was still here.

The night had been wild. He was exhausted. As he was climbing out from the backseat of a giant SUV, the clock on his last client's dashboard had read one thirty a.m.

The John was a middle-aged white guy with bad breath who wanted it all but was too cheap to spring for a room. Under normal circumstances, Dancer preferred a room over a car. It gave him a chance to shower afterwards if the John was amenable to it. But it was already late when Mr. Halitosis showed up, and Dancer was too tired to care. He just wanted to do the job and get home.

They agreed on a hundred and fifty bucks. Dancer had decided to stick him for an extra fifty because of the woodgrain dashboard and the suggestion of fine leather in the fancy SUV.

He snapped the lid from the bin and stuffed the wad of bills into a raggedy pair of cut-off jeans that doubled as his safe. The Milkman taught him to keep his money in something no one would want. He was sure his take tonight was around two-fifty, but he would recount it in the morning.

His usual thing after working was to watch a movie until he came down from the night. It was better to fall asleep thinking about the movie than work. However, without headphones, he didn't want to chance waking Tucker up. As nice as it was to have Tucker here, he was also not in the mood for conversation, knowing how Tucker felt about what he had done this evening.

He finished stripping off his clothes. With several baby wipes, he scrubbed under his balls and between his ass cheeks, wiping away whatever crap Mr. Halitosis used for lube. It would be enough until tomorrow, when he could get over to Chinn's for a shower.

All comfy in his navy-blue cotton sweats, he debated whether he would try to squeeze in next to Tucker or take the chair for the night.

He opted for the latter but then realized Tucker had all the blankets on the bed. He was about to peel a blanket from the bed but decided against it. The likelihood of Tucker waking up was too great.

Nestled down in his chair, his brain kicked into gear, thinking about his test tomorrow, Tucker's confession that he loved him, and his use of the word *boyfriend*. It had all happened so fast. In the blink of an eye, his life had changed. He flipped through a range of emotions but kept coming back to the same result: he was happy. It was harder than watching a good scary movie but better than thinking about what he had done for the last five hours.

He watched as Tucker shifted on the mattress. It was almost as if he was watching himself from afar, a little boy on that same mattress when the Milkman took him in so many years ago. From that day, that little boy had been safe, rescued by a schizophrenic man who collected milk crates. The Milkman was a better father than his stepfather had been. Dancer had thought he was okay with being alone in this world after the Milkman disappeared. Not much had changed until Tucker walked into his life.

"Robert." He purposely murmured the name out loud as his mind took him back into the house he tried to avoid.

He had just turned twelve when his dad died. It wasn't six months later that his mother brought home the boisterous stranger named Robert for the first time. He was larger than life, a one-man show that was introduced as his mom's new manager. Really, he was the scum of the earth, the shit that lay beneath the nastiest swamps in Dancer's hometown of Indian Waters, Mississippi.

The trips to San Francisco, New York, and London to market Mom's books—Robert paid for it all. It was money his father would have never spent. Robert changed their life from well-off to exceedingly wealthy. More money than a little boy from Mississippi knew existed.

He ignored the pain in his jaw from clenching his teeth. He hated everything about Robert: his hair, his breath, his grin. Robert had taken it all, including his mother.

*****

When Dancer's eyes opened, enough sunlight had crept in to signal that it was well past early morning. There was enough light that he saw Tucker was no longer on the mattress. In his place was a note written on a torn piece of a paper bag.

Most likely, Tucker had bolted because he finally saw the crazy that Dancer was offering him. Dancer shifted in the chair, not ready to get up, certainly not ready to read whatever Tucker had written that amounted to a goodbye. He shut his eyes again, hoping to appreciate the peace and quiet.

The words on that note called to him. The more he tried not to think about what they said, the more he wanted to know. When he couldn't take it a second longer, he jumped out of the chair and grabbed the note. He would read it and go back to sleep.

Good morning baby. You were too cute to wake up this morning. I went to visit Mattie. I hope you remembered today was family day. Be back shortly.

Tucker

Dancer reread the note as if he was going to read something different the second time. Tucker hadn't left him. He had only gone to visit his sister.

Relieved, he looked around for his tablet and then remembered it was under the mattress. He slipped it out and checked the time. It was almost one o'clock. He had to get up. His number one priority for today was to go to the clinic. His entire day hinged on this one thing.

He spotted Dottie across the camp. His legs weakened beneath him as if he saw death staring back at him. He hadn't known her when she was using; perhaps she was a different person then. Her heart was pure, and she often gave what little she had if she thought the person needed it more than she. Her face was sunken and haunted; death was coming for her. The muscles in his stomach shifted and tightened. Would his death be as lonely? Seeing Dottie made death seem imminent. It wasn't at all what he wanted, but what he wanted didn't seem to matter in life. He traveled up the narrow row of tents

135

and lean-tos and out of the camp. His mind searched for any symptom that indicated he could be HIV positive.

During the walk between the camp and the small storefront clinic, he was oblivious to everything around him. Inside the clinic, the nurse tried to be courteous, but he was not there for conversation. She went over the details of how the process worked, but he didn't want to hear any of it. *Just draw the goddamn blood and give me the results!*

An hour later, the nurse handed him a folded single sheet of paper with his results. He stood up. An unexpected churning in his stomach stopped him from unfolding the paper immediately. Not sure his legs would support him if he was positive, he sat back down. He resented the nurse for folding the paper.

His face rigid with tension, he scanned the one-page report as it shook in his hands. Columns of words, letters, symbols, and abbreviations, it seemed nothing but technical jargon. His breath hitched when his eyes landed on the letters *HIV* and, to the right, read *non-reactive*. His mouth formed a rigid grimace. What the hell did non-reactive mean? A metallic taste filled his mouth. Was he negative or positive? The muscle at the corner of his right eye quivered as he scanned the document further down. He reached the bottom of the report: *HIV Status—Negative.*

"Jesus." He mumbled as he exhaled the breath that had been locked in his throat. He was negative. He leaned back in the chair and exhaled. A lightness in his chest allowed him to take a full breath of air, followed by a slow and calming exhale. "I'm negative," he mumbled to himself. If he included the two-week window it took for the disease to incubate, he was still likely negative. He hadn't had unprotected sex in over a month.

There was a knock on the door. The nurse didn't wait for a response as she came in. "Would you like to speak with a counselor?"

Did she not know the results? He looked at the report again. Had he misread it? Sure enough, it still read negative. "Um, no, thank you," he murmured.

He couldn't get out of there fast enough. He had to tell someone. Out on the street, he wanted to scream but fought it off. Surely Tucker wouldn't be back at the house yet.

Dancer thought about Tucker, his charisma, dirty blond hair, and those beautiful blue eyes. Suddenly, life wasn't as cruel as he thought. Tucker hadn't appeared in his life as it was about to end. This might be the beginning.

He wasn't going to die. He hadn't lived a life so unimportant, surrounded by people who would never miss him when he was gone. Tucker said he loved him. He was important to Tucker.

The last twenty-four hours had been an emotional typhoon. Everything had been ripped from its foundation and tossed upside down. He wasn't sure he was thinking correctly, but he had a plan for that night.

*****

When Tucker walked into the shack that evening, he read Dancer's face before he had the chance to tell him. "You're negative! I knew it! You're negative!" An emotional combustion occurred as he leapt toward Dancer and yanked him off the ground. Tucker spun him around in the tight room until they tripped over the mattress. The fall sent their bodies plummeting, with Tucker ending up on top of Dancer on the mattress.

Intertwined, the two laughed. For Dancer, the feeling was exhilarating. He hadn't laughed this much in years. Tucker had given him so much. He had shut the entire world out to avoid getting hurt. Being with Tucker the last several days was like a rebirth. "Yes. Yes, I'm negative." He tried to pull away enough so he could at least see Tucker's face.

"Tell me everything! How did it go?" Tucker laid his head against Dancer's stomach, the gleam in his eyes endorsing his desire to hear the details.

"Well, there's not much to tell. It's a little clinic up on Washington Avenue. The same one I went to yesterday. I had to fill out an anonymous form that had a number on it. I didn't have to put my name on it or anything. They matched the results to my number. She drew blood and then had me wait out in the lobby. It took about an hour and then she came out, looked at my number, and gave me my results."

"Were you scared?" Tucker raised his ear from Dancer's abdomen.

His impulse was to say no. "A little. I didn't think I was positive, but I didn't know. I've had unsafe sex too many times to count. I can't believe I'm negative!" Although his test was negative, he had never felt so positive in his life. He brushed his hand across Tucker's hair, still amazed at how soft it was. It was the softest hair he had ever felt.

Tucker again raised his head. "You know, I've read about people who have a genetic mutation that makes them resistant to HIV."

Dancer had never heard of such a thing and wondered if Tucker knew what he was talking about. It didn't matter, though. He was negative. That was the only thing that mattered—that and, of course, Tucker. "Tell me about your day. Did you get to visit with Mattie and your mom?"

Tucker sat up cross-legged. "It was fun. Every Saturday, they have what's called Family Day. My mum can't leave, but we can visit all day. It was nice to see Mattie. She looked happy. They're doing good. My mum is clean. She has meetings she goes to all day. Mattie's still in school. They had lots of snacks to eat and they fed us dinner." Tucker bent down and rubbed his hand across Dancer's stomach.

"You had a nice time?" Tucker touching him reminded him of his plan. He couldn't wait. As much as he wanted to tell Tucker about this evening, he wanted it to be a surprise. It was brilliant.

Chapter Nineteen

With Old Man Gerhardt gone for three weeks, he was sure his plan would work. The apartment was the perfect place to take Tucker. They could shower, rummage through the refrigerator, and in that beautiful, lavish apartment, they would have sex on clean sheets in the king-size bed. The only hint that he gave Tucker about his surprise was that it was going to be a great night.

Dancer was sure he could get himself and Tucker into the apartment without being seen by the night watchman. About a month ago, during small talk, Gerhardt jokingly told Dancer about how the building's watchman got his nickname of Routine Ricky. Gerhardt shared that Routine Ricky took his dinner at nine every night and then took the Peterson's dog for its last walk for the evening. Routine Ricky then always came back and did a round of security checks before returning to the front desk. While he was gone, the only way into the building was by code.

Small talk had come in handy over the years of living on the streets. He learned to listen and discovered that people divulged things they weren't even aware of.

He pressed the sequence of numbers into the keypad on the wall next to the door. He said them aloud, just as Gerhardt's driver did every time he let him into the building.

With the sound of the lock releasing, he pushed open the door and ushered Tucker through the lobby, past the empty security desk, and into the elevator. Still in the dark as to what they were up to, Tucker dragged his feet, not understanding the urgency.

Once the elevator doors shut, Dancer knew they had made it. He used the same code to send the elevator on a direct path up to the penthouse. As the car shuddered and jerked up sixteen floors, Tucker studied the latest inspection report on the wall.

With its final ding, the metal door opened to a dark apartment. If the old man were here, the butterfly stained glass lamp next to his chair in the living room would have been on. He had never been in the apartment and seen the lamp off.

He crossed the room and turned the table lamp on. It didn't offer much light, but enough to illuminate the empty, overstuffed wingback chair next to it. A faint scent of furniture polish wafted past his nose.

Dancer knew the room well. The mahogany bookcase was filled with books and antiques from a life many years ago. Like the rest of the apartment, the dark wood floor in there was covered by several intricately patterned rugs. From this room, the entire skyline of Brierton was visible. It was a view that only wealth could buy.

"Wow!" It was the first thing Tucker had said since sneaking into the building. "Who lives here?"

It surprised Dancer that he hadn't had to reveal his secret to Tucker before now. "You remember that guy I told you about, Old Man Gerhardt? He's out of town for weeks. It's all ours for the night."

Tucker wandered deeper into the room, his hand brushing against the heavy drapery that hung from the high ceiling to the floor. He stared out the floor-to-ceiling windows into the dark sky. "Are you sure? What happens if we get caught?" His voice was low as if talking to himself. He pulled away from the window and walked behind the chair, again running his hand along the top.

"I wanted to bring you here. I wanted tonight to be special. You'll see. The place is nice."

"Where is he?"

"I don't know. I ran into his driver the other day. He said he was away on business or something. We can hang out here all night." Tucker's solemn demeanor threw him off. He wasn't expecting it.

"You brought me here to have sex, like you and him?"

"Huh?" Dancer's initial impression was right. Tucker wasn't as enthusiastic as he had hoped.

"I don't get it. This man is an abuser. What he does is sickening."

"What does that have to do with us?" Dancer asked.

"I don't know. It feels a little weird. Like if it wasn't for him, this place, we…"

"I wanted it to be nice." Dancer didn't want this to be about the old man. He had nothing to do with this evening. The night was theirs, a night to celebrate.

"Well, it's nice. But I don't need nice. Is that why you continue with him, because you like all of this?"

Dancer's plan had been shot out of the air. It had crashed and burned before he knew what happened. Tucker was making a judgement about something he knew nothing about. "Want to know what he does for me? He keeps me from having to walk the streets most nights selling my ass for five dollars less than the guy across the street."

Dancer moved closer to Tucker. He tried to tamp down his temper. "No matter how bad my life is, whatever is going on, every couple of weeks I get a moment where I can just breathe. I can smell something other than nasty soap from Chinn's. I get to close my eyes for a few hours in a real bed. I can shut my eyes and not worry about someone ripping off the money I just traded my body for."

"Has he told you he loves you?" Tucker walked up next to the bookcases as if he was admiring them.

Dancer followed him. "Of course not."

Tucker's head turned slightly. "Do you think he's in love with you?"

"How would I know?" Exasperated, Dancer didn't understand where Tucker was going. "I've never had a conversation with the guy to know. He could be!"

"Do you love him?" Tucker kept his back to Dancer.

"No! But if it weren't for him, I'd have been out there on those streets a hell of a lot more than I have been. If he hadn't taken me in, clothed me, did what no one else on this planet wanted to do, I'd likely be positive by now."

"Oh, Dancer, that is so not true." Tucker turned to face him. "He didn't do any of those things because he cares for you, he did them for his own self-gratification, to control you, to ensure you came back. That makes him a monster."

Dancer didn't want to talk about Gerhardt. Talking about whether the old man cared for him or not was stupid. "My skin crawls every time someone other than you touches me. I don't want to talk about him. If you want, we can go. I'm sorry, I thought you would like this." His eyes scanned the hallway and doors from the main living area as if someone was there. In all the times he had been in this room, he had never talked this much. He relived every single time he was here.

It started with a hot shower. Apart from the first time, Old Man Gerhardt never greeted him until after his shower. Each time, on the back of the door, new clothes hung for him. Dancer's source of expensive clothing. Dressed to look like any ivy league student, he would emerge from the bathroom and meet Old Man Gerhardt in the dining room.

The old man never ate with him but sat across the table and watched as he ate his meal. Initially, Gerhardt hardly spoke to Dancer at the table, other than to advise him to slow down, as Gerhardt too was dining, feasting on the beauty before him. However, lately he had been unusually chatty, talking about things of no concern to Dancer.

"Let's go." Dancer took Tucker's hand but felt the resistance.

The only sound in the room was the tick of a clock coming from somewhere nearby.

"No. I want to stay! It's the least he owes you." Tucker's voice revealed his resentment.

Tucker was mad, but maybe it wasn't at him. Could they salvage something out of this? Dancer had no idea. "We'll be fine. No one is coming up here this late at night." He needed to say something positive. Tonight was supposed to be for Tucker. He wanted it to be nice; it should have been nice.

He led Tucker down the hall and into the master bedroom. Dancer flicked on the light switch next to the door. His eyes glanced at the silver tray on top of the high boy dresser next to the door. If he was with Gerhardt this evening, the folded stack of twenties would have been there for his taking at the end of the night. With or without the money, the room was a reminder of who he was.

"Is it safe to have the light on?" Tucker stood in the doorway. His eyes scanned the room as if he was afraid to enter.

"We're sixteen floors up. Who's looking up sixteen floors and counting what lights are on? Relax." If he said the word enough, maybe he, too, would believe it. "Let's take a shower." They could both use the warm water to relax.

They entered the marbled floor bathroom that contained a bear-claw iron tub. "Or do you want a bath?" Dancer asked.

Tucker's eyes looked over the entire bathroom before settling onto the white tub. "Shower."

The two stripped off their clothes, leaving two piles of clothing in their path. Inside the tub, Dancer pulled the shower curtain from one side of the wall to the other side as he had done in the past. The difference now was that he wasn't alone.

"This is nice." Tucker snickered as the water hit him. His hand slid down Dancer's back and onto his ass.

Dancer turned to face Tucker. The flicker in Tucker's eyes confirmed that he was feeling more relaxed. He gave Dancer a light kiss. Wet and delicious, the crisp freshness of the water on Tucker's lips made Dancer moan.

Tucker inched in closer, their chests now touching. From the small of his back, Tucker pulled Dancer up against his erection.

Surprised that Tucker was already hard, Dancer wasn't ready to take it to that level. "Slow down, cowboy." They had all night. Pulling away, he reached around him and adjusted the water temperature. Coming back to Tucker, he handed him the bar of soap. "Here, let's get clean first."

Tucker scrubbed his body as if he was in a race. From his head to toes, he rubbed the bar of honeysuckle soap against his wet skin.

Dancer stood, waiting for Tucker to finish with the bar. His eyes admired his glistening, pale skin as the water stripped away the bubbles.

Finished with the soap, Tucker handed it to Dancer along with a delicate kiss. "Are we going to do everything?" Semi-erect, Tucker's penis was as beautiful as Dancer remembered.

"That depends on what you mean by everything." Dancer tried to maintain a straight face and not laugh at his lack of terminology.

Tucker's blue eyes sparkled. "You know what I mean."

Dancer tried to steady himself on one foot while he washed the sole of his other foot. "If you are asking if I'm going to let you fuck me, that would be a yes." He put his foot down and switched to the other foot. "In the bed, in the kitchen, in the den, but not in here." He watched as Tucker's ocean blue eyes turned to a storm that only wanted to devour him. He knew what he was doing to Tucker. He had years of experience.

Tucker grew to full attention again, his cock pointing straight up

143

against his abdomen. Dancer laughed; this was going to be like taking candy from a baby. Tonight might be fun after all.

Dancer was more excited than he expected about being Tucker's first. He wanted to pleasure Tucker and give him everything he wanted tonight. It was the one thing he knew how to do right. But for now, he had to get Tucker out of the shower before he exploded.

With Tucker safely out, Dancer positioned him in front of the large mirror above the counter as he patted him dry. He rubbed and caressed the towel down over Tucker's ass before sliding it in between his cheeks. He watched in the mirror as Tucker swelled to a full erection again. Dancer's own body responded at seeing this.

As naked as they had come into the world, they moved to the four-poster bed. He remembered the old man telling him that the bed once belonged to some famous person, a name he didn't recognize. It hadn't been important to Dancer then, and it surely wasn't important now.

Dancer pulled back the heavy comforter to the foot of the bed, leaving the ensemble of pillows in place. "So how experienced are you?" He asked as he climbed into the bed.

Tucker followed him on the bed. "Do you mean, what all have I done?" Tucker grinned as he positioned himself on top of Dancer.

"Yeah. Do you know if you're a pitcher or a catcher?" He slid a hand down Tucker's back to his ass. The soft pale skin that covered his ass was cool to the touch. His hands ventured across Tucker's ass, exploring, tracing the curve of his ass with the tip of his fingers, committing it to memory.

Tucker's body under the tips of his fingers felt amazing. Soft and hairless, his skin was as smooth as silk. His nose pressed into the side of Tucker's arm, and he took in a light, sweet scent of honeysuckle.

Lust glittered in Tucker's eyes as he stared down at Dancer. "Since I know you don't know shit about baseball, and I didn't just crawl out from under a rock, you mean am I a top or bottom?" Tucker squirmed, pressing his pelvis down into Dancer.

The feel of Tucker's erection against him forced an exhale. Light headed, he was surprised that Tucker knew the jargon. "Oh, do I have a quick study on my hands?" Dancer whispered into Tucker's ear before taking a nibble.

Tucker released a soft moan as his head rolled to one side. "Just like on the field, I'm a pitcher... *I think*." Tucker jammed his pelvis into Dancer as he smiled down at him.

Dancer couldn't hold back a snicker as he gazed up at Tucker's coy smile. He was an aggressive virgin who knew what he liked. Dancer was liking their naughty banter.

Tucker lowered his head and gave Dancer a delicate kiss. The taste of Tucker's lips pressed against his caused him to draw a long breath. It was his kiss that Dancer loved.

Tucker's hands caressed his body, gliding down his ribs, over his ass, resting on the side of his thigh. Dancer's body responded to every touch.

For someone who claimed to be a virgin, Tucker was a natural. Dancer's world disappeared, and for the first time, he wasn't thinking about anything other than Tucker's lips on his body.

Chest to chest, they moved against one another's erections, sliding up and down. As if Tucker's hands were eyes, they explored his body, turning up the heat between them. Their naked bodies rolled from side to side across the bed as they hungrily kissed one another deeper and harder.

In a marathon of kissing, they covered every inch of the bed as their bodies rolled back and forth, changing positions. One by one, pillows dropped to the floor as they made use of every square inch of the mattress.

Tucker's back arched, his shoulders leaving Dancer's body. His breathing was more like a pant as his head slammed back down, resting on the side of Dancer's neck. "I'm going to come." He muttered, his hot breath poured into Dancer's left ear.

Energy must have traveled through Tucker's body, shocking Dancer's own nervous system. Within seconds, they both cried out as spasms caused each of their bodies to tremor.

Dancer had never experienced anything like that. Tucker's touch, the taste of his mouth, the sounds he made as he drew close to climaxing; they worked in tandem to ignite a hunger inside him that he didn't know existed. Breathless, the tremors lessened into short pulses causing his body to flinch with each pulsation.

Dancer brushed back the tousled curls from his face as a tear slipped from his eye and rolled down the side of his face. He turned his face, smashing the tear into the one remaining pillow on the bed. Buried under Tucker's body, a warmth radiated throughout Dancer.

This was supposed to be about Tucker—it was the reason they were here. So why was he the one getting all emotional? With every beat of his heart, feelings kept bubbling up. Every sexual act from his past attached itself to what just occurred. But what just happened, whatever it was, it was different.

There were no mechanics in what happened. He wasn't in control. If anything, Tucker was. It wasn't important who had the control—it wasn't part of any deal that was made.

In their stillness, another tear fell from Dancer's eye and slipped onto the luxurious fabric that covered his pillow. He forced a hard swallow, knowing Tucker gave without asking for anything in return. Tucker's hand reached for his, and their fingers interlocked. Tucker rolled off him and to his side. "I love you," he whispered.

The tenderness that carried the words into Dancer's ear jolted his heart. It took a second for the words to register, the depth of what Tucker had just said. There was nothing in between the words, no conditions, no expectations, no exceptions. The power of the words *I Love You* stood solely on its own. What could he say to begin to measure up to what Tucker had just said? An adrenaline rush reached his brain, causing his thoughts to scramble.

He had never been drunk, but imagined its similarities to how he was feeling. Stampeded with thoughts of his Oma, his father, and even the good times with his mother, he wanted to laugh, shout, jump out of bed—all at the same time. His insides felt as if they were vibrating. He had forgotten what love felt like.

Chapter Twenty

"Freddy Krueger or Jeffrey Meyers?" Tucker's breathing had returned to normal.

Dancer thought about the silly question that led him away from his emotional thoughts of what had occurred between him and Tucker. "Do you mean *Michael* Meyers from *Halloween*?" Yes, everything about Tucker was endearing. He had never felt what he was feeling with anyone except him. Tonight, he wouldn't get nudged out of the bed, that passive dismissal from Old Man Gerhardt.

"Yeah, him." Tucker was propped on his side, staring at him with a fool's grin.

"What about them?" Dancer stretched his naked body across the bed as he wiggled his toes. He didn't have to be quiet.

"Who are you most scared of?" Tucker's arm draped over Dancer's stomach, and his fingers glided up and down Dancer's ribcage.

Dancer laughed. "I'm not scared of either one. They're not real."

"Okay, but if they were." The mattress shook as Tucker sprung onto his knees, his kneecaps pushing into Dancer's ribs.

In his head, he agreed to play. "I guess Freddy Krueger."

"Why?"

"I don't know, they're not real!" How long was this game supposed to go for?

"Cheddar or Swiss?"

Dancer's nose wrinkled. "I hate cheese!"

"All cheeses?"

Dancer nodded.

"Okay then, the ocean or the lake?" Tucker asked.

Dancer thought he had a handle on this game. "The ocean."

"Why?"

"Because it reminds me of your eyes." It was true. Every time he looked into Tucker's eyes, he thought of the ocean. Deep and infinite, there was always more to him. Every aspect of Tucker fascinated him.

Tucker's face softened. "Okay, an airplane or—"

"No, it's my turn!" Dancer rolled on his side to face his lover. He wanted to know something about him, something new, anything. "The mountains or the beach?"

"I don't know." Tucker lifted an eyebrow as his nose wrinkled.

Dancer was confused. His question was simple. Had he messed the game up somehow?

Tucker's nose crinkled. "I've never seen either one in real life."

How was it possible that someone hadn't seen either a mountain or a beach? Okay, maybe the beach, but mountains were everywhere. Dancer raised his head off the pillow. Was Tucker joking? "You've never been to the mountains?"

"No. We never went anywhere. The biggest thing we did was go to the local fair."

"Where did you grow up?" Dancer sat up.

"Here."

"In Brierton?" Dancer's voice couldn't contain his surprise.

"No, not Brierton, but about an hour from here. We lived in Saint Charles until my mum burned most of our bridges there, so we came here."

"You've never been camping?" Dancer was stunned.

"No."

That meant he never had catfish cooked on an open fire. Never had a tin-foil dinner or his granny's scrambled spam and eggs. Dancer wanted to share it all with him one day, an entire world that would awe him. Although he didn't know how to cook any of it, one day, they would go camping. "I can't believe you've never been camping. When my dad was alive, we camped all the time. Me, my dad and mom, and my Oma."

"Well, we never had much money."

Although Dancer had never been poor as a child, he understood now the definition of poor. "Okay. Steak, chicken, fish, or pork?"

Tucker gave a lopsided grin as if thinking. "It depends on how it's cooked."

"Oh my God!" Dancer was exasperated at Tucker's game. Why couldn't he answer the question! In a fit of laughter, Dancer pounded his hands into the mattress, faking a temper tantrum. "Just pick one!"

"Okay! Okay! Calm down!" Tucker threw his naked body over Dancer's, and the two wrestled on the bed. In a fight to get on top, they rolled off the bed and hit the floor.

Dancer's strength was no match for Tucker. Although he tried everything he knew, Tucker kept him pinned on the floor as he tickled him. "Say you're sorry!"

"Sorry for what?" Dancer was laughing so hard, he could barely get the words out.

"For yelling at me!" Tucker dug his fingers in harder as they jabbed at Dancer's naked flesh.

"I'm not sorry, I'm not..." Dancer couldn't formulate his sentence; the torture was driving him mad.

"Yes, you are. Say you're sorry!"

"Okay, I'm sorry. Stop! Stop!" Dancer screamed. He was about to pee on himself.

With Tucker's body pinning him down, he felt Tucker's erection touch his arm. Surprised that he was hard, he grabbed it as tight as he could.

"Oww! You punk, that hurt!" Tucker jumped out of his grip, and flipped his body, aligning it with Dancer's. Face to face, Tucker laughed, his warm breath penetrating Dancer's senses.

Tucker leaned down and crushed his mouth down into Dancer's. The kiss, hard and maddening, the passion fiery. Their tongues in sync, Dancer's hands gravitated to Tucker's hairless ass. Dancer used it to pull Tucker deeper into his chest. His skin was warm to the touch as their bodies meshed. Every place that Dancer's fingers touched evoked a moan from Tucker.

The faint smell of soap from their shower earlier wafted up as Dancer shoved his hair out of his face. His desire overrode all thoughts. Dancer imagined Tucker inside him; he needed Tucker inside of him. With no clothes to slip out of, Dancer pulled away and opened his eyes. Tucker was staring at him, doe-eyed. "Where's my backpack?" Dancer's words slurred as he looked around for his backpack.

Tucker spotted it first, and stretched his long arms out. He was barely able to reach it without getting up. He pulled the backpack up next to them.

Dancer scrambled to loosen the drawstring at the top. He dug around until he found what he was looking for.

With no words spoken, Dancer flipped the lid on the tube of K-Y and lubricated himself. Unsure if Tucker knew how to apply a condom, he did it for him, slipping it over his rock-hard cock. The muscles in Dancer's ass twitched with anticipation as he rolled onto his stomach.

Tucker ran his mouth across Dancer's neck as he eased into him. His lips brushed the back of Dancer's neck, forcing a moan deep in his throat. The weight of Tucker's body as his irregular and unpredictable thrust picked up to a full gallop was crushing Dancer into the floor.

"Slow. Slow, baby, slow." Never had it felt this good to Dancer. The sensation of every nerve being stimulated was maddening. Dancer's nails scraped at the rug on the floor, unable to grasp anything to hold on to. Had Tucker not heard him? Had the words come out of his mouth?

"Your ass!" Tucker thrusted deeper. It was only a few minutes before Tucker grabbed the back of Dancer's hair and pulled back. "I'm coming!"

Dancer was close as well when he felt the dead weight of Tucker's body collapse on him. No, he was too close. Dancer pushed his ass up in the air, lifting his pelvis off the floor. He took matters into his own hands and, with only a couple of strokes, he spilled, shooting his seed between his belly and the wood floor.

The two lay on the floor, sweaty and out of breath. After about a minute, Dancer was able to breathe enough to pull away from Tucker, allowing him to slip completely out of him. With one hand, he reached around, stripped the condom off Tucker, and balled it in his fist. Certain he couldn't talk without his voice failing him, he cleared his throat to make sure. "What the hell was that? You're a freaking rockstar." His voice faltered as he rolled to one side.

Tucker's breathing hadn't yet slowed. They lay there several more minutes before Dancer wobbled to his feet. His legs were like gelatin. He staggered into the bathroom and cleaned up before returning with a warm wash cloth for Tucker.

Tucker had moved to the unmade bed. His massive, naked body lay sideways, his long legs hanging from the side. His abdomen stretched as flat as a pancake.

"Here you go." Dancer handed Tucker the wash cloth. The clock sitting on the nightstand read one forty-six. He shifted his body weight, stretching his back as he waited for Tucker to finish. Dancer snickered and chided, "I think you broke my back." His eyes steadied on Tucker's incredible body.

Done with the wash cloth, Tucker hurled it over his head onto the other side of the bed. "Thank you."

Dancer returned to the bed and rested his head on Tucker's damp stomach. They laid in silence for several minutes, their lovemaking replaying in Dancer's head. He had been taken many times by men, none of whom had ever made love to him. In all those experiences, he never had anything to compare it to. Now he knew they didn't compare; they were as different as night and day.

Tonight was more than Dancer had dreamed. It was only supposed to be about sex, giving Tucker what he wanted. Freely, he had given more than just his body to Tucker. But he was also present the entire time they were making love. He hadn't run somewhere in the back of his head to escape what was happening. Tucker was the most amazing person he had ever met. He deserved someone who would be good to him, who would adore him until the end of time. A blissful grin covered Dancer's face. He wanted to be that person.

"When did you know you were gay?" Dancer asked the question to stop himself from getting emotional again.

Tucker hummed for a second. "I don't know, maybe when I was around ten or eleven. I was always into sports. When I was little, I played football, baseball, and soccer, so I was always around boys more than girls. Because I wasn't around that many girls, I thought it was natural. In about the eighth grade, it hit me I wasn't attracted to girls. How about you?"

"It was the opposite for me. I was always around girls. In dance, I was lucky if there was another boy in the class. I hated that the girls got to wear the tutu over their leotards and pink flats. Mine were always brown or black." Tucker's soothing fingers massaged his scalp through his hair.

"I'll always remember my dad telling me one day that, when I was older, if I wanted to wear pink flats, that I could. That if I was good at dancing, nobody would care what I wore. I wanted to be the best so I could have pink flats."

They talked about everything, from school, people in the encampment, to winning a million dollars, and their fears and dreams. Dancer wanted to know more about Tucker, everything.

It was almost four a.m., and except for peeing and getting water from the bathroom sink, they hadn't moved from the bedroom.

Dancer had rolled onto his stomach and, as silence fell between them, he drifted off to sleep. He hadn't yet reached a deep sleep when he felt Tucker straddle his ass. "What are you doing?" He kept his eyes closed as Tucker shifted his weight more to Dancer's thighs.

"Nothing." The tone in Tucker's voice suggested he was lying.

This wasn't Dancer's first rodeo, and he knew better. He bent his neck back to see what exactly Tucker was up to. He was surprised to see that Tucker had risen to the occasion and was trying to put a condom on. "Oh no!" Dancer laughed as he tried to squirm out from under him.

"Come on!" Tucker continued struggling with the condom while riding Dancer's bounce like a bucking bull.

Dancer was enjoying teasing Tucker as he pretended to resist. The divine thought of Tucker screwing him again ignited his own hunger. Tucker's plea was sappy and adorable, and it was going to get him what he wanted—there was no doubt.

"Come on. I came too fast. I want to do it again."

"That's your problem, Mr. Rabbit, not mine!" Dancer's butt cheeks clenched.

"Please!" Tucker begged.

Dancer couldn't let the man beg. He stopped squirming and made his proposal. "Okay, if you can put that condom on right—in the next thirty seconds—I'll let you fuck me again."

Tucker took twenty-eight seconds and was ready. For the third time, the two were intertwined and thrashing about the bed. Tucker had learned his lesson the first time. Truly a quick study, he was controlled and steady. He lasted far longer than Dancer had counted on.

Most likely unaware of what he was doing, Tucker had mastered the art of edging.

Chapter Twenty-One

It was after five a.m. when Dancer delivered yet another warm washcloth to his apprentice. Apart from dozing off for a few minutes, they had been up all night. The sun would rise in an hour. Tucker imagined sunrise would look far different sixteen floors up from where he usually experienced it. Not that he was a fan of sunrises, but he wanted to see it. "Are you hungry?" he asked Dancer, who was laying on his chest.

"A little. Why? What are you thinking?"

"I'm thinking we should go check out the kitchen and see what's in there."

The two were up and in the kitchen within minutes. With Dancer in his underwear and Tucker in his jeans, they combed through the cabinets, pantry, and refrigerator.

"We have eggs and a couple of slices of ham." Dancer's head was in the massive sub-zero refrigerator, scanning the contents.

"How about milk?" Tucker asked as he eyed the English muffins in the pantry.

"We have... S-o-y-milk?"

"How about cheese?"

"Check. We have cheese."

"Okay, give me the eggs, ham, milk, and cheese. No, never mind, not the cheese. I forgot you don't like cheese. Do we have green onions?"

Dancer combed through the small drawers in the refrigerator. "Nope."

Tucker picked through the seasonings, grabbing what he needed. "Look in the freezer. Does he have any hash browns, tater tots, or French fries?"

"What the hell are you making?" Dancer poked his head out of the refrigerator. "Damn! Do you know how sexy you are?"

153

Barefoot and shirtless, Tucker's jeans sagged below his waistline. A tiny trail of blond hair rose from his jeans to his bellybutton. "It's called a farmer's casserole."

"Never heard of a farmer's casserole." Dancer jerked the lower drawer of the massive freezer open. "Nope, nothing but ice cream, a box of Eggos, and some popsicles. The asshole never offered me a popsicle!"

"Gimme the Eggos!" Tucker answered. In no time, he mixed a dozen eggs with milk and poured the mixture into a baking dish. He was enjoying being in the kitchen. It had been a long time since he could cook like this. Second to baseball, it was a love acquired out of necessity. He had watched years of cooking shows, and with his mother being often gone the last two years, he had learned to cook for Mattie and had come to love it.

"I take it you've made this before?" Dancer's eyes followed his every move as Tucker diced the ham. "Yeah, twice. It's kind of like a quiche. If we had hash browns, I'd used those as the bottom layer, like a crust, instead of the Eggos."

Dancer watched as Tucker emptied the diced ham over the egg mixture and sprinkled a variety of seasonings over the top. "How do you know how much to put in it?"

"It's a feel. I just know." Tucker slid the nine-by-eleven baking pan from the counter to the oven. He played around with the buttons on the oven panel before appearing satisfied that he had set the timer. "In an hour, we can eat. Now it's time to figure out this coffee machine." The Jura Espresso Machine would be a challenge to figure out, but he wanted his coffee.

The machine turned out to be much easier than he had expected, and in less than a minute, he had the perfect espresso. "Are you sure you don't want one? You don't have to like coffee to love this." Tucker closed his eyes as he took another sip. "My God, this is good!" He held out the cup for Dancer.

"No, I'm good."

"Do you want me to make you tea? I saw tea in the pantry."

"I'll do it." Dancer hopped off the counter and sauntered over to the pantry. He slowed as he passed Tucker and gave him a light kiss as he ran his hand up his abdomen to his left nipple. With Dancer's gentle squeeze, Tucker let out a cry as his body shuddered.

"You're bad!" Tucker wanted to grab him but stopped, remembering what he had said about being grabbed. Did it still hold true? They had done more than touch in the last twenty-four hours.

Tucker's eyes drifted down to Dancer's ass as he walked away from him. He stared at the stretched fabric of Dancer's underwear, knowing that beneath it was solid muscle. The thought of what he had done to Dancer's smooth caramel butt sent heat curling down his spine to his groin. He couldn't stop smiling at the thought that he was no longer a virgin. Surging with the desire to have sex again, he licked his lips.

The sun peaked through the massive windows in the front room. With their warm drinks in hand, they stood at the windows, watching the sun as it peaked over the skyscrapers in front of them.

"I've decided I'm not going back out there." Dancer's voice quaked.

Tucker didn't understand what he was talking about. Had he heard him correctly? Was he planning to stay in this apartment forever? Surely not. "What do you mean?"

"I'm done. I'm going to find a real job." Dancer never took his eyes off the people below. "We need to get out of Camp Roosevelt."

"I thought you said nobody escapes." Tucker watched Dancer's eyes as they traced the people below them. Camp Roosevelt was his home. Tucker had no desire to live there forever, but it was where Dancer was, and he wanted to be wherever Dancer was.

"I'm HIV negative. You, Me... I'm tired." Dancer brushed his hair away from his face. "You know, I never realized he could see the camp from here." Dancer pointed to the east. "It's right over there."

Tucker looked past all the buildings, expensive store fronts, and people wrapped in coats on the streets. He was right; there was Camp Roosevelt.

"He knew I lived there."

How would the old man have known this? Was it a conversation, or had the man assumed? Tucker couldn't imagine that he cared enough to assume. "What would we do?" He didn't want to sound too eager in case this was simply a fleeting thought on Dancer's part.

"I don't know. I want to live like normal people. We could get jobs."

"Doing what? Tucker asked. It would be next to impossible for

155

them to get jobs. The last twelve hours, here in this apartment, was what normal might look like if they could. They could never afford anything this nice, but a real roof and walls, maybe a room for Mattie when she came to visit.

"I don't know." Dancer scratched at his chin.

Tucker's life hadn't been normal in so long. The closest thing he could compare normal to was the three-bedroom house they rented for a year back in Saint Charles. His mother was working at the time. He had his own bedroom, his own bed. He and his coach were even talking to colleges and making plans for him. At the time, he had no idea they were about to be evicted from that place too. "Normal would be nice. I think I could do normal with you very well."

Dancer walked away from the window and took a seat on the small leather couch across from the television. "I haven't watched TV in forever. Do you think you could figure out how to turn that thing on?"

Tucker joined him on the couch and examined the remote. Within minutes, the picture and sound appeared. "Anything particular you want to watch?"

"The news. What's going on in the world." Dancer hiked his legs onto the couch and across Tucker's lap.

Tucker was about to change the channel when Dancer yelled, "Stop!"

Tucker looked at the gigantic screen on the wall. A woman in a beautiful cream lace-detailed sweater dress that clung to every inch of her body was being interviewed by someone.

"That's my mom!" Dancer put both feet on the ground as he leaned forward to hear the interview.

Unsure whether to watch Dancer or the woman, Tucker chose the woman. Her hair and makeup were flawless. Behind her was a banner of what he imagined was her new book.

"Your mother, she's smoking hot." Tucker leaned forward. "Now I see where you get your looks. You guys are like models."

"Shh! I want to hear it!" Dancer took the remote and turned the volume up.

"*—Joaquina, your new novel,* A Black Rose in the Sand, *is set for release this Friday. This is the first book since your divorce from your second husband and manager, Robert Pick. Is it true that Robert is the rose you refer to in the book?*

Joaquina Ziegler dodged the question as well as the next two, which hinted that she'd had to pay her manager to get out of the seven-year marriage. She was in Chicago for the weekend promoting the book. She was less than an hour away from them.

They listened to the interview, Tucker afraid to say anything for fear they might miss something. When the segment ended, he waited for Dancer to say something.

It was several minutes before Dancer spoke. "Well, I'm glad she dumped that asshole."

Tucker was about to reply when an intrusive buzz from the oven timer sounded. His casserole was not as important as his questions or his boyfriend—it could wait. He didn't know what to say. The announcement that Dancer's stepfather was gone was unexpected. What did it change?

"Your timer's going off." Dancer turned to him. His eyes glazed.

*****

They ate in silence at a small breakfast table in the kitchen. Dancer picked at the casserole, nibbling on pieces of ham. Tucker tried to eat, but seeing Dancer's hollow expression, he lost his appetite. It was bland and should have cooled before they cut into it. He knew better, but he wasn't thinking. Dancer was the only thing on his mind.

The show had derailed their party. By Dancer's subdued demeanor, it was clear that he was deep in thought. He was unsure if he should interrupt Dancer, but the words just came out of his mouth. "How do you do it?"

Dancer scowled, "Do what?" A muscle in his jaw twitched.

"This... This life." Tucker gripped the arm of his chair as if he was on a wild roller coaster heading for a loop. To someone who may not have known Dancer, his expression may have appeared blank, but it was anything but. The wheels turning in Dancer's brain caused a tiny crease in the middle of his forehead.

Dancer pushed his plate away from him. "Sometimes life doesn't give you options. Sometimes you just have to swallow the shit that's jammed in your mouth." He picked up his fork and was about to use it before stopping. He tossed the fork onto his plate. "We should go."

"Okay." Tucker murmured.

"Let's take a shower and clean this place up before we head out." Dancer's tone lifted from two seconds ago. "Have you ever cut hair?" Dancer ran his fingers through his mounds of curls. "I look like a Shi Tzu with a bad perm. No one will hire me looking like this. Maybe you can cut my hair later?"

Did the wild, curly long hair really have to go? Tucker loved Dancer's hair. "I've never cut hair, but how hard could it be?"

After their shower, they tidied the apartment as best they could, bagging up the cum-stained hand towels into the bath towels and tossing them down the trash chute. Dancer knew it would be the last time he ever set foot in this apartment and that he would likely never see the old man again. It didn't seem fit to just walk out. He didn't entirely agree with Tucker that the old man was a user.

Dancer wasn't naïve, either. He knew the meals and new clothes came with a price and not out of the goodness of the old man's heart, although he was far politer than any of Dancer's other Johns. While Tucker was busy putting the last of the breakfast dishes away, Dancer scribbled out a note and left it on the old man's chair.

Sorry for any mess that I left
I am out of the business
Dancer

*****

Back in their tiny dwelling, the richness of last night had vanished. "What do you want to do today?" Tucker asked as he watched Dancer dig through one of his plastic bins.

"Right now, I'm looking for scissors. Do you feel like cutting my hair?" Dancer had been quiet for the entire walk home. "I can't believe I don't have a pair of scissors. I know I have scissors." He slammed the lid back onto the bin. "Fuck it! We can go to Walmart later and get some."

Dancer stood for a second with his hands on his hips as if assessing what to do next. "I think I'm going to just take a nap."

Tucker knew it wasn't the missing scissors that had Dancer upset. It was seeing his mother on TV that was causing Dancer to want to go to bed and pull the covers over his head. He knew that feeling all too well. "Okay. Do you mind if I lay with you?"

"Not at all." Dancer waited for him to remove his boots and then allowed him to climb into bed and move over toward the wall. When Dancer crawled into bed, Tucker took his arm and wrapped it around Dancer, pulling him in closer. He rubbed Dancer's shoulders, up and down until he felt the muscles relax, trusting that he was asleep.

Hours later, Dancer stirred first. The movement of the mattress dipping as Dancer got out of bed woke Tucker. The inside of the shanty was dim. Not ready to wake up, he rolled over to see what Dancer was doing.

"Hey, I'm going to Walmart to get those scissors. Do you want to go?" Dancer asked.

"No." Tucker tried to open his eyes, but he couldn't wake up.

"Okay. I'll be right back. Can you cut my hair when I get back?"

"Yeah," Tucker mumbled.

"Okay, I'll get something for dinner." Dancer kissed him on the forehead and headed out.

Tucker rolled back against the wall and fell back asleep.

When he woke up hours later, the shanty was dark. He stumbled to the bin with the lantern and found it. Looking at the time, he realized he had been sleeping almost six hours. Where was Dancer?

The realization that Dancer had been gone for hours shook him awake. There was no sign that he had been back and gone out again. Surely, he wasn't working. Had he changed his mind? Was it too much to expect that he could have left working the streets that easy?

Crossed between being concerned and pissed, Tucker put on his boots and headed out to look for Dancer. *Is he working? He said he wasn't going to do it anymore.* Tucker didn't know what he would do if he found him working. Could he accept it? He wanted to, but after last night and this morning, the lovemaking, the conversation, he was more than in love with Dancer, and there wasn't any part of him he wanted to share with strangers.

Tucker walked up to Washington Boulevard, where most of the gay sex workers were. Some chose a block on either side, but most of them worked a three-block stretch that ran from Fifth Avenue to Eighth.

It was a full moon out, and all the boys lined the streets watching the traffic. Tucker was amazed at how blatant and open the trade was as he weaved in and out amongst the guys working. He couldn't believe how young some of them looked. They were children, way too young to be out here.

He watched as they ran to cars that had pulled up to the curb. In most cases, it was only seconds before they were in the car and gone. Each one was Dancer, climbing in a car for the last time, before he disappeared forever.

The thought occurred to him that this scenario could be his mum as well. Did she do the same thing, working the passing cars? He spent many nights looking for her when she was out getting high. Most of the time, he could find her in one or two locations. Occasionally, when she wasn't at either place, someone there would point him to a third or fourth location. He found her every time. He had tried everything he knew to keep her sober, from hiding their debit card to flushing her stash. The latter got him an ass whipping when he was younger and taught her to hide her drugs.

Tucker saw someone get into a car at the corner. Could that have been Dancer? He picked up his step to a run, chasing down the car that had stopped at the light. It was dark inside; he couldn't tell. Without thinking, he ripped the door open.

The young guy in the passenger seat had a look of surprise in his eyes. "What the hell?"

It wasn't Dancer. "Sorry, sorry!" Tucker held out his hands as he retreated onto the curb. He watched as the car peeled its rear tires the second the light turned green. If Dancer was working, he could be anywhere. There was no way of knowing if he was even in the neighborhood.

Frantically, Tucker picked up speed until he reached Eighth Street. He walked one more block just in case. Dancer had to be out here. If he could find Dancer, he could fix this. But he had to find him.

Tucker walked the three blocks twice before taking on the side streets on either side of Washington Boulevard. When that proved unsuccessful, he started weaving in and out of the alleys that connected the streets.

When he turned up the alley behind New Beginnings, he saw red and blue lights flashing at the other end of the alley. Alarmed, he

160

picked up his speed to a run. He made it halfway down the alley before he saw it was an ambulance.

In a full sprint, he rushed up to the ambulance, but it was too late. The paramedic closed the door, and the van took off. Tucker stopped where the ambulance had been just three seconds ago. He looked around and then saw it: Dancer's shoe.

He rushed to the shoe and picked it up. Tucker was one hundred percent sure the shoe was Dancer's. He stood in the alley as the tail lights of the ambulance turned the corner. He forced himself to take a breath as his eyes stared at the flashing red and white lights. Was Dancer alive? Tucker wanted to chase behind the vehicle, but his feet wouldn't move. As if stuck in quicksand, he tried to push his upper body forward. He fought to push air down into his lungs as his breathing went shallow. He hyperventilated as his eyes chased the swirl of the red and blue lights. They soon blurred, and his body hit the asphalt, where darkness took over.

Chapter Twenty-Two

"Hey! Hey! Are you all right?"

The voice was unfamiliar, and Tucker couldn't understand why it was asking if he was okay. He tried to open his eyes, but they weren't cooperating. The pain in the front of his head was unbearable. He felt his body moving as if being lifted into the air. Was he floating? This was the last sensation he felt as he fell back asleep.

It was another three hours before he stirred. He slowly opened his eyes—the pain in his head said to move carefully. The room was dim. He lay there trying to figure out where he was. His brain wasn't releasing any information.

"Are you awake?"

Tucker squirmed at the voice as it reverberated in his head. Every muscle in his body pulled tight, the pain so intense that he wanted to scream, but that would take more energy than he had to give.

"Relax. Tucker, just relax." The sound of the voice was followed by someone's hands on his arm.

He knew the voice. His eyes tried to focus on whoever it was. Where the hell was he?

"You had a seizure."

His eyes strained as parts of the blurry figure came into focus. The face, then the eyes, the nose, and the mouth. It was Ian.

He lay in a daze; the sound of the blood pumping vibrated between his brain and his forehead. He tried to ask Ian what had happened, but his voice was missing. Disoriented, he closed his eyes.

After about fifteen minutes, Tucker opened his eyes again. Although nauseous, he was alert enough to try to sit up. "Where am I?" His tongue was swollen, causing him to slur.

"You're in my office. You had a seizure." Ian kneeled next to him.

Tucker's eyes scanned the room, looking for anything that was familiar. He was on the floor in front of Ian's desk. He recognized the office. The pain in his tongue increased. He must have bitten it.

The blanket that covered Tucker slid to his waist. He felt Ian push it up against his body. When he looked down, he realized he was naked. "Where're my clothes?"

Ian stood up. "Your clothes are in the wash. You soiled yourself."

"Um, oh." He was too groggy to be embarrassed.

"I went out to empty my trash can for the night and found you laying in the alley. What were you doing there?"

The alley? He couldn't remember why he was in the alley.

Ian was quiet for several minutes while Tucker continued to wake up. His head was killing him. It was a migraine.

"Did you get your prescription taken care of?"

"Um, yeah." Tucker's body swayed. "They're in my bag." Panic washed over him as he looked around for his bag.

"I got it." Ian pulled the backpack off his desk and handed it to Tucker.

Tucker opened the backpack to retrieve his medication to help with his migraine. Seeing his seizure medication, he couldn't recall taking it this morning. The morning was foggy.

"I sent someone to get Dancer. They said he wasn't in the camp."

Dancer, Dancer... "Oh, God!" The pain in Tucker's head exploded. "Dancer and I were... He was in the ambulance! They took Dancer in the ambulance!" Tucker tried to get up. He had to get to the hospital. "Where are my goddamn jeans! I need my clothes!"

"Okay. Okay. Settle down." Ian held out his hands. "I'll go see if they're ready. Wait here. I'll be right back."

Tucker tried to get up again. He wasn't coordinated enough to hold the blanket and lift his body off the floor at the same time. He took a deep breath, and more of his memory came to him. He and Dancer were in the alley. No, he had found Dancer in the alley. That wasn't sticking either.

He looked down in his bag. His brain was still foggy, but he was ninety-nine-point-nine percent sure he hadn't taken his medication today. *What was the day, what time was it? How long had he been out?* He looked around for his phone. A search of his bag proved negative.

Panic stricken, he forced himself onto his feet, using the corner of the desk to support his weight. The blanket dropped to the floor, his nude body exposed to anyone who walked in. He was too foggy to care.

He had just gotten his balance and was about to reach down for the blanket when Ian burst through the door.

"Oops!" Ian froze. "I have your clothes." He looked back out in the hall before closing the door. "Here. Can you do it by yourself?" He took two reserved steps closer to Tucker and held out his clothes.

"Thanks." Tucker leaned back on Ian's desk, his bare ass resting on its edge. "I can do it." His voice shook.

"There wasn't any underwear in the dryer."

"That's fine." There was never any underwear, but he didn't have the energy to share this. It took him a couple of minutes to get his pants on. "I have to get to the hospital. We have to find Dancer." A memory flashed: He had been looking for Dancer and seen the ambulance in the alley. As he approached, they were loading a body into the back of the ambulance. He only got a glimpse, but it was Dancer. The face was bludgeoned and bloody, but it was him. He tried to get to him, but it was too late. The memory of watching the flashing lights was the last thing he remembered. "How long have I been sleeping?"

"An hour or so." Ian stood against the door.

"Where's my phone? Do you have my phone?" Tucker struggled with the buttons on his shirt. He hadn't lined them up properly and had one button left without a hole. It wasn't important. He reached for his jacket. "My boots?"

Ian moved to the side of his desk and pulled out Tucker's phone from his top drawer. "I locked it up." He then produced Tucker's boots. "Here you go." He looked at the door and then back at Tucker. "Let me make some calls to see if I can find out where he's at. I'm sure they took him to Roosevelt General, but I want to make sure before we ride all the way out there." Ian moved to the other side of his desk and took a seat. He flipped through an old brown Rolodex and pulled a card from it. His eyes studied the card before he dialed the number.

After getting his boots on, Tucker slung his backpack onto his back. He wanted to hear Ian's conversation, but it was taking too long. Since Ian was unable to give an actual name, they transferred him to security and said something about someone named John Doe.

"I'm leaving!" Tucker couldn't stand there while Ian got nowhere with whoever he was talking to.

Ian slammed the phone down. "Wait! I'm coming!" He grabbed his coat off the rack, and the two fled out the door.

*****

It took forever for the Uber to arrive, but Tucker didn't have a choice. The fifteen-minute ride to Roosevelt General was a blessing and a curse. Tucker needed the time to get his brain cells clicking, but the wait was agony.

Tucker stood behind Ian as he spoke to the old man at the hospital visitor's information desk. He looked at his phone. It was after midnight, and he had twelve percent battery left. He couldn't understand why they were talking about John Doe again. *Is that Dancer's real name? How does Ian know his real name? What else does he know about Dancer?*

Within minutes, security arrived. One male and one female officer took Ian aside. They talked for several minutes as the female officer scribbled in a small note pad. What were they discussing?

Tucker watched as the female officer tucked her note pad in her breast pocket and then went over to a phone on the wall. She talked for a couple minutes before returning to her partner and Ian.

After several minutes, the officers walked away, and Ian returned to where he had left Tucker. "There's a John Doe that came in around nine o'clock this evening. He's still in surgery. They can't tell us much other than he's in critical condition."

"Can we see him?" Tucker was done standing around.

"No. He's in surgery." The color in Ian's face had drained. "Do you know Dancer's real name? Anything about his family? The officers need to identify him, get a hold of family."

Tucker didn't know his real name. He was Dancer. "His mum is Joaquina Ziegler."

"The writer?" Ian's eyes flickered.

"Yeah. But they're not talking. His dad's dead." Tucker racked his brain for more. "She lives in Mississippi. Oh! And she was on TV this morning. She's in Chicago for her new book!"

Ian scratched his head. "That show could have been taped days ago. Let me tell the officers." Ian walked back over to the help desk.

Tucker followed. He listened as Ian asked for the officers. The old man at the desk picked up the phone.

"Who's John Doe? Is that Dancer's real name?" Tucker asked.

Ian's brows narrowed. "No. It's what they call someone if they don't know who they are."

The old man hung up the phone and instructed them to have a seat. The officers were on another call but should be down soon.

For the first couple of hours, Ian texted and made what seemed like a gazillion phone calls, putting all his resources to work trying to find Ms. Ziegler. When the calls slowed and the texts became fewer and farther between, Ian dozed on and off.

Tucker remained awake throughout the night. He didn't want to miss anyone who came looking for them, like the officers who had yet to return.

He wanted to tell the officers everything he knew about Dancer. He could only hope they would have more resources than Ian and would catch whoever had done this.

The morning sun broke through the clouds. Sunlight filtered through the gigantic windows, bringing the hospital lobby to life. Staff hurried through the front doors. Most people were in scrubs and white lab coats, but several wore business attire.

The old man behind the desk had been replaced with a woman who looked to be in her early twenties. Tucker and Ian had not moved from their chairs all night. Tucker spent the night reliving the night before last. The sex had been amazing, but better than that was how much he had learned about Dancer through their conversation. Dancer hated cheese, loved to go camping, and adored his father. Tucker would never forget the look in his beautiful green eyes, the way they darkened to a deep green when they made love.

Tucker had waited long enough for someone to update them on Dancer's condition. He looked over at Ian, whose body was intertwined between two chairs, sound asleep. He wouldn't wait for Ian to wake up. He was more than capable of getting information himself.

Tucker approached the woman at the help desk, interrupting what sounded like a personal conversation on her cell phone. "Excuse me. We've been waiting all night for someone to come talk to us about my friend—"

"What's his name?" the woman stopped him. Her face scowled as she placed her fingers on her keyboard and waited.

"Dancer."

Her fingers hit several letters on the keyboard. "Dancer what?"

"Ziegler?" Tucker mumbled.

"I don't show a Dancer Ziegler." Her eyes scanned the monitor. "We have no one with that last name."

That didn't surprise him since no one had come back to talk to them to get his last name. "Well, look up John Doe then!"

Within seconds, Ian was at his side. "What's going on?"

"I'm trying to find out something about Dancer! She doesn't know shit about who's here!"

Ian grabbed Tucker by the shoulders and walked him away from the desk. "Okay, let me handle it. Sit down. I'll take care of it." Ian pushed him toward the chairs.

It was only a couple of minutes before Ian returned with two hospital passes. "He's on the fourth floor. Let's go."

Surprised, Tucker jumped up and took his pass.

The elevator rocketed them to their floor in a matter of seconds, opening to a sterile long hall. At the end of the hall was a double set of locked metal doors. There was a call button on the wall to the right of the door. Ian hit the button and stated that they were here to see John Doe, number nine-eight, in room four. The person put them on hold for a couple of minutes before buzzing them in.

They stepped into a large open area filled with glass bays. In the middle of the room was a round nurse's station with several people working. The smells of disinfectant and blood filled Tucker's nose. Noises came from everywhere, monitors beeping and alarms dinging from all sides. His gut rolled as he choked on a swallow.

A nurse pointed down the hall to room four. Tucker hesitated when he reached the door. Frightened, his eyes scanned the tiny sterile room. There was a young male nurse working at the bedside. Tucker's feet wouldn't carry him over the threshold. Monitors and equipment surrounded the body lying in the bed.

Ian motioned for him to step in.

Tucker stepped in and stood at the foot of the bed. The person in the bed lay motionless. IVs covered his arms, and his face was pale, swollen, bruised, and unrecognizable. His beautiful curls had been shaved off. He wasn't sure this was Dancer. The closer Tucker looked, the more equipment he saw connected to him.

"Hi, I'm Kyle. His nurse." Wearing a set of purple scrubs, the man's smile was genuine. "And you guys are?" His eyes bounced between the monitors and Ian.

Tucker looked at the nurse. He couldn't have been over five-six and all of a hundred and twenty pounds. Ian introduced them as a friend and a roommate.

"Well, your friend suffered an intracranial bleed in his brain. We have him sedated to keep him quiet."

"What's that?" Tucker's feet were planted firmly.

Kyle waved for him to step closer. "It means that his brain is bleeding."

Afraid to move, Tucker didn't trust his legs. He put his hand over his mouth as he muffled a cry. The person in the bed looked nothing like Dancer. A plastic tube that looked like a horn stuck out of the top of his skull. His eyelids were closed, shielding the distinguishing green eyes that burned into Tucker's soul when they looked at him. "Is he in a coma?" Tucker's voice vacillated.

"Yes. It's a medically induced coma. We need to slow down some of his functions to give his brain a chance to heal."

"Is that all that's wrong?" Tucker's arms remained next to his sides as he stared at the pallid face that lay in the bed. Tucker's memories of his own hospital stay flooded his thoughts. Long ago overshadowed by so much loss, disappointment, and strife, they now seemed like yesterday.

Kyle checked the IV bag and then pushed several buttons on a monitor before he answered. "Well, that's the biggest issue we're concerned with. His clavicle and radius on his left side are shattered and several ribs are broken. What's his name?"

"Dancer," Tucker mumbled.

Kyle nodded. "That's a cool name. Is that just what you guys call him or is that his real name?"

"I think it's a nickname," Ian interjected. "His last name is Ziegler. His mother is Joaquina Ziegler."

"The writer?" Kyle stopped what he was doing and looked at Tucker and Ian. "Really?"

"Yeah." Tucker reached down and touched Dancer's leg through the bed sheet. He then ran his hand up Dancer's leg, up his side until he reached his arm. Tucker's hand floated above the skin, unsure if he could touch his bare skin. There were needles and tubes everywhere.

"Do they live here?" Kyle asked.

"No. He's from Mississippi." Tucker's hand lowered until it rested on Dancer's skin, which was cool to the touch. His breath hitched. His heart was breaking into a million pieces.

"Oh. What brought him out here?" Kyle asked.

Ian moved around to stand next to Tucker. "Not sure. He's lived here for years."

Kyle started to say something when an alarm sounded above Dancer's head. The nurse silenced it and pushed several buttons. Another alarm sounded, sending Kyle to the other side of the bed. He pushed several more buttons before another nurse stepped into the room.

"Can I have you two step back into the lobby, outside the double doors?" Her tone was clipped.

Kyle was focused on Dancer, the lines across his forehead deep, his lips stretched thin as he worked. Another alarm rang as a third nurse entered the room, pushed them toward the door, and drew the curtain, shutting them out.

Chapter Twenty-Three

Ian and Tucker sat in the small waiting room of the Intensive Care Unit. The room was decorated with blue upholstered chairs over bumble-bee yellow carpet. The small flat screen TV mounted high on the wall was showing a golf tournament that neither of them were watching.

Near tears, Tucker tried to keep it together as the minutes passed into an hour. Had Dancer died, and no one had come to tell them? How long were they supposed to wait before asking to go back in? From where they sat, he watched as various hospital staff went in and out of the double doors.

"When was the last time you ate?" Ian stood up and walked under the TV.

Tucker's stomach muscles tightened under his lungs at the suggestion of food. "I'm not hungry."

"I didn't ask if you were hungry."

Tucker looked up at Ian. "I don't know." He racked his brain, but the time of his last meal eluded him. Right now, food was the least of his concerns.

"You need to eat something. Have you taken your meds?"

Tucker shook his head.

"Goddammit, Tucker! I need you to eat, and I need you to take your medication." Ian stood in front of Tucker. His eyes blazed down onto him. "Stay here. I'm going downstairs to get us something." Ian's phone rang in his pocket. He reached into his pocket and retrieved it. "I'll be right back." He turned and walked away as he answered the call.

Tucker watched as Ian walked out of the room and disappeared around the corner. Alone, he remembered a dream he'd had last night. He could see everyone standing around the casket at a gravesite. It was raining, and umbrellas shielded the faces of everyone dressed in black. He tried to block the dream from taking over his thoughts, but it kept rolling. In it, he pushed his way through the crowd to get closer to the casket. By the time he got up close, the casket lid had been shut. He needed to know who was in there. He slowly lifted the lid, and a pale face lay looking up at him. Nestled down amid ivory satin-padded fabric was Dancer, then he changed into Mattie, and then his mother. Faster and faster, the faces changed over and over in the casket, and then suddenly, the casket fell into a deep dark hole. It was gone. He was standing alone in the graveyard, just him over a hole in the ground.

Tucker stood up, attempting to shake the thought from his mind. A light headache caused him to squint. He considered turning off the light. The light between the hallway and the TV was plenty.

He paced the floor until Ian returned with two cups of coffee, two ham and cheese croissants, and two bananas. "Here."

Tucker took the coffee that Ian handed him and sat down.

Ian laid the wrapped sandwich and a banana on the side table next to him. "Did you take your medication?"

He had forgotten that quickly. Without answering, Tucker dug down into his backpack and found his meds. He took his seizure meds as well as medication for his headache. If he was going to have another seizure, at least he was here in the hospital that had his records. As he zipped the top of his backpack shut, it hit him. Where was Dancer's backpack? If it was laying in the alley, he would have seen it. Did the paramedics take it with him?

Ian sat down next to him. "When did you and Dancer become friends?"

Tucker didn't want to talk, but it would keep his mind from going where it shouldn't. He recalled when he and Dancer were downstairs last week. Dancer had waited for him, and now, he was waiting for Dancer. "Last week, I guess." He took a sip of his hot coffee. So much had happened in a week.

Ian took a bite out of his sandwich. With a full mouth, he continued. "He came to see me the other day, at the shelter."

It took a second for Tucker to register that he was talking about Dancer. "Oh, really?" He stopped short of asking why. Maybe that was none of his business.

171

"Yeah. It was the day he got his test results. He said you were visiting with your mom and sister. That he had to tell someone, and I was the only person he could think of."

That didn't make any sense to Tucker. Dancer hated Ian. Tucker took another sip of his coffee. *Was there no one else in Dancer's life?*

"Eat your sandwich." Ian took another bite of his. "He seemed happy. He and I, we weren't exactly friends, so I was surprised he came to see me. He's owed me some money for a while now. He said he needed help finding a job and that it was time he paid me back." Ian stopped again to take a sip of his coffee. "I get the feeling that you two are more than friends... No?"

Tucker debated how much and what he wanted to share about the two of them. He remembered what Dancer had said about him stealing the gift cards from Ian, and that he didn't like what Dancer was doing to make a living. "Yeah—we are."

"Aaah." Ian's facial expression didn't change. He took a sip of his coffee. "I kind of figured."

Was that it? Was that all that Ian was going to say? Tucker wondered about Ian's sexuality. He stared at him as if he would be able to see it on his face.

"Anyway, we talked. I feel for the kid. Said I'd help him next week with finding a job. What was he doing in the alley last night? Do you know?"

Did Ian know more than he was saying? "I don't know. He went to Walmart to get scissors and get dinner. When he didn't come back, I went looking for him. When I saw the ambulance, I knew. I was too late."

"Whoever did this, they didn't care if they left him for dead." Ian said.

Tucker's words shuddered in his stomach. "If I find the people who did this, I'm going to kill them!"

Ian's brows rose. "Oh?" He put his sandwich aside and stood up. "Um..." He scratched the side of his head as he paced for a second. "I'm going to check on Dancer." Ian walked over to the intercom next to the double doors and pushed it. After a short conversation, the door clicked, and he waved to Tucker to come on.

*****

Back in the room, Kyle was standing in front of a small rolling workstation.

"Hey." Kyle looked up from the monitor. "He's better."

"What happened before, with the alarms?" Ian asked.

"He had a sudden drop in his heart rate."

"Why? What happened?" Ian moved closer to Kyle.

"The heart and brain work together. When there is pressure in the brain from bleeding and swelling, it can cause your heart rate to drop. What we don't want is his heart to stop beating."

Tucker tried to contain his gasp. "Is he okay?"

"Yes. We caught it fast."

As the day progressed, Kyle continued with his questions. At times they were a little probing, but they felt sincere, as if he cared. He took a minute or two each time he was at the bedside to explain what he was doing and why.

Late in the afternoon, Kyle asked if Tucker and Ian could step out of the room for about half an hour. He had to change Dancer's dressing and clean him up a bit. "In about a half hour, check in with the station. They can let you know if I'm done."

Tucker followed Ian out into the waiting room. Each minute felt like an hour as Tucker paced the room. He looked at the clock on the wall. It had been twenty-eight minutes. Surely that was close enough. "Can you check if we can go back in?" He asked Ian.

Ian looked at his watch. "Okay."

Tucker watched Ian as he walked out into the corridor and over to the double doors and pushed the intercom. Within a couple of seconds, he waved to him to come on as the door buzzed.

They hurried back into the room, where Kyle was talking to an older African-American woman wearing a dark rose pantsuit and large hoop earrings.

The woman turned her attention to them. "Hi, I'm Rebecka Williams. I'm a social worker for Intensive Care. Kyle called and said you guys have some information on our patient here." Grim-faced, she balanced a clipboard under her arm.

Ian moved to the same side of the bed as her and Kyle. "Hi, I'm Ian Stephen, and this is Tucker…"

"Tucker Graves." He ran his hand through his disheveled hair before extending it to her. His hair was left standing to one side, tossed and twisted on the other.

173

"How do you know the patient?" she asked as she stared at his hand, refusing to take it.

Ian stepped in. "His name is Dancer. I run New Beginnings, the shelter down on Ninth, and Tucker is his roommate."

"I'm his boyfriend, not a roommate!" Tucker clarified.

Ian, Ms. Williams, and Kyle looked over at Tucker. Ms. Williams didn't hide the fact that she was less than impressed with either one of their credentials. "Well. Like I said, Kyle called me, and I had a chance to look over the report filed by security. There wasn't much in their report. My goal is to help identify him. To reach his family. Kyle told me that you said that his mother was Joaquina Ziegler?" She rolled her eyes as if she didn't believe it could be remotely true.

"Yes, the writer." Ian's tone was snappish.

The woman grimaced. Her posture stiffened. "Do we know this as a fact?" Her testy tone matched Ian's.

"Yes... no. It's what he told *him*." Ian nodded toward Tucker.

Ms. Williams scribbled on her pad of paper. "He didn't have any belongings with him. No wallet, phone, or anything to help identify him."

"What about his backpack?" Tucker asked.

The social worker looked puzzled. "The officers didn't say anything about a backpack."

"In his backpack was his tablet. Maybe there's something on that," Tucker said.

"I'll ask next time I talk with security. I'll try to reach Ms. Ziegler. Is there anything I can tell her to help determine if this is actually her son or not?"

Ian shrugged and shook his head. "I don't know."

"He has a big scar on his abdomen. He had his appendix removed when he was a kid." Tucker turned toward Dancer.

Kyle went to the bedside and lifted the covers. "Yes, it looks like he's had his appendix removed. He has the scar."

"He also used to dance! Ballet. He told me he used to live in Mississippi. His dad died of cancer when he was twelve. He wouldn't lie about who he was. That's his mother. He wouldn't lie."

"Okay. All of that is good information. We need to contact her." Ms. Williams stuck her pen in her pants pocket.

"What about the police? No one's come to talk to us yet. Have the police been notified?" Ian asked.

"Yes. Security filed a report with them. Once I hear back from Ms. Ziegler's office, I'll follow up with the police. But right now, he's still a John Doe."

"His name is Dancer!" Tucker's pulse quickened. "Do you guys care that someone nearly killed him?"

The social worker held her hand up dismissively. "I know you're upset about your friend, but yelling at me isn't going to fix that."

"Screw you!" The words flew out of Tucker's mouth before he could stop them. But he wouldn't have wanted to. She was a bitch!

Kyle turned to them. "You guys, I need you to keep it down. Dancer doesn't need to hear you fighting."

Can he hear us? That had never occurred to Tucker. His attention switched to Dancer as he moved as close as he could to the bed.

Kyle removed the empty IV from its hook and replaced it with a full one.

The social worker whispered something to Ian before exiting the room. Tucker didn't care what she had to say. He took Dancer's hand.

It was a little after six when Kyle announced that his shift was almost over. Shift change would take about an hour, and then they could come back in. He advised them to go get something to eat, go home, get some air, and that they could come back after eight.

As instructed, but against his will, Tucker followed Ian out of the unit.

"I'm hungry. Are you hungry? Can I buy you dinner?" Ian asked as he punched in their location into the Uber app on his phone.

It wasn't until Ian mentioned food that Tucker realized that he was starving. The burning in the pit of his stomach was a plea for food.

The Uber driver took them only a couple of blocks before pulling up in front of a fifties-style diner. Tucker looked out the window at the place. Was this where they were having dinner? His mind began to race—a real sit-down dinner? Would they even let him in a place like this as dirty as he was? He knew he stunk; he caught a whiff of himself every now and again.

After ordering their food, Ian sent a couple of texts before putting his phone away. "How are your mom and sister?"

"They're doing okay. Mum and Mattie are over at Family Ties. It seems to be working." Tucker gave a half shrug.

"I think it's pretty cool that Dancer's mom is a famous writer."

"Yeah. Well, they're not exactly talking."

"Do you know why?" Ian asked.

Tucker debated how much to say. "His stepfather was pretty abusive. I guess his mum didn't stop it."

"His real dad passed away?" Ian asked.

"Yeah. He was close to him." If Ian wanted to know any more, he would have to ask Dancer.

Ian was quiet for a couple of minutes. "You know, he and I have a lot in common. I could have been him, a long time ago."

Tucker looked up. He was intrigued.

"I grew up in a small town just outside of Denver—in a pretty abusive house. My mother didn't protect me or my sister. At the time, I didn't understand why. How she could love a man who beat his kids? I hated my mom for a long time, until I found out that she too was a survivor of abuse, by him as well as her own father."

Tucker looked down but kept an eye on Ian as he listened.

"I was lost for a long time. I made a lot of bad choices, choices that haunt me to this day. My life crumbled like a house of cards. That's why I was so happy when Dancer came to see me the other day. He was attempting to right a wrong."

"You mean that he wanted to pay you back for the gift cards he stole from you?"

Ian's brows rose. "Exactly." He stopped as the waiter put their dinners down in front of them. Ian salted his French fries and then removed the top slice of bread from his BLT. "I have to check. Sometimes you say no mayo, and they still put mayo on it. If I taste it, I'll puke."

Mushrooms did the same for Tucker. Dancer probably felt the same about cheese. He waited for Ian to start eating before he took a bite from his double patty cheeseburger. They ate for a while in silence.

"I'm glad he found someone. Everyone needs to know they are important to someone," Ian said as he tossed a fry into his mouth.

"What about you? Who loves you?" Tucker was hinting at the rumors of Ian's sexuality.

"Nobody at the moment. Somebody tried once, a long time ago, but I screwed that up. I cheated on him with an old ex of mine. The guy that I was seeing was crazy about me, and I ruined the one thing that was right in my life. I thought I knew what I was doing. I didn't know shit."

Tucker thought about him and Dancer. With what Dancer's stepfather had done to him, did they stand a chance? He needed to know that they did. "You guys couldn't fix it? Did you ever try to say you were sorry?"

"I did. He was…" Ian paused for a second. "Sebastian. His name was Sebastian, and he was the sweetest man I've ever known. He was willing to take me back. But at the time, I was just realizing how messed up I was in the head because of my childhood. I needed to work on myself, and I couldn't take the chance of failing this guy one more time. He was too good for that."

"So, what happened?" Tucker wasn't liking this story.

"I practically ruined this guy's life. It's a much bigger story than what I want to get into right now, but he ended up moving away and I did years of therapy."

"What about Kyle? He's cute. He was looking at you." Tucker was sure Kyle had set off his gaydar several times. There wasn't anything about Kyle that screamed that he batted on the same team; it was just a feeling.

"I'm not interested. I'm still in love with Sebastian." Ian's mouth twitched.

Hearing the sadness in Ian's voice, Tucker felt that Ian's sexuality was not as important as the hurt Ian was carrying. It was all just sad. Tucker went deeper into his own thoughts. His entire life had been nothing but grief. A father he never met, his baseball career cut short, the loss of his mother to drugs, his life now, possibly Dancer, everything was some sort of loss. Sadness surged in his throat, making it nearly impossible to swallow. He tried to push his dinner down before his thoughts overwhelmed him. Dancer couldn't die. His vision blurred as a tear bled from his eye. He fought hard not to cry. Men didn't cry, certainly not in front of other men. He took a drink of his soda, trying to push it back. His hand shook as he put down his glass. "Ian… is he going to die?" He didn't want to hear the answer. He couldn't deal with the truth if it was bad news.

"He's not going to die." Ian moved his hand over Tucker's and squeezed gently.

After dinner, the two headed back to the hospital and met Libby, Dancer's nighttime nurse. A mousy, petite older woman, this evening was Libby's first shift back after her days off. She was less talkative than Kyle but just as busy.

Exhausted, Ian lasted until about eleven o'clock. After several unsuccessful tries to get Tucker to leave with him, he gave up. Silence loomed over the room.

The entire intensive care unit was quiet. The hurried footsteps up and down the unit, the nurses coming and going, and the conversations were all reduced at some point in the evening to little more than white noise. The stillness left Tucker with time only to think as he went back and forth between the chair in the corner and the space beside Dancer in the bed. His mind raced with all the what-ifs. As he held Dancer's hand, he realized and came to know every line, scar, and callus. He noticed how his pinky bowed slightly out, how his nailbeds were flat. His nails were chewed and rough and short, though Tucker had never seen him chew his fingernails. He loved everything about Dancer just as Sebastian probably loved everything about Ian.

Chapter Twenty-Four

Tucker sat in the waiting room and watched the morning news as he chomped on a stolen apple. Earlier this morning, after being asked to step outside for the shift change, he had scooped up the apple from a food tray left unattended on a cart.

He had seen Kyle, Dancer's daytime nurse, come in about a half hour ago. Clean and refreshed, Kyle did not see him as he sprinted past the Intensive Care waiting room and through the double doors to start his shift.

Just seeing Kyle helped to calm him until he could get back into Dancer's room again. He didn't understand why he had to leave the room every time they had to do something and why it always took so long.

He waited another half hour after seeing Libby, the night nurse, walk out of Intensive Care before ringing the nurse's station and requesting to come in. He had quickly learned the routine of the Intensive Care Unit.

When Tucker walked into the room, he received a polite good morning from Kyle as he glanced up from his charting. Tucker moved close to Dancer and took his hand. He wanted Dancer to squeeze it, which would be a clear sign that Dancer knew he was there. He remembered what Kyle had told him yesterday about people in comas hearing everything in the room. "Hey baby. I'm back." Tucker whispered down to him. Although Dancer didn't squeeze his hand, Tucker held onto the notion that Dancer knew he was there.

He had been in the room for about thirty minutes when the phone on the wall buzzed. He listened as Kyle talked to the caller. By his tone, Tucker knew the caller was asking about him and that Kyle had told whomever it was that he was in the room. Kyle hung up the phone and rolled the workstation against the wall. "Your friend has another visitor coming in. I'm going to have to have you step outside."

Tucker was surprised. Who was here to visit? Was it Ian? Why was Kyle suddenly enforcing the rules? "Okay." Tucker massaged Dancer's hand before letting it go. "I'll be right back."

He stepped out of the room just as a woman was walking toward him. It took a second to register where he knew the woman from. It was Dancer's mother. He was invisible to her as she walked past him and into Dancer's room.

Tucker's heart was racing. She was here. He picked up his step as he left the Intensive Care Unit. What was he supposed to do? The thought of her being here scared him, and he didn't know why. He needed Ian. Tucker walked toward the elevator, unsure where he was going. He reached it just as the steel doors opened. Dancer's social worker stepped out. "Oh, good morning..."

"Tucker." He reminded her of his name.

"Yes. I was coming to find you. I received a message that Ms. Ziegler was en route." Ms. Williams smiled at him.

"She's here! In Intensive Care. She's in his room." He couldn't help but feel the softening in her demeanor.

"Oh, that was fast. Great." She looked as if she wanted to excuse herself and continue to wherever she was going. She rubbed his shoulder and wished him a good day.

Outside the hospital, Tucker realized that he was miles from Camp Roosevelt. He and Dancer had taken two buses to get here last week. Even if he could find the right bus, he didn't have any money to ride it. He could walk, but what was left at the camp to return to? Tucker looked around. This side of town was unfamiliar to him. He wasn't sure if he should start out to the left or the right.

A man in a black suit was walking toward him, talking on his cell phone. Maybe he could ask the man to call New Beginnings. Perhaps Ian would come get him. The man walked by as Tucker's nerves kept him from speaking.

He watched as a cab pulled around the circle drive and drop its passenger off. He thought about having the driver take him home. He could bolt from the cab a block away from camp. But he wasn't a thief. His only hope was that Ian would show up.

Tucker took a seat on the bench near the front door of the

hospital. What was Dancer's mother doing up there? Was she apologizing, crying, praying? Was her body draped over Dancer's as she poured out her tears? Was she sorry, or was she mad at him? Was Kyle as nice to her as he had been to Tucker and Ian? She wasn't as beautiful as she had appeared on TV. Would Dancer open his eyes for her? His mind raced with questions, none of which he had any answers to.

The cool air was refreshing after the stale air in the tiny waiting room. He looked up at the clouds. Was it going to rain again? They had gone two days without rain. A third would be nice. He pulled out his cell phone to check the time. It was dead. It didn't matter since he had nowhere to go.

After several hours of people-watching on the bench, Tucker's chin sunk into his chest as he fought to stay awake. He was set to close his eyes and take a nap, but he took one last peak at his surroundings first. Just as he looked up, Ms. Ziegler stepped out of the hospital. She was just as intimidating from afar. He watched as she placed her sunglasses on and hung her purse from the crook of her arm. She walked like a movie star in her fuchsia-colored heels, which matched her knee-length skirt.

She turned and walked away from him, down the path toward a large black sedan that was parked along the curb. He wanted to say something to her. Tell her who he was. His heart raced at the thought of speaking to her, and he couldn't pull himself off the bench. He watched a man step out from behind the wheel of the car and open the rear door for her. He couldn't let her leave without talking to her.

"Ms. Ziegler!" He stood up. "Ms. Ziegler!"

She was about to step into the car when she turned and looked behind her, her face expressionless.

He snatched his backpack and slung it over his shoulders as he tried to get to her before she disappeared. "Ms. Ziegler!"

"Yes?" She peered at him over the top of her sunglasses as the man stepped in between the two of them, his body language showing that he was more than a driver.

Open palms, Tucker held out his hands. "It's okay, it's okay. I'm Dancer's friend."

"Who?" Her expression hardened.

"Dancer, your son."

"Liam?" She tilted her head. "Oh, yes. I know who you are." Her expression hardened.

His name was Liam? And how did she know who he was? Baffled, Tucker choked on air caught in his throat. "You do?"

She removed her sunglasses. Her eyes, although bloodshot, were the same pale green as Dancer's. "Of course I know who you are. I've been in town a few days."

He remembered the interview with her that he and Dancer had watched the other day. "Your book?" he asked, still puzzled as to how she knew who he was.

"No, for my child. I'm here to bring Liam home." Her face was as cold as ice as she dug in her purse for a handkerchief. Dancer had had that same expression when Tucker first met him. It was haunting, looking at her.

He was about to ask how Dancer was doing when it hit him what she had just said. "What do you mean, take him home?" Tucker's voice shook.

"What's your name?" She shared the same southern drawl as Dancer. He didn't remember hearing it when she was on TV.

"Tucker. Tucker Graves, ma'am."

"I've been looking for Liam for a long time. I hired a private detective to find him. When I learned that he might be here, I came immediately. But then, the other night, we lost him again. I had no idea where he had disappeared to until I got the call from the hospital."

Tucker wanted to tell her that it was because of him—that he was the one who told them Dancer's last name. But that was insignificant compared to her saying she was taking him home.

"Do you have any idea why someone would've done this to him?"

"No, ma'am."

"Were you with him when he was attacked?"

"No, ma'am. If I were, he sure in the hell—heck, wouldn't be in that bed in there."

Ms. Ziegler's face softened as the corners of her mouth curved up slightly. "I have to go to the police station. Will you be here later?"

"Um, yes." He had nowhere to go. *Why is she going to the police station?* "Did they catch who did this?"

182

"No, not yet."

"His backpack is missing. Whoever did this, they took his backpack." It wasn't much, but Tucker thought that if they looked for the backpack, they might find who had attacked Dancer.

"I'll let the police know that. Thank you. We'll chat more later." Ms. Ziegler stepped into the backseat of the car, and her driver closed the door.

Tucker stood there as the black sedan drove down the circular driveway and out onto the busy street. How did she know who he was? How much did she know? None of it was as important as getting back up to Dancer's room.

He had been outside for hours. Maybe Dancer was doing better. He was moving as fast as he could without breaking into a full-on sprint.

Back in the room, Kyle and another nurse were doing something with a bag of liquid hanging from a pole. The liquid was being fed into Dancer through his arm. "What is that?"

Kyle didn't look at him as he continued to work. "It's an IV. This one here is saline."

There were several bags hanging from poles and feeding into his arms. "Is he doing better?"

"About the same. What we want is for the swelling of his brain to go down."

Tucker watched as the two nurses worked on adjusting an IV pump on the other side of Dancer.

After the second nurse left the room, Kyle charted for five or ten minutes before sliding the workstation out of his way. "Did you get a chance to meet his mother?"

"Yeah. I ran into her outside. She said she was going to the police station. Do you think they caught whoever did this to him?"

"I don't know. I heard you were here all night. Do you live close?"

"Not really." Tucker hesitated. "We live over in Camp Roosevelt." Kyle didn't react upon hearing that Tucker was homeless. Had he already figured it out?

"Over where the old hospital used to be? That's a ways away."

Tucker nodded.

"I figured since you didn't leave last night, you might need stuff

183

to freshen up." Kyle nodded toward a brown paper bag sitting on the only chair in the room. "I snagged you a patient overnight kit. It has some stuff for you to clean up with."

Tucker looked at the bag. "Thank you." Was Kyle being nice, or did Tucker stink so bad that he had to do something for his own sanity?

"There's a small employee bathroom down on the second floor that has a shower stall. If you're quick, I bet you could get in a nice hot shower. The code is seven, four, nine, eight. Don't tell anyone I told you. There are towels stocked in there." Kyle glanced at him before continuing his work.

"Oh—okay. Thank you." Tucker looked in the bag. There were tiny bottles of shampoo and conditioner, a bar of soap, mouthwash, toothpaste, a small toothbrush, and trial-size deodorant.

Taking the bag, Tucker set out to improve his hygiene.

*****

By the time Tucker returned from his shower, it was shift change. The nurses were handing off reports, which meant it would be an hour before he could go back in. Was Libby on duty again this evening? He took a seat in the waiting room with three women who were chitchatting. He stared up at the waiting room TV. A show about cupcakes was on, but he couldn't hear it over the women yakking.

His worry about Dancer dying was now compounded by Ms. Ziegler's revelation that she planned on taking Dancer home. Could she do that? Surely Dancer would have a say in that and wouldn't go. He and Dancer had plans. They had talked about moving and having their own place. It was going to be a real apartment with a bathroom, its own kitchen, and bedroom.

Through the chatter of the women, Tucker was able to surmise that it was the smaller, heavy-set woman's husband who was a patient in Intensive Care. The woman to her right sounded like either her sister or her husband's sister. The woman on the left was much younger than the other two. Through a series of glances, he concluded that she had to be one of their daughters.

The judges were evaluating the fancy cupcakes on TV. Tucker

184

was now into the show, and he didn't notice Ian until he was right in front of him.

"Shift change, huh?" Ian took a seat.

"Um, yeah. They should be done in a second." Ian's presence was comforting. The day had been long without him.

"How's he doing?"

"About the same. His mum's here." Tucker looked toward the double doors.

"They found her. That's great!" Ian held his stare on Tucker. "No?"

"Yeah. She said she was here to take him home."

Ian grunted but said nothing. His silence validated Tucker's fear that it was a real possibility. "Can she take him like that?" Tucker asked.

"Well, I'm sure she didn't mean she was taking him home like that." Ian's brows rose as he nodded toward the double doors. "Maybe she meant that she hoped she could bring him home eventually. He's an adult. Unfortunately, like he is now, he doesn't have a say in it. She could have him transferred to another hospital closer to home... I guess."

Ian's words did little to reassure Tucker. He stared up at the TV, but nothing on the screen was sinking in. He prayed that when they walked into Dancer's room, he would be sitting up, smiling at them as they walked through the door.

Tucker wasn't religious, but if God gave him this one thing, he would try to be better at acknowledging God. He was granted no such prayer; Dancer was in the same state when they got to the room. Tucker looked at the surrounding machines. Was Dancer alive or had the machines taken over?

"How's he doing?" Ian asked.

"About the same." Poker-faced, Libby's answer was clipped.

Tucker went to his bedside and took his hand. It was warmer than earlier. He looked at his face, which was swollen and bruised. His Dancer was somewhere under all that bruising. He touched his cheek. Dancer's skin felt like a water balloon.

In the silence, the conversations that he and Dancer had were running through his head. He was thankful that neither Libby nor Ian could read his mind as he recalled them making love. The sounds that Dancer made, his green eyes as they stared up at him, the way

Dancer's ass molded around his cock made Tucker's flesh tingle, sending warmth throughout his body. In that moment, they had been one. Their bodies were connected, an awareness that their heartbeats and thoughts were in sync. Afterwards, there was a closeness that he had never felt with anyone, an awakening into a deeper sense of this other person, and of himself.

There was nothing he wouldn't do for Dancer, including exchanging places with him right now. Dancer deserved to live more than he did. What was he going to amount to anyway? Likely nothing. But Dancer, he was a fighter.

Anger boiled in Tucker at whoever had done this. It must have been more than one person to cause this much damage. He tried to stop his mind from playing out the fight, of Dancer being beaten and left for dead. Why—why would someone do this to Dancer?

The phone in the room rang. By now, Tucker was used to it being someone from the nurse's station. Libby's conversation was less than twenty seconds long. "Hey, guys. He has another visitor." That was their cue to leave. It had to be Ms. Ziegler.

They met her at the double doors as they stepped out. Tucker introduced Ian, hoping he would facilitate a conversation with her regarding not taking Dancer away.

She shared that the police were involved and that a detective was being assigned to his case. Tucker was grateful to hear that it was a case now.

She added that she had also talked with his neurologist, who said that they wanted to keep him sedated a little longer and that the major concern was if he had sustained any permanent brain damage.

This was Tucker's first realization that Dancer might never be Dancer again. Even if he didn't die, he might be like a different person. It hit him like a train, blowing every ounce of air from his lungs. He closed his eyes, trying to fend off the emotions that rapidly bubbled over. He was angry, angrier than he had ever been, more than when he realized he would never play baseball again. He wanted to punch the wall, knock as big a hole in it as he could.

The entire exchange was only a minute or so long, but it changed Tucker's world once again. Hope kept slipping from his grasp. Ms. Ziegler disappeared behind the double doors as they closed and locked.

Ian shoved his hands inside his coat pocket. "You know, his mother will probably stay all night. You can share a ride with me back to the other side of town if you want."

Tucker's impulse was to stay. He should stay.

"Have you eaten?" Ian asked.

"Yeah," Tucker lied, knowing Ian would try to feed him if he said no. He wanted to be alone.

Chapter Twenty-Five

Barking dogs and the highway traffic were white noise in the camp during the evening. Everyone was tucked away in their shelters awaiting the next storm, due in the next couple of hours.

The ride with Ian in the Uber was a blur. Dropped off at the front of the camp, Tucker walked toward their shanty. As he got closer, he saw the door was lying on the ground. The realization set in: someone had gone inside.

He went in prepared to fight, but it was empty. Whoever had been there was gone. He felt around in the dark, looking for the lantern that sat on top of the bins. It wasn't there. His eyes adjusted to the dark, but everything was still shadows. There was a bin missing. He looked around, hoping to see it. The camping stove was missing as well. He shuffled across the room to the mattress. The blankets were gone. "Fuck!" He continued looking for the lantern along the walls of the shanty. It wasn't here; they had taken it. "Fuck! Fuck! Fuck!" He thrust his fist in the air.

His suitcase sat at the foot of the mattress. He sat down and dug through his bag. Tucker had nothing of value other than clothing, none of which was worth taking. He brought his knees up into his chest and folded his arms around his legs as he buried his face in his arms. Tucker wanted to cry, but that would change nothing. Dancer was still fighting for his life, and now, they had been robbed.

A surge of anger caused his leg to kick out, sending his suitcase spinning into the middle of the room. He collapsed onto his back and covered his face with his left arm. There he lay for hours, until his body gave way to sleep.

*****

The howl of the wind as it crashed down onto the shanty startled him awake. Curled in a tight ball, he had been shivering for hours. He had forgotten to seal the door last night, allowing the rain and wind to pierce the inside of what was once a cozy, tiny room.

He opened his eyes as he stretched his long legs across the mattress. Groggy, he stared at the opening where the white door was supposed to be. The door was still laying on the ground outside. The rain bounced off it as it pelted down from the sky.

A jagged flash of light filled the doorway followed by an explosion of thunder. It rattled the shanty as it passed through his eardrums, down into the floor. He pulled himself up. If nothing else, he had to put the door back up.

Between the dark clouds and the closed door, the room was reduced to near total darkness. Tucker fell back onto the mattress and dug his phone out of his pocket. He pushed the button, hoping there was enough power to tell him what time it was, but remembered it was dead.

Tucker lay there, thinking about the walk to the hospital. It would be a bitch in this storm. In the dark, he tore apart one of the disposable razors Dancer had bought him, and freed the blade from the plastic. First, he carefully sawed most of his hair off with the blade. He then used his last disposable razor and the nearly empty can of shaving cream to shave the rest off. In less than twenty minutes, he was as bald as Dancer.

Tucker looked around the room and found Dancer's silver North Face jacket laying on the floor next to the bins. He wasn't sure it would fit. His arms were much longer than Dancer's.

As he guessed, it was a tight fit, but having Dancer's jacket on consoled him. He sniffed the arm of the jacket, hoping it smelled like Dancer, but there was nothing. His eyes fell to a toy—a small brown plastic dog. He hadn't seen it before. Was this Tamale? He picked up the toy and stuffed it into the jacket. He looked around for another piece of Dancer before going into the bins along the wall. The bin of clothes that the thief left behind was filled with nice clothing, all folded and stacked in order. In the other four bins appeared to be junk. He remembered Dancer saying that those were the Milkman's.

He layered his own coat over Dancer's jacket. He felt like the abominable snowman wrapped in cellophane and doubted the combination of coats would work. It was either abandon Dancer's jacket or his own.

He did neither. Having Dancer close to him outweighed being uncomfortable. Moving the door out of the way, he looked around outside for the thief. There were only one or two people out, neither of whom looked capable of making a haul like that.

Debris caught in the wind sailed above Tucker's head, causing him to look up at the thick charcoal clouds. They covered the skyline. He pulled his lapel across his mouth, trying to shield his face as he set out for the long walk to the hospital.

The violent wind whipped across his face, causing him to keep his head down. It was much colder without his hair. Several times, the wind forced him to turn his body sideways and lean into the wind to keep moving. Occasionally, he looked at the river of water flowing in the gutter as it raced toward the first available drain. This was the mother of all storms, but it was not enough to stop him from getting to the hospital.

Two hours later, soaked and exhausted, he arrived. The cold had reached the bones in his hands and feet. He was too wet to go inside, but he had no other option. A clock on the wall read that it was almost noon. He went into the first bathroom he could find and used paper towels and the hand drier to dry himself as much as he could before heading upstairs to Intensive Care.

When he pushed the button in front of the double doors, he was told there was already a visitor in the room. It had to be Ms. Ziegler. He would have to wait until she came out. He was forced to take a seat in the waiting room.

He sat watching TV until five o'clock, when the evening news came on. He watched as they covered the top news, the weather, and then sports. When the news returned from a station break, a reporter was standing outside the hospital and launched into a breaking story: *"The estranged son of the world-renowned romance writer Joaquina Ziegler has been admitted into this hospital, Roosevelt General, and is reportedly clinging to life. Sources close to the family have confirmed that Liam Ziegler had been living on the streets in Brierton, Illinois for the last couple of years. On Monday, he was admitted after an apparent mugging in the alley on Sixth and Gettysburg. It has been reported that his family is here at his bedside in his final hours. Police are looking for two men caught on surveillance cameras exiting the alley moments before an unidentified person called 911.*

The news station flashed a grainy black and white video clip of two men in hoodies running from the alley. Tucker studied the grainy snippet but didn't recognize the men.

They moved on to the next story, but Tucker continued staring at the television. They were talking about Dancer, but they called him Liam Ziegler. He was estranged, she was renowned. They were here at his bedside... *in his final hours?*

Tucker exited the waiting room and pushed the button to talk to someone.

"Hello, yes?" the crackling voice asked.

"Can you please tell me how Da—Li-am," his tongue tripped over the word, "Liam Ziegler is doing. I know his mother's in there, and I can't come in. I wanna know how he's doing."

"Hold on, Sir." The mic clicked off. She was gone for several minutes before coming back on. "Sir. Are you still there?"

"Yes!" Tucker's adrenaline kicked in.

"Someone will be out in a minute to talk with you."

"Oh... Okay, thank you." That didn't sound promising. Would they ask him to leave? Would that 'someone' be security? Tucker looked down the hall toward the elevator. Would they be coming for him?

He waited next to the door for almost twenty minutes before Ms. Ziegler exited from the double doors. "They said you wanted to speak with me?"

No, he didn't want to speak with her. He wanted to see Dancer. "Um, I saw on the news that... Is he dying?" He barely got the word out. The muscles in Ms. Ziegler's jaw twitched.

Her expression sobered. "He's not dying." She shifted her body weight to her right leg. "I met with his doctors this morning. The swelling has reduced. We're hoping to wake him up tomorrow."

"That's good, right?" Tucker's expression softened. "Can I see him?"

"Of course. I'm glad to know he has you as a friend. He was never much for friends. Once he's stable, he'll be transferred to UCSF Medical Center in California. Maybe you can visit once he's better and at home."

"Transferred? Why?" She *was* taking him.

"Why? Because he's my son." Her words were snappish.

"But..." Tucker had no rebuttal. All he could think about was Dancer being taken away. It didn't seem fair. This was his home. The fiery look in her eyes dared him to argue. He had never backed down from a fight, but those four words had an air of finality to them. She had smacked him down like a pesky fly in the air. "But..."

Ms. Ziegler didn't try to hide her emotions. "Look, Liam's been gone for a long time. It's time he came home. I love my child and only want the best for him. Please dispose of that long face before you go in there. He doesn't need the negativity in his space." She pressed her lips together as she drew her purse in.

She stepped around him and only got two steps away before Tucker exploded on her. From zero to sixty, he was in full fight mode as his rage boiled over. "Excuse me!" He whirled around. "Don't take him from his home. For once, try putting his needs before what you want. Don't do that to him again."

Her stare caused him to look down at the floor. It said that she, too, was a fighter. His eyes shot back up to her. A fighter didn't look at the floor, they stared down their opponent. Tucker cleared the trapped air in his throat. "I'm not much. In fact, I'm probably nothing to you, but I've never let him down. I've never chosen someone else over him. He's in every thought of mine, and I love him." His words spat out with the ferocity and intensity of the raging storm outside.

Ms. Ziegler's nostrils flared as her hands rested on her hip. She was silent well after he had finished.

"You love him?" Ms. Ziegler asked, placing her other hand on her left hip. "You love my son? Well, guess what? So do I. This is not about what I want to do. I want my son to live. I want the best treatment for him, and I think I'm the best person to judge that."

"Respectfully, did you want the best treatment for him when you let your husband climb on top of him when he was just a boy? Did it take you six years to find him, or are you here to replace your husband with him? Respectfully, he could live a lifetime without having the kind of love you have to offer."

The color drained from Ms. Ziegler's face. "You have no idea what you're talking about. I think we're done." Her nostrils flared as she turned and stormed off.

Tucker's body trembled, adrenaline pouring into every ounce of his being. It had been the most important fight of his life, and he had lost.

Chapter Twenty-Six

It was six o'clock, and Ms. Ziegler hadn't returned. Shift change was about to happen, and if she showed up this evening, Tucker might never get a chance to see Dancer again. In Intensive Care, he rubbed the back of his hand against Dancer's cheek. "It's shift change, so I have to go for a bit. If I don't come back tonight, know that I'm just outside the double doors." He guffawed, knowing Dancer hadn't seen the doors he was talking about. "I love you."

Tucker stepped back and looked at Dancer's silver jacket, which he had hung on the chair, the only piece of furniture in the cold, sterile room. He remembered the plastic dog he had brought with him. He retrieved the toy from his pocket and laid it on Dancer's chest. "Tamale said to get well."

Kyle looked up at him and then looked away.

Tucker pushed a hard swallow down. Was Dancer dying in here? He didn't look any different than he had two days ago. Was that why Ms. Ziegler wanted to move him? He wiped a tear from his eye before it hit his cheek.

His plan was to sit in the waiting room until he could get back in. He would take his chances that she wouldn't be back. "Do you know where his mum went?"

Kyle looked up. "Um, she said she was going to her hotel."

"Did she say if she was coming back?" He braced for the answer.

"I think so. I'm leaving in about ten minutes. Don't worry, he's strong."

Kyle wasn't saying anything he didn't already know, but it was nice to hear it. "His mum said you might wake him up tomorrow. Is that right?"

Kyle stopped what he was doing. "We'll see how tonight goes.

194

They'll run more tests in the morning. If it looks good, the doctors may wean him off the pentobarbital."

"Then how long will it take for him to wake up?"

The lines around Kyle's mouth softened. "It depends. It's not like waking someone up in the morning. His brain was damaged. He may open his eyes and kind of appear to still be sleeping. He may not follow directions or communicate the way he used to because of the injury. We won't know to what extent until some of the medicine is out of his system."

Just then, a male nurse that Tucker had never seen walked into the room. "Hey, Kyle. Ready to go home?"

"Hi, Chris." Kyle looked up and nodded at Tucker.

Tucker stuffed Tamale down into his pocket. "Have a good night. Oh, and thank you."

After combing the other floors for food left on dinner trays, Tucker returned to the Intensive Care waiting room with two dinner rolls, a package of wafers, and an orange. This evening, the waiting room was full. In it were some of the people he had shared the room with over the last three days, but there were also several new faces. Tucker wondered if their loved ones were as badly hurt as Dancer.

He ate his dinner, waiting for his chance to go back into Dancer's room. Would Ms. Ziegler return before he could get back in there, or worse, would she forbid him from ever going in there again? He remembered when his grandmother was dying and all the fighting in the hospital between his mother and her sister. He had been furious with his aunt, who was trying to stop his mother from seeing her. It was the last time he'd seen his aunt. Would Ms. Ziegler do the same thing to him?

He tried to focus on the TV, but the volume was too low. With the room full, the sound had been reduced to garble.

Ian pushed his way through the people standing in the doorway. His eyelids sagged, revealing dark circles under them. "How are you?" His hand rested on Tucker's shoulder.

"Fine." Tucker was anything but fine. He never understood why people said they were fine when it was a complete lie. "I got into it with his mum today."

"Oh?" Ian removed his hand from Tucker's shoulder and folded his arms across his chest.

195

"She told me she is having him transferred."

"When?"

"She didn't say. To California." Tucker looked up at the sound of Ian releasing a large sigh.

"What happened between you? What was said?"

Tucker didn't remember everything. He was so mad at the time that his words had spewed out. "I told her I thought it was bullshit that she was moving him. That she was only looking out for herself and not him."

"Uh-huh." Ian took a seat next to Tucker.

"I thought she was being selfish, and I told her." He watched Ian's eyes, hoping they would reveal that he agreed. "I told her I loved him."

"You did?" Ian's brows lifted. "And?"

"She didn't say anything. She's a bitch!"

Ian laid his hand on Tucker's thigh. "She's his mother. She's as scared as you. It's not going to do you any good to fight with her."

As if timing was everything, Ms. Ziegler appeared as she approached the double doors and rang the buzzer.

"There she is." With her back to him, he eyed the dripping mid-length honey-colored trench coat that was pulled around her waist. Tousled by the storm, her long black hair curled down into her coat.

Ian followed his glance. Stooped down, she was talking into the speaker.

The sight of her made Tucker's stomach tighten. He needed to apologize for the way he had spoken to her. Would she talk to him? Worse, would she kick him out, forbid him from seeing Dancer? That alone was reason enough to repair the damage. Tucker decided to just do it before he lost his courage. He was up on his feet and made his way to her before he could change his mind.

"Ms. Ziegler." He called out as he walked toward her.

She turned toward his voice, her expression carrying a thousand words as her eyes rolled and her lips set a hard line across her mouth. Her eyes were glassy and bloodshot. She had been crying. He had been insensitive, not realizing what she was going through. He floundered in his discomfort. "Um, I'm sorry about earlier."

Ms. Ziegler's sniffled as she shook out her hair from under her coat. "Thank you."

She looked younger than his own mother. Her piercing green eyes, trimmed by long, gorgeous eye-lashes, were impossible to look away from. Her high cheekbones against a flawless olive complexion said that she didn't have to try to be beautiful. Like her son, they were gifted with natural beauty.

Nevertheless, his saying sorry and her saying thank you didn't change what she was planning to do. He was still losing Dancer. "I'm sorry for being disrespectful, but..." He remembered someone once telling him that sorry didn't come with the word 'but' in it. "I love Dancer and would do anything for him."

Ms. Ziegler's shoulders fell. The muscles in her face relaxed. His body mimicked hers. He unclenched his fists as his own shoulders fell.

"I was a little surprised earlier when you said you loved my son. It is no surprise he turned out gay." She said it with no expression or sign of feelings.

Turned out gay? Tucker bit his tongue. That was not a fight he wanted now.

"Does he love you as well?" Her eyes looked at him, searching for the answer.

Dancer had never said the words to him, but he was sure he did. "Yes." He was certain he could speak the truth for Dancer. "If things were different, if I wasn't homeless, a high school dropout with a mother who is a junkie and a father who cheated fatherhood; if I wasn't eighteen and didn't know shit about life; if things were different... I might not have met your son, and that is far worse than anything I can think of." The tightness around his jaw relaxed the moment he took a breath.

"I have no business asking anything from you, but..." He wasn't sure this was a good idea. "Can you look at me?" He held his hands out, palms up. "I am perhaps the one and only person in this world that loves Dancer as much as you. I want you to see me and know I'm real. I'm here."

Ms. Ziegler and Tucker moved against the white wall to let a couple pass. When the doors opened, Tucker's eyes peered into the Intensive Care Unit until the doors closed. All he wanted was to see Dancer.

"My mother once told me that boys do what's easy, men do

what's right. I never knew what that meant until now. Your son, well, he's everything to me. There is nothing I wouldn't do to protect him," Tucker said.

Ms. Ziegler released a long-controlled breath. "You said some things earlier that were difficult for me to hear. I've failed my son many times over. It was hard hearing it from you. I don't know you, but you know me, and that's a little intimidating and a little unfair."

Again, Tucker couldn't stop himself. "I don't know what you mean about this being unfair. You're the one holding all the cards here. It seems neither Dancer or me have any say in what happens to him. That's what's unfair." He fought back a tear. He turned toward the waiting room to shield his face. Through the crowd of people, he could see that Ian was still in his chair. His eyes were fixed on them.

Ms. Ziegler pushed her purse higher onto her arm. "Thank you for talking to me. I appreciate it, I do." The door opened again and several nurses walked out. She caught the door before it closed. "I'd like to check in on Liam. Give me some time with him, and then why don't you come in, and we can sit together for a while."

Tucker was taken aback by her offer. Her words felt like a ton of weight had been lifted off him. "Okay. Thank you."

In the room, Dancer's nurse had commandeered another chair, so both Tucker and Ms. Ziegler could sit. Although neither was in their chair at the same time, it was nice not having to leave the room.

A little after nine o'clock that evening, Dancer was transported down to radiology for a new CT scan of his brain with the hope that the swelling had decreased.

While he was out of the room, Tucker discovered that Ms. Ziegler was a nervous snacker. She asked him to join her in raiding the waiting room vending machine, where they bought prepackaged sandwiches, chips, M&Ms, and sodas.

While waiting for Dancer to return, Ms. Ziegler shared bits and pieces of Dancer's early childhood. She told stories of him and his father, how much he adored dancing, his strong tenacity. Some of it, like the fact that his favorite food was fruit, any kind of fruit, was of little importance, but Tucker still wanted to know it all.

She asked Tucker many questions. In the beginning, his answers were short with little detail.

"Are your parents together?"

"No."

"Are they both living?"

"I never met my dad."

"What does your mother do?"

"She's in rehab."

He must have said more than he realized. She asked. "So, who takes care of Tucker?"

At first, he took the question literally. "No one takes care of me."

Her eyes softened as her brows raised. She didn't say a word. She didn't have to for Tucker to know he had misunderstood what she was asking. Still, his answer still wouldn't have changed. He would be alone in this world without Dancer, and she would be responsible.

*****

By early morning, the doctor arrived in Dancer's room. Exhausted, Tucker stepped to the back of the room as Ms. Ziegler and the doctor discussed the plan of care. Because his CT scan showed that the swelling had reduced, she explained to Ms. Ziegler what to expect as her son came off the sedative that was keeping him in his induced coma.

Tucker listened, knowing he was not a part of any plan being discussed. He kept his head down, eyes on the floor, hoping he had disappeared into the wall.

Kyle went to work implementing the doctor's orders as soon as she stepped out of the room. Tucker watched as Kyle explained the straps he was fastening to the side of the bed. "These are restraints. When Liam wakes up, he'll be groggy and one of the first things he will try to do is pull the tube from his mouth. It's a natural response, and it happens fast."

"He's not going to like that!" Tucker eyed the restraints. The irony was not lost on him that they looked like something out of a horror movie.

"I know. We'll only keep his hands restrained until he wakes up enough that he understands that he's still on the ventilator. Once he wakes up enough, we can see about taking that off."

"No, he's not going to like it!" Tucker looked at Ms. Ziegler for help. Surely, she wouldn't be for the restraints either. He eased over to the bedside to get a better look at them. They were as bad as he thought.

Ms. Ziegler wrapped her arm around Tucker's waist and brought him in close to her. "It's just until he wakes up. They know what they're doing," she whispered to him.

The prospect of Dancer opening his eyes any moment was overshadowed by the fear of him realizing they had tied him down. It could take days, but the doctor also said it could happen within minutes.

He and Ms. Ziegler watched as Kyle secured Dancer's wrists to the bed frame.

"Talk to him, like you've been doing. Sometimes a familiar voice can help stimulate the brain to respond," Kyle suggested as he finished strapping Dancer's wrists down.

Tucker waited for Ms. Ziegler to say something. His eyes moved back and forth from her to Dancer as he waited.

"Hey, honey, the doctor said you can wake up. You've been sleeping awhile now." Her voice was low and sweet, like a mother holding her baby for the first time. She rubbed her hand up and down his arm as she whispered to him.

Two hours passed before Dancer's head rolled slightly to one side as if he was waking up. Tucker was sitting in his chair, half day dreaming when he saw it. Before he could say anything, Kyle was already next to Dancer. Both Tucker and Ms. Ziegler stepped to the head of the bed with Kyle standing on the opposite side of them.

Within a few minutes, Dancer's left hand twisted. The restraint tightened. Kyle took Dancer's hand and placed his hand in it. "Liam… Liam… Can you squeeze my hand?"

Nothing happened. *Come on Dancer, squeeze his hand*, Tucker begged silently.

"Can you squeeze my hand?" Kyle repeated.

"Come on baby, squeeze his hand." Tucker placed his hand over the top of Dancer's other hand. "Come on baby, wake up."

Dancer's right hand moved under Tucker's. Then it pulled itself from underneath Tucker's hand and onto the top of his hand. There was a light squeeze. "He squeezed my hand!" Tucker was sure.

He took a half step over as Ms. Ziegler moved in closer. She put her hand on the top of theirs. "Liam, darling, it's Mom. Wake up, honey."

Dancer's hand flexed as if trying to signal he heard her.

It was another fifteen minutes before Dancer moved again. This time, both hands yanked, but the restraints held them in place. His head dropped to one side as his eyelids fluttered. Within a few seconds, his eyes opened and fell to his wrist.

"They're tied down. You have a tube in your throat." Tucker took Dancer's hand, stopping it from jerking against the restraints.

Chapter Twenty-Seven

The voices sounded as if they were coming from above him. Dancer tried to open his eyes, but they were too heavy. His throat was throbbing. Swallowing was next to impossible. He tried to raise his hand to scratch his throat, but his arms wouldn't move. He tried the other hand, but it wouldn't come up either. Whatever was in his mouth was stopping him from licking his lips.

"Liam… Can you hear me?"

Dancer turned his head toward the female voice and nodded. It took a second, but it sounded like his mother. He again tried to open his eyes. The bright light caused him to squint before closing them again.

"It's Mom, I'm here. It's okay, relax. You're in the hospital."

In a foggy state, Dancer couldn't understand how his mother could be in the room. He had mostly drifted back to sleep when he felt someone take his hand and shake it. "Hey buddy. You awake?"

Dancer didn't know the male voice. He turned toward it. The figure in front of his face was blurry and took a second to come into focus. He didn't know who this person was. He turned his head to the other side, and he knew it was Tucker standing over him. Next to Tucker was… *Mom?*

"I need you to wake up for me. I'm Kyle, your nurse. Open your eyes, so I can get your breathing tube out. Then you can talk." Kyle rubbed Dancer's shoulder, jiggling him awake. "Nod your head for me. Can you nod your head?"

Dancer nodded.

"That's good. Can you open your eyes for me?" Kyle asked.

It took a second, but Dancer's eyes opened. He was semi-awake.

Within minutes, Kyle had Dancer sitting up. "Hey there. I'm Kyle. I've been taking care of you the last couple of days while you've been sleeping. Your mom and Tucker are here." Kyle stepped to the side for a second.

Dancer tried to look over at them but everything was blurry.

"I understand you go by Dancer," said Kyle. "What would you like me to call you? Dancer or Liam? Just nod. Dancer?"

Dancer wasn't sure if his head was moving.

"Okay, Dancer it is."

Drowsy, he tried to keep his head up and his eyes open. He tried to listen as Kyle talked to Tucker and his mother. He was sure they were discussing him.

"It will take time for all the drugs to get out of his system and for him to wake up all the way. You might also notice that his memory might be a little foggy. Most of the time, patients regain all of it, so don't panic if you see this." Kyle fluffed the pillow behind Dancer for him.

His head was as heavy as a bowling ball as he fought to hold it up. He tried to talk but nothing came out. He stared at his wrist as he tried to pull his hands up to his face.

"No, baby," Tucker told him. "They tied your hands down. You have a breathing tube in your throat." Tucker's hands rubbed against his. Dancer hurt from his forehead down to his legs.

"Hi, honey. I'm here."

Dancer turned toward his mother. As she came into focus, the corners of his mouth curved upward. He again tried to talk, but nothing came out. He barely moved, and a sharp pain radiated in his shoulder.

Within twenty minutes, he could hold his eyes open. Everything was in slow motion. Unsure what had happened, he was surprised his mother was here. His eyes moved from Tucker, to his mother, and to Kyle, who was doing something with the needle in his arm.

A petite woman came into the room. He didn't know who she was, but she was wearing scrubs like Kyle. She walked over to Kyle, and the two chatted for several minutes.

"Hey, Dancer. This is Cathy. She's a respiratory therapist. You've been breathing well on your own. You're not relying on the ventilator to breathe for you anymore. We want to remove your breathing tube for you. That way you can talk. Does that sound all right to you?"

Dancer nodded at both Kyle and Cathy. He would do anything to get the tube out of his mouth.

It took Cathy and Kyle less than five minutes to remove the tube. Other than the feeling that someone had jammed a shoe down his throat, he found he could breathe normally. Each time he swallowed, pain shot down this throat. "Can I have water?" His voice was scratchy.

"Not yet. But I have ice chips here for you." Kyle walked over to the sink in the room and washed his hands. He scooped ice chips out of a plastic bag into a tiny cup. He handed them to his mother. "Just put one or two in his mouth and let him suck on them."

Ms. Ziegler stepped up and held the first chip to his mouth. She rubbed the chip across his dry lips, moistening them first. Her own lips parted as Dancer's lips glistened, and he released a low moan of satisfaction.

The cold ice soothed his chapped lips. He let her feed him another one before he was sure the pain wouldn't prevent him from asking his question. "What happened?" Dancer closed his eyes again. The pain in his throat was unbearable.

"You're in the hospital. You got jumped." Tucker moved to his mother's side. "You've been sleeping for days."

Dancer's gaze was fixed on the wall as he processed what Tucker had said. His throat and mouth were dry. He tried several times to swallow, hoping to lubricate his throat so he could speak. "Aha" was all he could muster as he took ahold of Tucker's hand. His grip was weak, but he squeezed Tucker's hand as hard as he could.

Tucker kissed him on his forehead. They both glanced over at his mother. She appeared unfazed by their affection. He still couldn't believe she was here. How had she found him? Dancer tried to sit up, but his shoulder was in too much pain. It was all too much to wrap his brain around.

Ms. Ziegler waited about a half hour before giving him a few more ice chips. He closed his eyes and moaned at the coolness of the ice against his lips.

Once he could bear the pain of talking, he moistened his throat the best he could before beginning. "What's wrong with me?" His eyes fell to his left shoulder, which was killing him.

Kyle slid his workstation out of the way. "Well, you had swelling in your brain. That's the reason we had you sleeping for so long—to help keep you still while your brain repaired itself. Also, your left shoulder was fractured as well as your wrist. The pain you're feeling from breathing is because of several ribs that were fractured. When you came in, you were in bad shape." Kyle cleared his throat. "You're doing great now, though."

Tucker took Dancer's hand as he grinned at Kyle. "He's been amazing. He's been taking care of you almost every day since you've been here."

"Yes, and this will be the last day you'll see me until next week. I'm off for the next couple of days." Kyle's face muscles relaxed.

Ms. Ziegler rubbed her hands together. "Well, I hope you have something planned that's fun. You have been amazing. I can't thank you enough."

"I do." Kyle's expression brightened even more. "My girlfriend lives up in Chicago. She's a nurse at La Rabida Children's Hospital. The lake is beautiful this time of year."

Girlfriend? Dancer took another look at Kyle before looking over at Tucker. They both grinned at each other, conveying to each other that neither were convinced the 'friend' was actually a 'girl'.

"I know. I was there last year about this time for a festival and fireworks show on Navy Pier. Cold but beautiful. What is that, about a two-hour drive?" Ms. Ziegler asked.

"Yeah, if the weather's good." Kyle pulled off his latex gloves and tossed them in the trash.

The room suddenly became quiet. It was as if words escaped everyone at the same time. The sound of water rushing through the pipes under the counter echoed through the room. The stillness gave Dancer a moment to recall that he had been attacked.

A doctor arrived an hour later and congratulated Dancer on his recovery. He stated that it was likely they could transfer him out of Intensive Care and onto the floor by morning. Dancer gave the doctor a lopsided grin as he lost the battle against sleep. His eyes drooped shut as he listened. He tried to open them again, but it was too late.

*****

Late that evening, Ms. Ziegler had the hospital staff move Dancer to the twelfth floor, a private floor reserved for VIP patients.

He was asleep when they came to get him. He was told that Tucker and his mother would be waiting for him up there. Dancer shut his eyes as he traveled several floors up to the VIP wing of the hospital.

It was morning when he opened his eyes again. Light streamed in through the large glass windows. He remembered being moved. His eyes scanned the warm birch-colored walls in the large room.

His new room overlooked the city in the distance and was furnished more like a hotel suite than a hospital room. Beneath the giant window was a small couch, a coffee table, and a leather recliner. Tucker was curled up on the couch with a blanket over him.

Just seeing him was better than anything in this enormous room or its spectacular views. The sheets, pillow, and mattress were all an upgrade from the floor below. But what Dancer wanted was to touch the man on the other side of the room.

He lay awake until the door opened and a woman in pink scrubs walked in. She smiled at him once she saw he was awake. "Good morning, Mr. Ziegler. My name is Daraja." Her accent was thick. "I'll be taking care of you today."

She fixed his pillow behind his head and adjusted the bed's height. He looked at her name tag, hoping to read her name. D-a-r-a-j-a—RN. "Good morning." His throat hurt but felt a thousand percent better than yesterday.

Tucker stirred before flipping the covers off himself. He stretched his long body on the couch as he looked at Daraja and then Dancer.

"How are we feeling this morning?" Her accent as well as her bright white teeth against her dark skin made him think she might be African. She began her morning assessment as she talked.

Dancer watched Tucker as she poked and examined him. Dancer wanted her to leave; he wanted Tucker next to him.

"Dr. Reed should come in some time this morning." Daraja continued talking, but either her accent was too thick or his injured brain wasn't processing what she said. Her voice sounded like something coming out of a drive-through speaker.

She made one last adjustment to the bedding across the lower section of his stomach before turning to Tucker. It sounded like they were discussing food. She smiled at him before exiting the room and closing the door behind her.

Tucker rose out of his chair. "She seems nice." He balled up the blanket he had slept under and laid it down in the chair. He walked over and kissed Dancer. "Oh my God! Your breath stinks!" Tucker exclaimed through laughter as he pulled up. His blue eyes gleamed down at him. "How are you this morning?"

"I hurt. Everything hurts." Dancer looked down at his wrist. Even breathing caused him pain.

"You scared me. I thought… that I might lose you." Tucker used his finger to trace over Dancer's cheek and chin. "I love you so much."

With no hesitation, Dancer repeated it back. "I love you too. I don't think I've ever said it to you." He paused and thought about it for a second. "I knew it the first night you and I slept in the Milkman's chair together. You held me all night, and I fell in love."

"Really?" Tucker looked surprised at Dancer's declaration.

"I don't think I've said it to anyone. I wasn't sure what love felt like until that day." Sure, it could have been the drugs that were making him emotional, but he didn't care. He meant every word of it.

Tucker chuckled. His finger dropped to Dancer's heart. "I'm sure you told your mum and dad and your Oma that you loved them."

"Yeah, as a kid." A sharp pain surged through Dancer as he tried to reposition himself in the bed. Bad idea.

"That counts." Tucker took hold of his hand.

Tucker's hand was warm. His breath probably did stink, but he wanted another kiss. "Was I really sleeping for four days?"

"Yep. Me and your mum were right here the whole time." Tucker sniffled as he wrinkled his nose. The whites of his eyes turning pink, he rubbed his hand across his face.

Then Tucker's face went from jovial to a somber, stoic expression. "What's wrong?" Dancer asked.

Tucker's expression dulled. "I don't know what to call you."

"What do you mean?" Dancer tried to sit up. Something said this was serious. He used his one good arm and tried to push his body up higher onto his pillows. Pain shot through his ribcage, causing him to stop.

"Are you okay?" Tucker asked.

"Yeah, yeah. What do you mean, you don't know what to call me?"

207

Tucker's face flushed. "Dancer or Liam? Is Liam the real you? I want the real you. Dancer feels like…"

Dancer had to digest for a second what Tucker was saying. "Dancer is the real me. I like the name Dancer. It's my Oma's nickname that she called me. It means everything to me. Liam is a name my mom and dad gave me. I had no say-so in it. It means nothing."

"Okay." Tucker's head nodded as if he wasn't convinced and was still mulling it over. "Can I ask you one more question?"

From the haunted look in Tucker's eyes, Dancer wasn't sure he wanted to know the question.

"What were you doing in the alley?"

The scared look on Tucker's face told Dancer exactly what Tucker was thinking. "I was looking for dinner." He racked his brain to make sure he was remembering everything. "I'd just left Walmart and was cutting through the alley on Sixth to go behind Sammy's Deli and Market. They dump a ton of food on Sundays." He couldn't remember if he had made it to the dumpster or not.

"Oh." The lines in Tucker's face relaxed.

All the talking had irritated Dancer's throat. "Can I have water?" he asked.

"Yeah." Tucker looked around the room before heading to a small refrigerator tucked in a counter along the back wall. Within a few seconds, he was back with a glass of water and a straw. He smiled as he held it to Dancer's lips.

The cool water moistened his mouth and throat. "Slow down, Mr. Ziegler." Tucker laughed.

Dancer tried not to laugh as he swallowed the water he had been savoring in his mouth. "Don't ever call me that again." Laughing hurt. Tucker calling him Mr. Ziegler—what people had called his father—was just too weird. He looked at Tucker's bald head. Yesterday was a blur, but he remembered being surprised that Tucker's head was bald. "Your hair. What happened to your hair?"

Tucker grinned as he ran his hand over his bald head. "I wanted it all off." His cheeks turned a burnt rose. "They shaved all of your hair off. I loved your hair. Do you remember we were supposed to cut our hair that night?" Tucker rested his hand on the sheet covering Dancer's legs. "If you were going to be bald, then I wanted to be also."

Dancer looked about the room. "Where's my mom?" He took another sip of the water Tucker was holding for him before laying his head back down on his pillow.

Tucker put the glass next to his bed. "She's at the hotel. After we got you up here, she took off." Tucker's entire face lit up.

"What? Why are you smiling?" Dancer knew that grin.

"Your mum. Last night, she asked me back to her hotel room." His voice teetered on a laugh.

It took a second, but then Dancer got it. "Oh my God, don't be stupid!" He tried not to laugh, knowing it would hurt. "You're so stupid." His laugh was sending pain all around his ribcage, but he didn't care.

"No, really." Tucker's voice was a full-on laugh. "Like mother, like son. I guess you Zieglers find me irresistible."

"Shut up. You're grossing me out!" Dancer pleaded.

"Okay. She knows everything. She offered to get me a room. But I couldn't leave you. This floor is so nice I was also afraid that if I left it, they wouldn't let me back up here." Tucker pulled at the front of his dirty sweater.

"What does she know and how?" A nervousness washed over Dancer.

"Well, for starters, she knew you lived here. She had a private eye or someone like that looking for you. You know the man we kept seeing? Well, that was her private eye following us. She was already here then, but when you got jumped, he couldn't find you. It wasn't until the hospital called that she knew where you were."

Dancer gasped. "Really, a private investigator?" Air rushing into his lungs sent a sharp pain against his ribcage. "What else does she know?" He was afraid to ask.

"She knows I'm your boyfriend." Tucker kissed him again.

Was it the kiss or hearing him call him his boyfriend that sent a flutter through Dancer's belly? It sounded nice. He had never been anybody's boyfriend. "So how did she know we were together? The guy following us?"

"No. I told her." Tucker's face frowned. "We kind of got in a fight. It slipped out."

"A fight?" He was about to ask for details when the door opened and Daraja walked in with a tray.

209

"I have breakfast for you two." She sat the tray down on the wet bar.

Whatever it was, it smelled wonderful. Dancer hadn't been hungry until she walked in. He watched as she removed the metal dome over a plate. "Here you go, Mr. Graves." She placed a plate of waffles, bacon, and scrambled eggs with bell peppers on the coffee table. "Juice?" She held up a small glass of orange juice.

"Yes. Thank you." Tucker stepped away from the bed as Daraja approached the bed with a tray. "And for you, Mr. Ziegler, I have some warm broth."

"You've got to be kidding me." Dancer looked across the room at Tucker's breakfast. "Did you order that?"

"No. I told her I wasn't hungry." Tucker answered.

Daraja slid Dancer's bed tray over his lap. "Let's start with this. See how well you do. If you can hold it down, we can try some Jell-O for lunch."

"Good Lord! Jell-O? I can't wait!" Dancer had zero appetite for the broth or Jell-O.

Daraja gave him some meds and left the broth on the tray in front of him before leaving the room.

"Can I have some of your bacon?" Dancer begged.

"Nope." Tucker never slowed or looked up from his plate.

It wasn't long before Dancer's eyelids grew heavy. His pain meds were kicking in. He closed his eyes as bits of his memory came to him. There were two figures walking toward him. As he always did, he remembered pulling his hoodie down across his forehead as he approached them. One guy said something as he walked past them.

Dancer tried to remember what the guy had said. Maybe he never knew. Maybe the guy was talking to his friend. The next thing he remembered was feeling a blow to the back of his head. A sharp pain and a bright light flashed before his eyes. He tried to keep walking, but it was as if his feet were off the ground, as if he was floating. His memory stopped there, as the medicine took over, sending him into a deep sleep.

Chapter Twenty-Eight

He woke up three hours later to the sound of his mother's voice and a room full of people. Tucker, his mother, Daraja, and a man and woman in lab coats were all standing in the room.

Daraja helped him sit up as the two strangers introduced themselves as his physicians. They talked to him, but in third person as they took turns running a series of tests, reviewed his records, and charted. The female physician went over a host of problems to look for and issues he faced in the coming days, weeks, and months of his recovery.

"I'd like to see you go home in a few days. But you won't be feeling all that great. Your recovery is just beginning. You will need plenty of support."

Ms. Ziegler nodded her head in agreement. "I have that taken care of. I'll hire a nurse to stay at the house."

Tucker's heart dropped. *A nurse? The house?* She was still in charge.

Dancer scowled. "What are you talking about? The house?"

"Well, honey, you can't go back to the camp. It's unsanitary. You need professional help."

Dancer looked at Tucker. She obviously knew about Camp Roosevelt too.

"What are you talking about? The house?" The inflection in his voice caused it to screech. "I'm not going with you!" Dancer tried to sit up, but it hurt too much. In the shape he was in and the pain, there was little chance he could get back to his place, but this was his decision, not hers.

Ms. Ziegler jutted out her hips. "Honey. We can talk about this in private." She turned to the two doctors. "How soon do you think he'll be able to travel?"

211

The male doctor took the lead on her question. "I imagine light travel in five days."

"San Francisco?" she asked.

"Oh. I think I'd like to see him in my office at least once before that—next week. I have colleagues in the city that I can contact to assist you with him." He reached under Dancer's covers and pressed on his abdomen in several spots.

"I'm not—" Dancer sucked in a breath. With two fingers, the pressure the doctor applied to Dancer's abdomen sent pain to the back of his head. His fight not to black out ended the conversation, for now.

Within a few minutes, both doctors and Daraja completed their work and left the room. Tucker looked to be leaving the room as well.

"No! Stay!" Dancer's pain had subsided enough that he could talk. He didn't want to be alone with his mother. He needed Tucker to stay. Dancer's blood was boiling at the way his mother and the doctors had been talking over him as if he wasn't even there.

His mother's face softened. "Honey, we need to talk." She fumbled down in her purse and pulled out a twenty. "Here, Tucker. Why don't you go downstairs and have lunch?"

"No!" Dancer demanded. Again, his mother was dismissing what he wanted.

Tucker looked as if he didn't know what to do. His brows rose high, but he didn't say a word.

"Tucker. Don't leave me!" Dancer's voice was low and gruff.

Tucker's shoulders dropped. "I'm not." He moved in between Ms. Ziegler and Dancer and took Dancer's hand.

"Okay." Dancer's mom lifted her chin. "I want you home."

Dancer's eyes rolled. "What the hell are you talking about? I hate you! I ran away from you. Why would I go with you?" He thought about the last six years of his life. Men had abused him over and over. He had chosen to be on the streets, selling his ass to strangers, instead of having it taken for free from someone who supposedly loved him. "Who the hell do you think you are that you can just march in here after six years and tell me what I want or need? You don't know me, you don't know anything about me! Tell me why I left! Tell me... say it!" Dancer's upper body rose off his pillow.

"I didn't know." His mother's voice cracked. "I suspected." The color drained from her face as she placed her fingers over her mouth. Her eyes filled with water. "When Tucker confronted me, he confirmed what I knew but had blocked out." Ms. Ziegler pulled a handkerchief from her purse. She dabbed the silk cloth against her cheeks trying to wipe away the tears. Her sniffle was the only sound in the room.

Dancer turned his head away from his mother. He refused to watch her stand there and play the victim.

Ms. Ziegler cleared her throat. "I don't know where to start. It took two years to find my way out of the pain enough to say 'no more'. That's why I'm here. To say I'm sorry. For years, I cried myself to sleep wondering if my son was alive."

"You need to get the hell out of my room. Now!" The words were caught in Dancer's throat but loud enough to be heard.

"I turned a blind eye to what was happening in my own home. After losing your father, I was so lonely. Deeply depressed and turning a blind eye to it allowed me to be loved. The worst part was that I knew I'd made a mistake marrying Robert, and yet I couldn't let it go. After Robert and I split up, I started seeing a therapist. She helped me realize the damage I'd done to our family with the very bad decisions I'd made."

Just hearing his name caused bile to swirl in Dancer's gut. He didn't want to talk about Robert. He closed his eyes, trying to shut her—no, the world—out. It was as if he was fourteen again.

Nothing had changed. *Whatever she says goes.* When his dad was alive, he had played the peacemaker between Dancer and his mother. He quelled the arguments and made it all better once he separated them. Every conversation ended with his dad making it all better. But his dad wasn't here. He closed his eyes as he squeezed Tucker's hand tightly. He had no words to say.

"I may never earn your trust or love again for what I did. I'll take this permanent sorrow to my grave with me, knowing I failed to protect you, my son. I am the person who brought you into this world, and I failed." Her voice trembled.

A lump in Dancer's throat threatened to suffocate him if he didn't swallow it down. When he opened his eyes, she was standing right next to him and Tucker. Her eyes were bloodshot, her face drawn. It killed him to know she had been in so much pain as well. "I was a boy."

"I know, sweetheart. None of this is your fault."

Dancer broke his gaze, choosing instead to rest his eyes on the wall behind her. In the beginning, he had believed it was his fault. He was just coming into his own sexuality. He blamed himself, thinking that he must have been the reason Robert did what he did. Robert made himself look like the victim in all of it. For the last six years, he had hated his mother for loving that man.

"I was fourteen," he muttered. For years, he believed she had stopped loving him and his dad and, instead, loved this other man. He had been grieving not only the loss of his father but of his mother. At the time, as a child, it was all so dark. It was suicide or run, and he had never looked back. He watched as a tear trickled from the side of her cheek before falling onto her blouse. She wiped another one away with the back of her hand just as it formed at the bottom of her eye.

Dancer's heart pulsed through his bruised ribs. Tucker's hand caressed his. He avoided eye contact with them as he stared down at the white sheets that covered his legs.

Silence dominated the room for a few minutes before two hard knocks on the door broke the silence. Ian walked in smiling. "Wow! Nice room."

He stopped inside the door. The look on his face said he knew he had walked into the middle of something. "I'll come back."

Tucker's eyes bounced back and forth between Dancer and Ian. He patted Dancer's hand several times. "You and your mum need to talk. I'll step out for a minute with Ian." Tucker released his hand and ushered Ian out of the room.

Dancer waited until the door closed. He questioned if he wanted to continue talking. His mother stood next to the bed. Her eyes were hopeful that he would speak. He didn't know what to say. He looked at the heavy white cast covering his forearm. His bone was broken, and the cast was there to protect it, hold it steady until the bone could mend. His physical injuries where clear to anyone. No one could see his emotional injuries and scars, and the pain that hadn't eased in years.

He was tired of hurting, tired of being angry. He was just tired. Before all of this happened, he had known he was ready to leave the streets, tired of men using his body for their own sexual gratification. He was tired of being cold, hungry, and alone, but he hadn't dealt with any of the pain that had caused it all. He had spent six years hiding from life until Tucker. Camp Roosevelt was very much like the cast on his arm, there to help him to heal, but over time, it had become his cage. "Mom." His voice trembled.

Ms. Ziegler looked up. Her eyes were filled with grief, regret, and a tiny bit of hopefulness as she waited for him to speak.

"I love Tucker. I can't leave him." How had so much changed in the blink of an eye? This week had obliterated his concept of normal. Every aspect of his old existence no longer worked with what he wanted.

Her expression softened. "Then you both can come home. Come to San Francisco. You'll love California."

"When did you move to California?" he asked.

"Right after Robert and I split up. I couldn't live in that house a second more." His mother laid her hand over the top of his. "Really, I want both of you to come to California."

Dancer knew that wasn't possible. Tucker would never leave his mother and Mattie. He would put them before anything. He put everyone before himself. There was so much about Tucker that his mother didn't know. "I'm tired, Mom." His wounded brain was on overload. Dancer closed his eyes, wanting all these decisions and changes to go away.

"I know you hurt, and I'm sorry that I'm the cause. I'm far from perfect. My greatest catastrophe in life is failing you." Ms. Ziegler moved her hand onto Dancer's forehead and stroked the light stubble that once was beautiful locks of hair.

He squeezed his eyes tighter, trying to lose himself in the darkness behind his eyes.

Chapter Twenty-Nine

Dancer sat in the billowy chair in the corner of the large hotel suite that his mother had gotten for him and Tucker. He and Tucker had been arguing for the last hour about moving to California. It had been three days since they had discharged him from the hospital. Three days since his mother had proposed that he and Tucker move to California. Three days since he asked Tucker to come with him, and three days of agony when Tucker didn't say yes.

"You don't understand." Dancer repositioned his body in the chair, looking for a comfortable position. "I feel like I have to go with her. There's so much that I have to work on. With myself, with her, with life. I don't think I can do it, at least right, without addressing my issues with her. She's the only love I have besides you, and it's all messed up. I have so many unresolved issues with her, and I have to figure those out so I can love you the way you should be loved."

"And I feel like I have to stay here, to take care of Mattie and mum." Tucker pushed back.

"Tucker… I don't think it's the same." Dancer didn't want to fight. He didn't have the strength. "I feel like my anger toward my mom is intertwined with love. Like I can't separate the two."

"But I still don't understand why you have to move all the way out to California."

"Because that's where my mom's at—and anyways, where would we live? I can't simply go back to the way things were. I just can't." He was frustrated that he couldn't better explain his feelings to Tucker so that Tucker would understand and want to go with him. "It can't be fixed over emails and telephone conversations. I'm not even sure it can be fixed. But I gotta try. You deserve so much, to be loved as much as you love. I don't feel like I can do that without addressing some of the crap I have in my head about people hurting

216

me. She's the start." It felt like he was being forced to make a choice. Tucker's not agreeing to go felt like a rejection, another wound. Could he have really misgauged what he and Tucker had? Yeah, going to California wasn't their original plan. He and his mother had done nothing but talk for the last three days. Yes, he was still hurt over her abandonment, but he was also tired of his existing life, selling his body to survive. It was the only money he knew how to make, and he didn't want to do it anymore. But no matter what Dancer said about moving to California, Tucker pushed back. He watched as Tucker paced the room. His silence spoke volumes. His only remaining tactic was to pin Tucker down for an answer. "Either you are or you aren't."

Tucker released a gasp of air from deep within his gut. "I have to see my mom. Tomorrow's family day. I need to see her and Mattie. California's a long ways away." It was what he had been saying for the last three days.

"I don't understand. You don't need to ask her for permission to go." Dancer wanted to scream. All he wanted was for him to say yes. But if Tucker didn't go, what were his options?

Tucker gave a half shrug. "I... I want to see them." He stopped as if he was going to say something but had chosen not to at the last second.

Dancer wanted to get up. To go to him and hold him. He had to convince him somehow to go. He lifted his wrist cast to reposition his body in the chair without moving too much. It was his rib cage that caused him the most pain, mainly when he moved. "I can't make you go with me. I want you to go. I love you."

"I love you too, but—" Tucker moved over to the coffee table in front of Dancer's chair. He sat on the edge of the table, facing Dancer. "What if Mattie needs me? What if my mum relapses? What if—"

"You're the one who once told me I was hiding." There was no need to listen to all the what-ifs. Tucker was dropping excuses. "You can't fix her. She's an addict. She's where she is supposed to be right now. What are you going to do, sit around and wait for her to relapse? Maybe she'll be fine. Why do you always put them first?" Would Tucker always put his family before him? Once again, he wanted a love that was being offered to someone else before him.

"I have always put them first. I'm here because I put them first. Why would you think it would be different now?" Tucker asked. "I feel like shit. Last week, while you were still in your coma, I had an argument with your mum. I told her I thought she put your stepfather before you. I think I even called her selfish."

"To her face?" Dancer's brows rose. "You got balls." Dancer loved the cute little smirk that turned the corner of Tucker's mouth upward. Even while fighting, he was in love with Tucker.

"But now, are we doing the same thing?" Tucker paused for a second. "You're choosing your mum, I'm choosing my mum."

"But that's it!" Dancer cut him off. "I'm not choosing. I want you both. I need you! I want you!" Dancer's head lowered into his chest. He could feel the tears coming. Dammit, he wasn't a crier, especially in front of people. He sniffled, trying to hold back his runny nose. He was asking Tucker to leave his family so that he wouldn't have to give up anything. Dancer knew what he was asking wasn't fair, but what other options did they have? "Tucker, what do you want?" Dancer couldn't look at him. Tucker's answer would hurt more than his injuries. He leaned forward in his chair as if reaching for the desired answer. "I know that you want to protect them, but I almost feel like you're trying to save them. Like if you're here, you can stop something from happening. But you can't!"

"But if I'm all the way out in California, what happens if she gets kicked out or something? I know I can't save them, I get that. But I also can't just abandon them either. I have to think about Mattie."

"Can you hear what you're saying? It's one what-if on top of another. She took Mattie with her because Mattie's not your responsibility. She's hers. I get it, you want to protect her. But sticking around here won't change anything. Come to California. My mom wants us to finish school. Maybe you could play baseball again. There's nothing here for us to grab a hold of to even begin to build a life. This is our chance to escape Camp Roosevelt. This is it." He had given Tucker his whole heart, his love, everything he had to give, and it didn't seem to be enough.

He buried his face in his hands as Tucker made a low growl in the back of his throat. Dancer shook his head before bringing it up out of his hands. "Do you have any idea what you're asking me to do?"

Tucker asked. He was rooted on the edge of the coffee table, his face flush. A deep sadness clouded his blue eyes. "When you were in the hospital and I first met your mum, she said something about taking you home. It was when you were still in a coma. The thought of you leaving me, her taking you away, scared the shit out of me. I was so pissed at her for saying it. But now look, she's taking you anyway."

Tucker was only a foot away from him, but it felt like miles. Dancer was losing him. Tucker's lack of eye contact said so. "She's not taking me anywhere. I want this, for the both of us. This is our chance." He looked over Tucker's shoulders at the plastic toy dog Tucker had brought to the hospital.

His dog, Tamale. Dancer's only memory of love was this plastic toy. Would Tucker be a memory one day too? Emptiness ran through him. A memory, a choice that would be remembered for eternity. He had to choose one or the other. Someone had to lose. If Tucker said no, and he stayed here with Tucker, what would change? They would be stuck in Camp Roosevelt forever.

"We can either both stay here, in misery, or escape. This is it— we may never get this chance again. Our moms suck, but mine is offering us something, a chance to change our lives." He looked around the incredible suite they had been holed up in for the last three days. It amazed him how quickly this had become normal to him. It was a reminder of a life he once had, that he had forgotten, buried under six years of living on the streets, having men do things to him he would never forget.

Three days in the hotel had brought a normalcy to him. For the first time, he knew he deserved better than a life on the streets. But no matter what he said to convince Tucker that he, too, deserved better, it did not work.

*****

The city lights shone through the sliding glass door of their twenty-first-floor balcony, softly illuminating the suite. Dancer lay in bed next to Tucker, his injuries not allowing him to get comfortable. Flat on his back, he used his good arm to caress Tucker's bare upper chest as he listened to him sleep.

They had talked until there was nothing more to talk about. Tucker had made it clear that any decision he made would come after seeing his mom and sister in the morning. That was hours away, and what if he said no, he wasn't going? Would this be the last night they spent together? He tried to picture what life would look like without Tucker in it. Weeks ago, Tucker hadn't even existed, and now, he was all that mattered. So much so that Dancer had to sort out this mess in order to love him the way he deserved to be loved. He knew he couldn't love Tucker that way with all the anger from his past still bottled up. The only way to free himself of it was to understand it, and then and only then could he set the anger free. If this was to be his last night with Tucker, would it have been better if none of this ever happened between them? A part of him said yes, but he knew that was a lie.

He could hear his mom's TV in the room next to theirs. She had started sleeping with the TV on after his dad died. After she remarried, the TV stayed on. Hyperaware of everything, he could smell the remnants of the dinner they had ordered. A loss of appetite left most of his hamburger uneaten. Tomorrow was light years away.

The tip of his finger circled Tucker's nipple. The more he touched it, the harder it got, which stirred his own arousal. If this was going to be their last night, possibly the last night he would ever love again, he wanted one last night with the man that didn't want him enough to go with him. He needed to feel that closeness after they made love, the deep connection, an intimacy that connected their souls. He needed it now more than anything.

He ran his hand down Tucker's chest until he reached the covers across his waist. His hand slipped under the covers, down to Tucker's groin. It wasn't long before Tucker's body responded to his careful caressing.

He wasn't sure what he could pull off. Intercourse was out of the question as was most everything else he thought about. His fire continued to smolder, the need to make love. It was the only thing that would satisfy what he was feeling. Lost, lonely, and abandoned, he needed the closeness that came with making love.

Tucker's heavy erection in his hand was what he most desired. He needed Tucker.

The pain in his side shot up through his stomach when he turned to nuzzle his face into the side of Tucker's neck. He lay still for a second until it eased.

Tucker moaned as his body twisted. His eyes opened, falling on Dancer. "What are you doing?"

"I want to make love."

"Are you sure?"

He had Tucker's hard dick in his hand. He was sure.

Tucker positioned his body over Dancer's without putting his weight on him. He pressed his lips against Dancer's. His mouth tasted of chocolate from the Almond Joy he had eaten before falling asleep.

Dancer's mouth relaxed, allowing Tucker's probing tongue total access. Dancer inhaled Tucker's scent, wet and delicious. A mixture of body soap and lotion, a bouquet of fresh flowers and spices penetrated Dancer's senses.

He wanted more. He wrapped his arm around Tucker, laying his cast on Tucker's back. It was awkward, but there was little he could do to change it. Tucker's pelvis rested on his, their erections pressed together.

"I love you." Tucker whispered through their kisses.

"I love you too." Dancer pressed his pelvis tighter into Tucker. He wanted all of him. He squirmed, knowing that, if he moved wrong, he could be flooded with intense pain.

Tucker's lips pressed against his neck. Tiny kisses against his skin sent heat throughout his body as he begged for more. With his one good hand, he gripped Tucker's ass. If he could, he would cut the cast off right now to have both of Tucker's ass cheeks in his hands.

He put the cast to good use as he pressed it down onto Tucker's shoulders and tried to push Tucker's head down to his erection.

Tucker resisted. "I don't want to hurt you."

Dancer ignored him and pushed harder until Tucker gave in.

Tucker flipped his massive body, aligning himself so they each had access to the other's genitals without Dancer having to move. The sensual touch of Tucker's warm mouth proved to be too much for Dancer. He let out a slight moan as his breathing became labored. He wasn't going to last long at all. A moan from Tucker said he too was getting close. As predicted, it wasn't long before the muscles in Dancer's ass stiffened as his back arched. He uttered a gasp that was almost a cry as he shuddered his release. Intoxicating waves of ecstasy were still surging through his body when Tucker climaxed seconds later.

Completely spent, Dancer carefully rolled over onto his back. His arms stretched out across the king size bed as if they were wings. His breathing ragged, Tucker startled him as he came up and kissed him. He tasted himself on Tucker's lips.

Dancer knew that, as incredible as the sex had just been, it didn't change anything. Tomorrow had to come. But at this moment, he felt as close to Tucker as ever. Their bodies snuggled together, Tucker held him in his arms.

Chapter Thirty

Tucker was one of the first to arrive at the rehab center for Family Day. Staff had set out tables and chairs on the lawn. There was another table filled with breakfast muffins, donuts, coffee, and juice. The weather was better than it had been during last week's visit. Outside temperatures couldn't have been much above fifty degrees, but Tucker acknowledged and savored the morning sun's meager warmth on his back.

Last week had been cold and rainy, and Family Day had to be moved to the visiting lounge. It wasn't all bad. He had been so hungry that he ate four muffins and washed them down with two cups of coffee and an OJ juice pack.

Today, Tucker and his mother talked as they watched Mattie on the swings with another little boy who was also a resident. Tucker smiled, seeing her laughing and screaming like little girls do. Every time she squealed, it made him laugh. It warmed his heart seeing that his mother looked one hundred percent better than she had last week. There was a clarity in her eyes. The old Sarah Graves from years ago was back.

"How long are you going to be here? Did they say?" Tucker asked. It was the beginning of his probe before he brought up his plans.

"Between six months and a year. I'd rather not be here that long, but we'll see. It's all about working the program, one day at a time." Sarah rubbed at the blond peach fuzz that had come in on Tucker's head. "What happened to your hair?"

His knees bounced nervously under the table. There was so much to tell her, and yet they were talking about her. "I cut it off. Tired of it."

"It looks good. It makes me think of your father." Sarah ran her

223

hand back and forth across the top of the table. "Brings out the blue in your eyes."

Tucker wondered how much he looked like his dad. The conversation stalled as he thought about the man, whom he had never met. They sat for a few minutes, staring at Mattie across the way.

Sarah broke the silence. "What have you been up to? Are you still staying with that guy?"

That guy. She didn't know his name. "Dancer. Yeah." He stopped short of telling her they were in a suite at the 'W' Hotel. She definitely didn't need to know that he'd had the best two-patty bacon cheeseburger and make-up sex of his life last night.

"What do you do all day?" Sarah asked.

Did she care or was she just making conversation? "I don't know. Nothing."

"You need to find a job." Sarah's voice took on a more parental tone. "Save money so, when we get out of this place, we can get a house of our own. Maybe move back to the old neighborhood."

"Yeah, maybe." He wasn't sure which of the old neighborhoods she was referring to.

"Look, I'm not busting my ass every day in here to take care of you when I get out of here." Her hand slid back and forth across the top of the table.

"I never asked you to take care of me. I can take care of myself." This was the Sarah he knew. Within ten minutes, she had pissed him off. He folded his arms across his chest.

Sarah rolled her eyes. "How you goin' to do that with no job?"

"Don't worry about it!" He couldn't forget the misery of his job hunting.

"You need to do something with your life. You're eighteen years old. You need to get out of that place. It's dangerous."

He had enough of her standing on her soap box. Who was she to lecture him on anything? "Well, we're not there anymore. We got a hotel room."

Surprise flashed across Sarah's face. "A hotel? Where'd you get the money for that? Christ, please tell me you didn't steal it or something. If you get caught, I ain't got the money to bail you out. You'll have to stay there."

"I didn't steal shit!" Tucker's cheeks turned pink. "His mum.

She's in town. She got it for us." He tapped his fingernails on the table.

"What's she like?" Sarah's mouth twisted. Her tone was riddled with jealousy.

"She's nice." He was about to tell her who she was and that she was stinking rich and lived in San Francisco. That would have been a big mistake. His mother would have schemed a way to latch on like a bug on a windshield.

"Tucker! Tucker!" Mattie charged across the lawn yelling his name.

She was there before he could twist his long legs out from under the picnic table. "Hey, baby girl." Tucker grabbed her and gave her a smothering bear hug.

Mattie broke loose from his grip and took her seat at the wooden picnic table. Unaware of the tension between Tucker and their mom, she broke off a tiny piece of the blueberry muffin she had left on the table earlier. Her presence provided enough of a distraction for him to reset his mood with his mother.

Tucker searched for the words to tell her he was leaving them. He wanted Mattie to hear it from him. He swallowed as he looked down on his little sister as if she held the answer.

"Mum." He stopped as Mattie's arm bumped her cup, sending her red punch across the table.

"Dammit! Watch what you're doing!" Sarah pulled back from the table as the punch drained in between the wooden slats.

His annoyance flared again as his mother's outburst over a simple accident stopped him cold. There was anger in her eyes. "It was an accident." Tucker tried to smooth over her harsh tone as he used a tiny white napkin to soak up the red punch. The thin napkin turned red as it tore apart and disintegrated. He dabbed harder, but the napkin was no match for all the punch.

His mother was like the punch, and he was the napkin. She would win every time. She soaked the life right out of him. Until today, he had never recognized it as such. The sense of defeat, the lack of motivation to reach for something more with her around. She was poison, and it was killing him.

Dancer made him happy, gave him hope. He was in love. Heat radiated through his chest knowing that his choice was Dancer.

225

Dancer made him feel alive. "What I wanted to tell you was that his mother is here. She wants him to move back to California with her. I want to go too."

Sarah's face tightened. "California?" She leaned back and crossed her arms over her breasts. "What's in California?"

His answer was Dancer, but he'd never come out to his mother. There was never a reason to. He chuckled. Mattie knew. He had never come out to Mattie—she just knew somehow. The anger in his mother's eyes told him she wasn't worth the energy. "I don't know… Maybe a fresh start. I need…" He thought about what she once told him: boys did what was easy, men did what was right.

Tucker wanted to be a man and do what was right. As hard as it was to leave Mattie, he couldn't take Mattie with him. His mother would never allow that to happen. Nor could he save his mother from herself. He wasn't abandoning Mattie, he told himself. He would make a life for himself so he could be there for her if something happened. Right now, he couldn't even take care of himself.

"You're going to leave me and your sister?" She tried to pin him down with her eyes.

Mattie's little eyes looked up at him. "Where're you going?" Her question caused them to look at her.

He rubbed the back of Mattie's hair. Long strokes all the way to the end. His breathing became shallow at the thought of leaving her. "To California. With my friend Dancer and his mum."

Mattie's bottom lip pouted out, but he knew she didn't understand. "Do you have to ride in an airplane to get there?"

"Yep. But I'll be back to visit you. And you and mum can come visit me." He tried to lie as cheerfully as he could to make Mattie—and himself—feel better about what he was saying.

"Yeah!" Her little legs kicked up and down in the air as if someone just told her she was going to Disneyland.

"I just… feel like I need to go." He looked around at everyone around them. They were oblivious to the family drama playing out at their table. He had learned a long time ago that he couldn't win with his mother. She was toxic, and this was all part of her cycle. She would only get louder or storm off. Either way, it wouldn't change anything. There was nothing else for him to say.

"You're going to go?" Sarah broke the few seconds of silence.

Tucker shrugged. "What do you want me to do? You're the one who told me to go be a man! I'm trying!"

"Yeah, go be the man. Just like your father. Go fucking run!" Sarah rolled her eyes as she squeezed her legs out from under the table. "Watch your sister! I have to go to the goddamn bathroom."

He watched as his mother stormed off and into the building. Exasperated, he blew out a puff of air from his lungs. Thoughts swirled in his head. What was he supposed to do? If he stayed, how was that helping any of them? But if he left, was he running like his father? Was he abandoning them? Why did it feel wrong?

He lowered his eyes toward Mattie. She was going on and on about some boy that was making fun of her and what she had told him. Her words faded in and out as he gave her an occasional "Uh-huh" to show that he was listening. He was miles away, lost in a sea of disappointment, failure, and uncertainty.

*****

By the time Tucker made his way back to the hotel and up to their room, Ms. Ziegler and Dancer were standing among several piles of clothes. She had spent hours shopping for him and Dancer. He walked into a room full of shopping bags and new clothes draped over every piece of furniture in the suite.

"What the heck is all of this?" He didn't need to ask, but it seemed like an appropriate question to start with.

"Mom thought she needed to go shopping for us." Tucker knew that the bright expression on Dancer's face wasn't about the clothes—he was happy Tucker was there.

Even with his beautiful locks of hair shaved off, Dancer was stunning. Tucker was in love. With Dancer, he could survive anywhere. His anywhere was Dancer.

He met Dancer in the middle of the room, where the two exchanged a small kiss. "Really?" He looked down at the stack of shirts and pants on the bed.

"Those are all yours." Dancer pointed to the two piles of clothes on the bed. "And these are mine." As if awarding a prize on a game show, he extended his hand to the piles of clothes on the couch, chair, and desk. "Mom's been busy. And look, new shoes too."

"I figured you kids deserved something new. New clothes always make me happy." Ms. Ziegler took a seat in the desk chair and crossed her legs.

Tucker looked at Dancer, trying to get a read on the situation. Dancer had been on a roller coaster of emotions since he woke up from his coma. Tucker had done everything he could to help, but he was fighting with his own demons. The thought of him and Dancer not being together was inconceivable; the thought of leaving Mattie had been heartbreaking. He had gone over to New Beginnings after leaving Family Day and spoken with Ian. His heart-to-heart talks with Ian always brought him clarity and, in this case, gave him the push to do what it was that he really wanted. Ian encouraged him to go, reminding Tucker of the great love he himself had let go and had never gotten over. He lived every day with the 'what-if'. Ian even promised to keep an eye on Mattie for him.

He lifted the top shirt in his pile and looked at the one under it. Okay, so the second shirt was super cute. He looked at all the other clothes on the bed. He had never had so many new clothes at once in his life. Back to school shopping was two pairs of jeans and three shirts. "I guess I need to look as fancy as you guys in California." Tucker smiled as he casually slid the news out that he was going with them.

It seemed to take a second for it to register with Dancer what Tucker had just said. "Um, you mean…" A huge smile swept across his face. "You mean it? You're going to go?"

"Hell yeah! I'm not passing up on these clothes." Tucker laughed as his eyes shifted to Ms. Ziegler.

Tenderly, she smiled at both of them.

"But you'll keep your boots, right?" Dancer chuckled.

Tucker looked down at his raggedy boots and laughed. "Yeah, I'll keep the boots." He flipped through the rest of the shirts, checking out the sizes. He stopped when he came to a Gucci blue denim embroidered sweater. "There is no way I'm wearing this."

Dancer looked at the sweater. "Yeah, Mom, I'm not sure what you were thinking."

Ms. Ziegler stood up and walked over to the bed. "Really? Neither of you like it. I thought it was cute." She picked up the sweater and examined it. "I love this sweater!"

228

Both boys broke out in laughter as they scrunched their faces. The sweater was the worst kind of ugly.

"Okay, try on your pants." Ms. Ziegler suggested. "If they don't fit or you don't like them, we can return them with the sweater. Get something you like."

Dancer held up a pair of his new pants. "They'll fit."

"Dancer, try them on so I can see." She pleaded.

"Okay, okay." Taking the pants with him, Dancer disappeared into the bathroom.

"I'm glad you're coming with us." Ms. Ziegler spoke in a low voice as they waited for Dancer. "I was concerned, one, that he wouldn't go if you didn't, and two, he would blame me for splitting you two up. The truth in the matter is that, if he and I are going to fix this, he'll need you and the love and support you'll provide."

Tucker pushed down a lump in his throat. "Thank you. I love him and can't imagine living without him."

"Thank you for loving my son as much as you do. Can I have a hug?" she asked.

As the two embraced, Dancer exited the bathroom. "Hey, what's going on out here?"

Tucker and Ms. Ziegler burst into laughter at the sight of Dancer standing there in his new slacks that stopped two inches above his ankles. Two sizes too small, the bulge in his crotch showed everything.

"Oh my God, please take those off!" Tucker screamed in laughter as Ms. Ziegler shielded her eyes with the back of her hand.

Chapter Thirty-One

Tucker and Dancer had been in San Francisco for two months. They arrived with Dancer's mother after spending another week in Illinois and getting his doctors to sign off on the okay to fly.

The morning they flew out of Brierton, the limousine made a quick stop at Camp Roosevelt. Dancer was prepared to leave his entire life behind. He was taking the only thing in his life that mattered, and that was Tucker; but he had to say goodbye to Dottie, knowing he would never see her again. He asked a couple of people as to her whereabouts, but no one had seen her in several days. He started toward his old place, wondering if there was something inside that he wanted. But, before he reached the shanty, he saw that a new squatter had already moved in. It was just as well. There was nothing in there that he needed, just bins filled with memories that he would rather leave behind.

At the airport, Dancer had a private laugh when life revealed its sense of humor. They exited the limousine and were standing on the curb, checking in their bags. He felt eyes staring at him and looked up. It was Old Man Gerhardt. Their eyes met. The look on Gerhardt's face at the sight of Dancer in his navy-blue slacks and Canada Goose Expedition Parka, carrying his mother's designer luggage and stepping out of a limousine, was priceless.

Never in his wildest dreams had Dancer seen himself living in a four-thousand square foot, 1922 Spanish Mediterranean home on a cliff overlooking the ocean. Perhaps it was the incredible views of the Pacific Ocean and Baker Beach or the peacefulness that dwelled within the house that made him believe this was somewhere he could call home one day. It was not the home he had run away from so many years ago and not the home that had stolen the last six years from him, but the home of an earlier time in his life. There was so much about their new life to figure out, but there was no urgency to any of it. Every day, he woke up feeling safe. With Tucker curled under his arm, the world wasn't half bad any more. In fact, it was pretty freaking good.

This morning, when Dancer woke up, he found Tucker sitting in the bed reading a text message. Ever since his mother had gotten Tucker and his mom cell phones, they had been texting each other almost every day.

"Good morning, sleepy head." Tucker laid his phone down and gave Dancer a kiss.

Dancer savored the taste of Tucker's lips. He would never tire of them. "Good morning. How long have you been up?"

"About a half hour. I was just texting my mum. She sent me a text and a picture of her and Mattie. I guess her school is on a field trip to the zoo, and my mum went." Tucker showed Dancer the picture on his phone. "They look so good."

"Yeah, they do." Dancer smiled at the cute picture of the two of them standing in front of an elephant. "What time is it?"

Tucker looked over at the clock on his side of the bed. "Nine." He went back to looking at the pictures of Mattie and his mother.

Dancer lay his head back on his pillow. "How are they doing?"

"Good. She is all excited about some sober mother-daughter dance this weekend at the center." Tucker used his free hand and rubbed Dancer's bare chest.

It made Dancer feel good to know that Sarah was doing well without Tucker. The separation had seemed to improve her and Tucker's relationship. They were able to stop feeding into each other's weaknesses and insecurities and enjoy what they each had to offer. Dancer knew she had a long way to go, but in all her apologies to Tucker, she conveyed how badly she wanted a new life. She was just as happy for him and his new life.

"Okay, it's time for me to get up." Tucker bent over and kissed Dancer before leaving the bed. He walked over to the heavy curtains and pulled them open. Light flooded into the room and onto his naked body. Tall and lean, his ass was pale against his now honey-brown skin. This was proof that they had officially become beach bums, visiting the local beach every day.

"I love your little Speedo tan." Dancer admired his boyfriend's

231

beautiful pale butt from across the room. "Your ass looks like a sugar cookie."

Tucker snickered. "And I know how much you love sugar cookies. I wish I was as brave as you and could lay out there naked too." Tucker moved over to the door and grabbed his robe from the back of the door. "I'm heading down for coffee. I think your mum's up already too." Tucker covered himself and tied the sash around his waist.

"I'll be down in a little bit." Dancer wasn't quite ready to leave his warm bed as he stretched the comforter up around his neck. He dozed for another twenty minutes, thinking about Sarah and Mattie. He planned to ask Tucker his thoughts on inviting them for Christmas, which was a little more than two months away. He knew that, in another month, Sarah would be able to leave the rehab center on passes. It was really Ms. Ziegler's idea to fly them out, but she had left it to her son to ask Tucker.

From his bed, he stared out at the fog that clouded the Golden Gate Bridge. Just the tips of the two towers were visible, but if he watched long enough, the morning airstream would push the fog out, unveiling the bridge in all its orange majesty.

He could hear Tucker and his mom laughing down in the kitchen below him. Tucker and Ms. Ziegler had fallen into a routine of morning coffee, chopped fruit, and bagels at the breakfast bar that looked out into the manicured English garden on the side of the house.

Dancer rolled over onto his back as his mind drifted. He and Tucker were making plans to return to school for their diplomas, at the San Francisco Adult Education Center in the Fall. Tucker had also expressed an interest in joining the local baseball league. In a million years, Dancer had never imagined being in love with a jock.

He still couldn't wrap his brain around all that had changed in such a short time. From that first day that he saw Tucker in Camp Roosevelt, his life had never been the same. Being alone wasn't so bad until that moment he met Tucker. Tucker caused everything Dancer believed to be true to collapse, and exposed the truth. He was never safe; he had been trapped by fear. Fear had controlled him.

After breakfast, he and Tucker walked down to the beach, which was less than a mile from the house. It had become their morning ritual. Barefoot in the sand, Dancer inhaled the fresh mixture of saltwater and seaweed. They held hands and talked as they made their way to the far end of Baker Beach, where the gay and nudist community hung out together.

In the mornings, this section of the beach was virtually empty. Other than the occasional nude sunbather, the only constant was an eclectic group of men that came together for the morning volleyball game. It was Tucker who made friends with this group first, and he excelled at the game. For Dancer, the sound of Tucker laughing and arguing with the guys was as soothing as the rhythmic waves and seagulls behind him.

The ball was next to impossible to hit over the net for Dancer, so he chose to sunbathe instead of playing. In the nude, he lay on his blanket under the warm morning sun and read his mother's books. He couldn't believe how talented she was. In each book, he read parts of his own life as a child and came to understand so much about her that he never knew. Every man that the heroines in her books fell in love with contained different aspects of his dad.

Things Dancer had read in her books were the springboard to many conversations, helping him shape his feelings into words with his therapist. The three of them had started seeing a therapist in individual and group sessions. In each session Dancer grew to understand himself better, as well as his damaged relationship with his mother. The sessions were also strengthening his and Tucker's relationship. He smiled, remembering a profound thing that his therapist had said to him last week. It was as if a light switch had been turned on. *It is from your past that you gain strength, courage, and confidence, but only when you consciously omit fear as an option.* Life was going to be a work in progress, but with Tucker, he felt as if anything was possible.

Once Tucker's volleyball game was over, they hiked up through the rolling hills of the Presidio. The narrow dirt trail curved up and over the Pacific Ocean to a former military post. The two boys stood at the cliff's edge, looking out toward the sea. The whistling wind blew across their faces, carrying a light scent of the sea into their noses. The cold, crisp air had turned Tucker's cheeks a bright pink.

"Lake or ocean?" Dancer asked.

"Ocean, definitely the ocean." Tucker beamed as his eyes moved from the sea and looked at his best friend and lover.

233

"I was right." Dancer leaned in and gave Tucker a kiss.

"About what?" Tucker brought Dancer in closer, holding him by his waist.

"I was right about your eyes. They are as deep and tranquil as that ocean out there. I could swim in your blue eyes forever and never touch the bottom. I see forever when I look in your eyes. I see peace, and I know that, whatever life throws at me, I'll be able to handle it. If it knocks me down, it won't keep me down. I have some pretty amazing reasons to get back up."

READING GROUP GUIDE

1. Escaping Camp Roosevelt is about the relationship between young men who have essentially different experiences with surviving heartbreak. Talk about what Dancer learns from Tucker and vice versa. In what ways do Dancer and Tucker surprise each other? Have you had someone come into your life and change it forever?

2. Dancer and Tucker are both homeless and appear to be in economic equivalence. Discuss the hidden class differences between Dancer and Tucker. How do family origins affect the characters' ambitions?

3. Dancer is a loner, content with living by himself. Tucker is needy and wants to please people. Talk about the ways that traumatic events in one's childhood can shape who they become as adults.

4. Trust plays a large role in the novel. What did you see as the pivotal point in the book that allowed Dancer to let go of years of mistrust and allow Tucker into his heart?

5. Tucker and his mother have a complicated relationship. Did you empathize with Tucker's character and his struggle with leaving Mattie behind? Was this the right choice?

6. At the end of the novel, both Dancer and Tucker had to make difficult decisions not only regarding their own lives but the lives of others. Do you think they made the right choices? Talk about the way Dancer and Tucker's relationship would have played out if their choices had been different.

7. By the end of the book, had your opinion on homelessness changed?

8. The novel is about finding love in the darkest of places. Discuss the ways love is explored by each of the characters. Do you think Tucker moved too fast? Have you experienced something like this in your own life?

About The Author

Bryan T. Clark is a LAMBDA Literary finalist and Rainbow Award winning author of gay romance and contemporary books. He is also a funny, loving, family-oriented, and proud member of the LGBT community. In his work, he is known to push the boundaries with brilliantly crafted stories of friendship, love, complicated relationships, and challenges all woven into a hard-earned happily-ever-after.

Behind his computer, working on his next novel, Bryan writes Male/Male Romance with an emphasis on *moral dilemma*. His multicultural characters and riveting plots embody real life, filled with challenges, personal growth, and, of course, what we all desire—love.

When Bryan isn't writing, he enjoys traveling, lying by a body of water soaking up the sun, and watching a good movie while snuggled up with his husband and their loyal companion (Nettie the Sheepadoodle) on the couch.

Born in Boston, Massachusetts, Bryan has made his home and life in the Central Valley of California.

E-mail-Bryanbrianx2@yahoo.com
Website-www.btclark.com

If you've enjoyed *Escaping Camp Roosevelt*, I'd love to hear about it. Honest reviews on Amazon, Barnes & Noble, and Goodreads are always appreciated. If you would like to explore some of my other novels, follow the links below.

Ancient House of Cards
https://www.amazon.com/dp/B00JGZHSH1

Before Sunrise
https://www.amazon.com/dp/B01BU6F430

Come to the Oaks
https://www.amazon.com/dp/B01N5XNP2S

Diego's Secret
https://www.amazon.com/dp/B079HB64WC